WOLF CRAIGS

GWEN GATES PARKER

To Mother,
who raised an army of her own

FOREWORD

First Minister's Emergency Press Conference
9th April

"First Minister Andrea Taylor, it is a week since the bombing of the Louise Weiss Building of the European Parliament in Strasbourg and so far 101 people have lost their lives. This morning, we all heard the shocking news that the New Nationalists, the ruling party in Westminster, were behind the bombings and that arrests have been ..."

"Let me first start by saying how shocked we were by the deaths of so many people in the Strasbourg bombing. Our thoughts and prayers were with the families of all those involved during our two-minute silence this morning."

"Yes, of course, but can you tell me Holyrood's position on the revelation that anonymous sources within the New Britain government went directly to Commissioner Francois Janvier to lay the blame at Westminster's door ..."

"And can I just say how very professional and accomplished the emergency services were and how their actions, I'm sure, helped to save many lives."

"First Minister, what is your position on the explosive claims this morning that the Westminster ruling party, The New Nationalists, were involved in the Strasbourg bombing? How does this affect our position in New Britain?"

"We in Scotland must hold together as one nation against the darkness of the rogue Westminster government. We are being held against our will by those diminishers of democracy, and it is up us to honour the people's choice to leave New Britain in the Independence Referendum in December last year. They cannot hang on to us any longer!"

"First Minister, we are aware of the problems around The Home Secretary, Marcus James' ongoing lack of recognition of the second IndyRef. But do you think there is any truth in the claims that the NNP were behind the terrible bombings?"

"We voted with an 81% majority to leave New Britain in December 2023! Our voices must be heard! Ulster's Independence Referendum in 2022 was recognised and they immediately began the transition to join the Republic of Ireland and the EU. This took them a year, end to end. Our second Independence Referendum was declared null and void and the result unrecognised within two weeks of the result. Why? What is it that we have, that desperate far right New Nationalists need up here in Scotland?"

"First Minister, as a result of this incredible revelation about the Strasbourg bombing, we are now under threat of serious sanctions from the EU, which sit alongside the no-deal Brexit and the 2021 Travel Ban Covid controls already in place. People are already struggling. What do you have to say to them?"

"I would first like to congratulate Northern Ireland First Minister Timothy Craft and Taoiseach Seamus Weir for their smooth and successful joining of the Republic of Ireland and Ulster, with few problems. However, the injustice of our unrecognised Referendum leaves much to be desired, and we hope to join our Celtic brethren soon as a free state. We are prisoners of the terrorists! We must fight back! The EU must recognise our status as a nation in chains!"

"First Minister, please! People are beginning to starve. The NHS has all but collapsed, the police force is shored up by Security Forces manned by thugs and anyone who can leave the country has left. There are warships in the North Sea from Denmark down to France! As a nation, what are we going to do?"

"Give me six months. Give me freedom to rewrite our constitution. Give me your taxes. I can save us. You have to trust me. You have to trust in a free Independent State of Scotland."

CHAPTER 1

November 9th (8.10am)

Lewis Sinclair pulled his lapels closed against the freezing wind, dragged himself up the stone steps and placed his key fob to the plate which opened the door. He pulled it open with a well practiced tug and stepped into the cold, dank corridor. A few more steps saw him at the bottom of the stairs and he took them wearily, one at a time as he fumbled his keys into his pocket and juggled his bag and coffee cup. Lewis was only at work because his girlfriend, Izzy, made him come. If he was out of the house, they saved on fuel. He'd already had to give up his car so Izzy could use their petrol allowance to get to the hospital but he hated going on the bus. It was always stuffed with people who had long since run out of washing powder and deodorant and there was always someone with a hacking, wet cough and an excuse not to wear a mask.

By the time he reached the top of the third flight of steps his old leg injury had begun to throb and he was breathing hard although he tried not to show it as he walked past two of his students, huddled together for warmth. He was embarrassed about his poor fitness but was usually in too much pain and too lazy to do anything about it, even though he now considered once more his promise to Izzy to dig them a vegetable patch. He passed the lift shaft covered in yellow and black warning tape and glanced into the darkness where the lift should have been. For a year it had been out of action but no-one had been to fix it, and now there was no-one left to complain to.

Lewis pulled open the door to the science department and had to adjust his eyes to the dimness. With no windows in this hallway and no bulbs left overhead, Lewis and his colleagues had to almost sense one another as they passed. He saw a shadow up ahead and called out to him.

"Morning," he said, more of a reflex than a greeting.

"Morning," came the mumbled response. It was Don Jack, the chemistry teacher. Don's shadow moved into the staff room and Lewis followed a moment later.

He threw his bag onto a chair and in one movement picked up the kettle, filled it with water and set it to boil. He opened his coffee cup, drained the last of the dregs and began to refill it with granules from a nearby jar. He looked at the sugar bowl. Empty, which came as no surprise.

It was Monday. First of the month. Lewis had another reason to be here today besides drawing his shrinking wage, although neither he nor anyone else could bring themselves to admit it. Even teachers got hungry.

They both sat on their usual seats, although there were many more available, their hands clutched at hot coffee mugs. Lewis' darkened eyes and pale skin hovered above the steam as his frozen fingers defrosted with the first warmth of the day. They sat in silence waiting, not quite sure what another day would bring. Don reached into his pocket and pulled out a loaf of homemade bread.

"Here. For you and Izzy." Don said.

"Magic, Don, thanks," Lewis eyed the fresh loaf and doubted if any of it would make its way home to his girlfriend.

The air bristled as an unfamiliar siren emerged through the stiff breeze outside. It got louder until it tore at the air inside the room before it stopped abruptly. They heard the sound of slamming doors and heavy footsteps outside before silence settled back into the room. After a while, Lewis spoke.

"I don't recognise that one," he said, staring at the bread. Nope. Izzy would not be getting her share.

Steam continued to rise from cooling drinks.

"Me neither," Don agreed with a small frown. He coughed and tugged at his sock inside the heavy boot on his foot.

The light in the room imperceptibly brightened as snow began to fall against the window. Don looked up at the ceiling with old, tired eyes and sighed. He leaned behind his chair, picked up a stack of red buckets then handed one to Lewis on his left, placed one on the floor on his right and one on the coffee table. They both watched as water began to drip from the broken ceiling tiles.

"There's a new security service in town, to stop the looting. That's the third new group in six weeks." Lewis said, then rubbed at his sore leg. His old motorbike accident left him with several plates down his left leg, and none of them liked the cold. "They have blue vans and yellow flashing lights."

"Black uniforms?" Don asked.

"Black uniforms," he nodded. "I saw them outside Tesco Foodbank. They had dogs. They shot a man last week. I think he jumped the queue."

They both thought about this in silence. Voices outside began to rise.

Lewis and Don craned their necks to watch impassively from their seats as below their window, Aaron Barr from 6J was pushed to the ground, cuffed and then marched off the school grounds and into the van. This was the third boy in a month to be arrested. The siren wailed once more as Aaron was driven away.

"I suspected that was for Aaron," Lewis said.

"What did he do?" Don asked.

Lewis sniffed. "Poor bastard. He took the old tea towels from room 23. But Mrs Bush said he could have them."

"So what's the problem?" Don asked. He was incredulous but had no intention of assisting Aaron. Now that would be a stupid move.

"The old bitch in the office said she wanted them back so kicked up a fuss yesterday. Said Mrs B had 'no right to give away school property.'" Lewis paused, then said sadly, "Poor kid wanted them to make nappies for his baby sister."

"Poor lad," Don murmured but nothing more was said. Snow threw itself at the window and the red buckets echoed with drips.

They finished their drinks.

"Shall we?" Don asked, eventually, as he looked at his watch.

They both rose and left the room, headed to their individual classrooms.

Lewis opened the door to his room and flicked on one light. Behind him, a gaggle of students slouched in to take seats and behind the,m a gossiping group entered with a little more energy. Their voices blew little clouds into the frigid air. Slowly, his registration group grew. Lewis opened his diary and picked up a pen. Since the school had failed to pay the electricity bill last year, they were on energy restriction so only had one computer per department and it was kept centrally. No more electronic registers or tracking, everything was done by hand.

"Ok," he began, the tone of his voice indicating the need for quiet. "Do we have ... Jack?"

"Here."

"Nathan."

"Here."

"Daniel."

"Yup."

Lewis noted the next three names as absent; neither Talia, Shana nor Pramila had been seen for weeks and it was presumed they were not going to return.

"Gracie?"

"No, sir," came a few murmurs, "The family got their ... you know, papers."

"Visa? It finally came through?"

"Yeah, sir, they moved on the weekend."

"But I saw Gracie's dad on the bus this morning," Lewis said.

"They couldn't all go. It's her and her two sisters. Mum and dad weren't allowed to leave."

Lewis nodded sadly in understanding. The three teenagers would be lucky to ever see their parents again. But healthcare workers just weren't allowed to travel outside New Britain. He moved on.

"Fraser?"

"Here."

"Jennie?"

"Here."

"Chloe." Pause. "No Chloe?" he asked and peered into the class. It was dim, he couldn't be sure if she was out there somewhere.

"No, Sir," Sophie McCall replied from the back. "Lucky bitch."

"Sophie! Language!" he chastised mildly, then asked, "What do you mean, 'lucky'?"

Suddenly there was a wail and another girl burst into tears. The two students beside her made sympathetic noises and tried to comfort their friend. Lewis gritted his teeth. Despite his enforced role as guidance teacher, he was never keen on counselling teenage girls. He wasn't good with other peoples' tears and emotions; it was just too much effort. If he was honest, girls scared him. He'd better ask though, he thought.

"Jessica, what's wrong?" he asked and glanced at the rest of the class, searching for an answer. They all shifted in their seats, unwilling to catch his eye. In the end, Sophie McCall rolled her eyes at him and spoke once more.

"It's Chloe. She married Tomasz and his family took her to Poland with them. That's why she's not here."

Lewis made a surprised face. "Oh! That was … not what I was expecting. Married? Wow." He frowned, then asked quietly, "Wasn't Tomasz going out with Jess?"

"Yes!" Sophie spoke with irritation, making a 'duh' face at him, "But her dad couldn't afford the … the dowry," she finished quietly. Jess sniffed again.

Lewis let out a long breath as he finished the register. No Tomasz Wozniac, then, he presumed as he noted the last absence. These were the fewest kids yet.

There was no bell but Lewis knew it was time to go as he glanced at the old watch his father gave him since his mobile phone died. The students moved off to different rooms and began the first of several independent study periods of the day. There just weren't enough people to cover all the lessons so only core subjects were taught, with practical tutorials slotted in when the expertise was there. Today, Don's presence meant some of them would benefit from survival techniques, honed over many Duke of Edinburgh qualifying expeditions. Lewis' sociology tutorials were less popular; the students were too busy working out how to stay alive.

Instead of teaching in the classical sense, Lewis spent a lot of time mitigating the heart-breaking aftermath of Post Traumatic Stress disorder in kids as young as 11 years old. They arrived at his door pale and wordless or crying and hysterical as the reality of life in Post Brexit, Post Pandemic, Post Sanctions New Britain sank into the fabric of their lives. He heard tales of uncles shot for taking food in a desperate attempt to feed now orphaned cousins, and families split apart as the lucky few were granted passage to a new life overseas.

In reality, he had nothing to tell them. There was little hope in the current political climate. What did the future hold? Where was the bright spot in their situations? It was all he could do to help them hang on in there. The EU sanctions imposed six months ago had really taken their toll. He listened in dismay as the wails and sniffs coming from Jess disappeared down the corridor.

In the last four years, his kids went from dealing with boyfriend troubles and falling out with friends over social media to basic survival. The drinking water in the taps was only just guaranteed clean but the foundation of everything else they knew suddenly shook. Food shortages, energy rations, blackouts, lockdowns, internet blocks and the curtailment of fundamental freedoms quickly became the norm. Every day something else happened to take the population of a modern Scotland further from what they knew. The Security Force Act was the worst; they took away the legal right-of-way over land, for fear that people may steal livestock and in turn be shot by desperate farmers. The powers of the state grew from that until now, every small infraction - usually an attempt to feed a hungry family - was a detainable offence. Since the armed thugs of the Security Units had landed in the streets, Lewis had seen five dead bodies, just lying there after some minor misdemeanour. Aaron Barr from 6J was just the latest visible victim.

Lewis took the chance to refill his coffee once more and headed to the staff meeting, where they would find out if they qualified for the monthly canteen handouts. This was the real reason he'd turned up today. The students got the first choice of out-of-date food to take home to their families, but if there was anything left, the teachers also benefitted. Last month, the volunteer cooks made chocolate cake with some of the old beetroot and rapidly spoiling milk left over from the last farm co-op donation.

Downstairs in the main staff room, the radiators were on. As each teacher entered the room and the warmth hit their faces, they breathed a sigh of relief and joy. The mugs didn't steam in here and woollen socks and sweaters began to itch and lose their appeal.

"Nice one," Lewis cried as the warmth hit his face, and he loosened his scarf. The snow pelted against the windows here too, but there were no buckets on the ground floor. Not yet anyway. Don sat next to him, not completely relaxed knowing this morning's news might not be good. With few working phones, limited radio coverage and a ban on all print media, the morning briefing now included local, national, and global events, in case anyone missed them. This was how many of the teachers found out about the Strasbourg bombing.

After a while, others joined them on the old, fraying seats, and the room filled up. Still, there were notable gaps in the faculty.

Lewis scanned the room and made a mental note of the ones who were there.

"Where's Luisa? And Clara?" he asked Don, but he shrugged. "For that matter …" he paused, "… I don't see any of the modern languages department, do you?"

Don scanned the room. "No," he replied. "Or IT. There's no IT department, either."

Don twisted in his seat to talk to the man behind him then turned back. "Bill's gone, Stuart just told me. Back to Australia."

"He's not Australian," Lewis said.

"His wife is," Don replied.

Lewis nodded in understanding just as the headteacher hurried into the room, still in his overcoat and hat.

"Morning, all," he called as he pulled off his coat and placed it over the back of his chair.

"Morning, Brian," came a chorus of replies.

Lewis and Don exchanged looks. The rapidly reducing role, the disappearing faculty, the cold, dim rooms and suspension of the timetable; could the school even carry on? This meeting could shape not only the rest of their school year, but the rest of their lives. The last thing they needed was to be out of work.

Brian Sergeant, the headteacher, sat down with a sigh and unfolded a small sheet of paper. He looked at it then looked at his remaining staff be they loyal or reluctant. Lewis sensed his distress. As it turned out, this would be the hardest meeting he ever had to chair since the New Britain borders closed.

CHAPTER 2

November 9th (8.35am)

Fran MacDonald eased herself into her cold leather chair and glanced at the name badge on her desk. *Minister for Europe, Migration and International Development* - it had been a title she had been proud of once. She began to open the morning mail. Six letters and a package. Since the government's disastrous attempts to privatise then restrict the internet available to all New Britain citizens, the access to email had been patchy at best. Where it used to be a source of endless information and communication, it was now home to nationalistic propaganda, government adverts and long periods of just being 'off'. So the 'snail mail' had become popular once more.

She kept all her paper copies now, to file the old-fashioned way and she lodged all her mail, phone calls and duties into a large, blue leather-bound book. She opened it now and began writing notes, recording her morning so far, eyeing the large envelope beside her, but determined to leave it until last.

The internet problem was an issue, but far worse was her secretary who just last week discovered an Irish connection through her grandparents. She had rushed through a new passport and a ferry ticket with the last of her savings and disappeared within days. Sometimes Fran wondered why she bothered to turn up herself now that the compulsory pay cuts meant her salary barely covered her bills.

Subsequently, there had been no applications for the vacancy of secretary to the *Minister for Europe, Migration and International Development* in Holyrood, mostly because even Fran's job didn't really exist anymore. Since the sanctions slammed down on them after the bombing, she was a minister for a place they could no longer communicate with, regarding migration that didn't happen and development which in turn simply couldn't happen. An assistant to a nobody was not a terribly appealing position, it would seem.

Fran finally ripped open the last letter. It was larger than most, weighty and thick. It was from Steve Lister, under-secretary of State in the Scotland Office in Westminster, and it contained the information he had gathered on the Strasbourg bombings. She settled to read; this was what she had been waiting for.

With little else to do, Fran had to justify her pay cheque. She made it her business to gather all the details of the Strasbourg bombing. If she could nail down the evidence that the New Nationalists had actually done the deed, maybe Andrea Taylor, First Minister and formidable potential ally, if you were worthy, would finally embrace Fran into her inner circle. Fran was kept in the loop by sympathetic and thorough colleagues across the EU but as they were no longer a part of the European Union she had no say in the direction of the research. She was only involved once the facts, such as they were able to compile, had been established.

What she did know was that the incident would have been far worse if the second device had detonated correctly, and more lives lost. So, she was grateful for that. She so desperately wanted to work it out first, be applauded, be significant. However, when the New Nationalists were implicated back in April, Fran wasn't so sure – why would they do such a thing? Now, reading the reams of information from Steve Lister in the Scotland Office, she frowned. It didn't make sense.

Fran scooped up the phone as it began to ring.

"Fran MacDonald," she said brusquely into the receiver.

"Fran, it's Steve."

It was Steve Lister himself. Based in London, he was Fran's greatest source of information outside Edinburgh. "Did you get it?"

"I just opened it. I was about to call you."

"It's all I have, Fran, sorry, I'm not sure you'll find what you're looking for in that lot."

"Give me time, I'm sure there's something I can use."

There was a pause.

"Fran, what exactly are you looking for?"

Fran switched the receiver into her other hand and licked the tip of her finger to turn another page from the pile in front of her.

"Honestly, Steve? I don't know until I find it. Is there anything else you can send?"

"Hell, no! Jesus Fran, it was practically a James Bond film trying to sneak all that lot out of the office!"

"Ok, thanks, Steve, talk soon, eh?" she made to put the phone down.

"Fran," he said swiftly. "There's another reason for my call. I'm getting intel down here about some major fallout from the High Court's repeated blocking of the second Independence Referendum. The Home Secretary, Marcus James, is getting very twitchy and wants to know what's going on. Holyrood has gone radio silent on us. You must know what Taylor's next move is?"

Fran sighed and dropped her head into her spare hand. Outside, the trees waved in the breeze and the top of Arthur's Seat began to turn white.

"I know, Fran," he heard her sigh, "But they're killing me down here. If there's anything you can tell me …"

"Steve, I …"

"They're so disturbed by what they are hearing, they're threatening to terminate my position and send me, and the rest of the Scotland office back to Holyrood. And then where will we be? There are questions, Fran! Questions I can't answer!"

"Believe me, Steve, I have way more questions than answers, too."

"We already have a limited say in New Britain after the Indy Ref, and if I go, anything we need Westminster to hear will essentially stop at Berwick. I have to throw them something, Fran, please! What the hell is going on up there?"

"Ok, Steve, let's just calm down." She took a deep breath, "Scotland, in the light of successive governments denying us the chance to act upon the successful outcome of our second Indyref, is currently considering its position within the union ..." Fran began the well-rehearsed speech.

"Fran, I know the 'official' position, but that isn't enough. There hasn't been an official peep out of Holyrood for weeks and Westminster is getting itchy. Do you know how tricky it is being a Scotsman in London?" Fran could almost hear sweat trickling down Steve's cheeks.

"... and as long as we, and the rest of New Britain are being held to ransom by the New Nationalist Party, we will play hardball," Fran spoke quickly and quietly now. She would not be pushed by the bullies in parliament.

"What power do we have, Fran? We have nothing to threaten Westminster with! They hold all the cards. They said they're not letting Scotland go quietly and they mean it! If they're the ones who bombed the European Parliament building in Strasbourg, look where that got us all."

"That's still not proven."

"As good as."

"I ... I still don't know, Steve. I think Andrea has some options ..."

"Yes, fine! But if they think something untoward or illegal is going on in Holyrood, they're the ones who could bomb you too!" Steve cried.

"What the hell ...?" This was the first talk of a direct internal threat.

"Yes, Fran! Think about it! What do they have to lose? Who would come to our aid? The EU and UN sanctions on New Britain don't discriminate between Scotland and England and if Westminster sees fit to bomb insurgents in Holyrood, then who's going to stop them? The best we can hope for is Médecins sans Frontiers to come in and clean up the bloody mess!"

"And what would be the point, Steve?"

"What is the point to any bombing?" Steve spoke through gritted teeth. "Or war? It's always power, control and resources. Especially, in our case, resources. Listen, up there have everything we need, right? Hydroelectric power, wind farms, oil rigs, clean water, right? If we choose the independent route, as much good as it'll do us now, how long do you think before the grabbing begins? We have everything they need."

"I know." Fran spoke slowly. "But we ..."

"But we also have Faslane, Fran. The nukes."

Fran swallowed, but her mouth was suddenly dry.

"If push comes to shove, Westminster will not want the subs at Faslane under the control of a bunch of difficult, separatist, left leaning, EU sympathising Scots!" He paused, knowing that there was every possibility that this call was being recorded or monitored. "So if you're going to do something drastic, I'd do it sooner rather than later, Fran. In terms of Scottish-English relations, I don't think we have much time left."

There was a silence which neither of them filled. Finally, Steve spoke again.

"Fran, why did you want all my intel on the bombings? Do you know something we don't?"

"To fill some ... gaps."

"Is it what you were looking for?"

"I'm not sure, I have a lot to sift through. But thank you."

"No problem. Fran, help me out here. Please."

"I will, don't worry."

Fran put the phone down and stared out of the window. Something drastic. Little did Steve Lister know that drastic measures were already underway and by the end of the morning, the Scotland Office in Westminster would be deserted.

There was a soft knock at the door and Todd Horton, minister for Rural Affairs and the Environment, slipped into the room.

"Fran, we need to talk. This cannot go on," he said, "I think Taylor is out of control."

Fran held up her hand to stop him.

"Not now, Todd, I am very busy, can't you see?"

"I'm not sure I like what I've been hearing recently, and I know she has been slipping under the radar. Fran, we have to take a stand."

"For goodness sake, Todd, I have more important things to think about than your paranoia!" she said with irritation. "And rest assured there is nothing 'going on'."

Todd paused and regarded her, but then left with a shake of his head. As the door closed, Fran smiled. She knew exactly what was going on. She was on the edge of the inner circle. She was significant. Todd and all the rest of them would find out all he needed to know when the time was right.

CHAPTER 3

The old Volkswagen creaked into a parking space behind the hospital and Izzy pulled out her keys. All four doors opened and there were groans and sighs from the occupants as they hauled themselves out into the cold. A lift into work was a rare pleasure, and Izzy was one of the few people left with a car. Izzy wrapped her coat around her, donned her mask and darted for the main doors.

"Thanks, Iz," they all called and each person disappeared down a different, dark corridor. Izzy pushed her name tag to a door sensor and entered her ward. It was a warm place to work, at least, with some peace in the early morning when patients were still drowsy and sedated and not calling for help which never came fast enough. The few doctors left had to drag themselves from their messy cots in the clothes they wore from the day before.

Izzy exhaled, stress already prickling her cheeks.

She took a seat at the ward reception desk, stabbed on her computer and kicked her bag under the table. After a moment, the screen glowed and Izzy realised that the system was up and running once more after last week's black out. They had resorted to paper filing to keep track of patients, medication and treatments. So today her job had doubled as Izzy had to input all last week's data along with anything new. Thank goodness the NHS was no longer completely free to everyone, otherwise her job would have been impossible. Before she could begin, however, Izzy picked up the phone and dialled an internal number.

"Sexual Health Clinic," came a stiff voice at the other end.

"I have a surgical appointment today," Izzy said, her hand cupping the receiver, "Is the doctor in today?"

"Not today. Try tomorrow," the clipped voice replied.

"But … but … I've been trying for days now, it'll be too late soon. Is anyone else there who could do it?"

"How many health credits do you have?"

"Well, none, my boyfriend used them for his leg surgery. But I…"

The voice sighed. "If you had credits, I might have been able to persuade the nurse practitioner to fit you in. But no credits, no real chance. Sorry."

"Can I get pills? Induce it?"

"Hah!" the voice snorted. "Pills went long ago. You're lucky I've answered the phone. My best advice is to come down and wait for a surgeon. First come, first served."

"I can't afford the time to come and wait all day!" she hissed.

"Choice is yours," the voice shrugged.

A dark blue figure arrived at the desk in front of her and Izzy looked up. Silhouetted in the only bright lights left in town, was Callie Sharp, the Charge Nurse. She dropped a substantial pile of files into Izzy's in tray and sighed deeply. Around her neck was a stethoscope and her uniform was crinkled and stained. Izzy replaced the receiver and forced a smile.

"Hi, Cal. Aren't you going home soon?" Izzy asked. It was way past handover time for the shift workers.

"There's no-one to cover. I have to stay." Callie yawned and tried to pin her hair back into its bun.

"You need to sleep. Little Josh needs you at home." Izzy spoke softly but was unprepared for what came next.

Callie burst into tears. Izzy jumped up and led the older woman to a seat beside her and offered a tissue.

"No he doesn't!" Callie sniffed, "They left last night. My husband took him to Belgium." She spoke quietly into her mask, almost a whisper.

"But, how?" Izzy asked, quietly. The border with Belgium was the tightest of all.

Callie burst into fresh tears and covered her face. From beneath her fingers she mumbled, "Trafficked. We paid someone."

Izzy gasped. "But … why?" then realised what a silly question that was. "Isn't that really dangerous?" she tried again but once more realised too late the insensitivity of her question.

"Yes, it is," Callie wiped her nose. "But we had no choice. Josh's insulin isn't covered anymore. We had to ration it and he got so sick. So we took the decision for them to leave. I couldn't go. I couldn't leave my other boys." Callie also had two teenage sons, both at work in the co-op croft just outside town. She relied on them for most of her food now. "They will be ok. They'll claim refugee status when they get there."

If they get there, Izzy thought as Callie got up once more and began her rounds. With no doctor in sight and a nurse shortage again this morning, she had to diagnose, prescribe, treat, feed, care for and discharge all the patients in this ward and the one next door. Izzy watched her go and admired her ability to just keep on going. Every life in here was in her hands.

Another visitor loomed into Izzy's view. "Help you?" she asked before she looked up.

"I've got a patient for you," came the gruff reply. Izzy peered at three men in front of her. The one in the middle was slumped, his eyes swollen shut, blood trickling from his lips. On both sides, were armed guards who usually stood outside the main doors. Drug and equipment theft was now a 'shoot on sight' crime and the guards were busy men. They were holding the middle man up, one under each arm.

"Holy shit!" Izzy cried, as she stood up, "Callie!" she called, "Callie! Blood!"

Callie hurried round the corner. "What the hell are you doing?" she yelled, "Take him to A and E!"

"Can't," said one guard as he dropped the injured man into a plastic chair, "They're full."

"Already?"

"Only one doctor, one nurse and all the triage beds are full from last night. They told me to bring him up here."

Callie wiped her face. "Ok, get him into a bed, over there, room 13. Izzy, can you come help me please?" and she raced off to get an emergency supplies trolley.

The two guards hoisted him unceremoniously from the chair and dumped their cargo into an unmade bed and made to leave.

"Whoa! Just a minute!" Izzy called, "What happened to him?"

One man shrugged. "Car drove up outside, door opened, and they shoved him out. The usual. Happens all the time. Don't want to pay a hospital bill so they ditch the unfortunate bastard and leave." Both guards left the ward as Callie returned with gloves and aprons and a bowl of water.

"Sir? Sir? Can you hear me?" she asked as she pulled on blue gloves. The man groaned and drew up his legs to his middle. He was conscious, then.

"Do you know where you are?" she asked. He shook his head, eyes still closed.

"You're in the infirmary, Edinburgh. You were found injured. What's your name?"

"Steven," he managed to whisper.

"Steven, do you know what happened to you? Can you remember?" Callie moved through a series of well-practised tests, checking for consciousness and injury.

"They jumped me. Beat me up. Three or four of them." Steven croaked. His eyes fluttered open.

"Do you remember who it was?" Izzy began wiping blood from his face.

"It's usually banter, but not today. Not after … ow!" Steven jumped as Callie gently manipulated his nose. It was most likely broken.

"Sorry," she said but continued. They was little time for sympathy.

"After what, Steven?" Izzy asked.

He sat up slightly, rubbing his chin. "Little bastards, they are, in the warehouse. Rangers' fans. We have a joke about Man 'U' and how my guys would destroy Rangers any day, and we have a laugh." His voice was hoarse and faltering.

"So did your team beat them or something?" Izzy asked. She wasn't football's biggest fan.

"No. Haven't you heard?" Steven's voice caught and he cleared his throat and coughed up bloody phlegm into a bowl.

Callie and Izzy exchanged looks. "Heard what?" Izzy asked.

"I'm English," Steven pointed out.

"Yes, I can tell that," Izzy replied, nonplussed.

"I think you need to turn on the TV. What channels can you get here now?"

Callie reached for the remote and clicked on the TV over the bed. It blinked into life, the familiar face of Europe Minister Fran MacDonald beside the First Minister Andrea Taylor and other suited and uniformed officials. "I don't see ..." Izzy began but he shushed her. "Listen," he said.

"... have made it clear that there will be very few exceptions to the rule. Deployment of troops will begin as soon as possible to secure not only our country but our very existence."

"What the hell have they done?" Callie asked as a cold shiver gripped Izzy's spine.

CHAPTER 4

9th November (8.45am)

Lewis watched as the headmaster took a seat and cleared his throat. The room fell silent almost immediately, as if they knew something was not quite right.

He began with a catch in his throat.

"Now, things are a bit different here from a couple of years ago, I'm sure you'll agree."

There were murmurs from his staff.

"And I'm afraid I'm not here to make it any easier today."

Tuts. Grumblings of 'now what?' and 'couldn't be much worse'.

Brian began reading.

"From the Office of the First Minister, Holyrood, to all national, regional and local government staff," he began, in a shaky voice. The room fell silent.

"In light of the no-deal Brexit result of 2021, Covid infection controls imposed by Europe, compounded by the sanctions for terrorist acts against the European Union in Strasbourg in April, Europe has completely closed its doors to New Britain citizens. In addition, the newly formed government of The United Republic of Ireland, since Ulster seceded from the UK, as was, in 2023, have also closed the sea borders to New Britain and have been detaining all New Britain citizens at their point of entry, processing them either as illegal immigrants or now, as refugees."

"Lucky bastards!" someone called.

"What, the Irish or the refugees?"

"Both," came a grumbled reply and several people nodded agreement.

Brian took a deep breath, took off his glasses and looked around the room.

"Hasn't been such plain sailing for us, huh?"

More murmurs. "Yeah, how come Ireland get their IndyRef and get out of the UK almost immediately? We voted out a year ago and got taken to court. What gives?" Murmurs, tuts, agreements.

"It's because of the rough deal they got in Brexit, isn't it? Border controls in the sea. And the Republic of Ireland were willing to take them in. And all the violence," came one reply.

"And they've got Europe to back them up."

"They've got more balls than us…"

"More guns too…"

More murmurs.

"New Britain is hurting." Brian explained, patiently. "Westminster have lost Ulster and are not prepared to let go of Scotland that easily. We're in a frosty period, to say the least. When the Irish parties left Westminster and with Scottish parties barely engaging with London, we all knew what would happen, with the rise of the New Nationalists. We don't know if it was actually The New Nationalist Party in Westminster who ordered the bombing in Strasbourg, but look at all the sanctions they've slapped on us; trade, movement, arms, even food."

"We know all this Brian, basically life is a pile of crap and everyone has deserted us. But what's this got to do with …"

"I'm getting to it. So now we are under sanctions, with everyone with a claim on foreign residency running for the exits. We've lost so many students and staff, friends and colleagues to this situation, that I have stopped counting. Even with London legally 'reserving' some jobs and tightening exit rules, people are still leaving in thousands, legally and illegally. Who would have thought *that* would ever happen, huh?"

More nods and murmurs.

"*Reserved occupation* just means political prisoner, Brian, and they know it!" called an angry voice.

"Thank God the government never cared about teachers," Lewis called and a few shrugged. "This is having a real impact on the kids, Brian," he continued, "We've got parents getting passage for kids and sending them off alone to new countries. This morning I heard the word 'dowry', for God's sake, just so someone could get their daughter out! When's it going to end?"

"Yeah, I'm pretty tired of my wages getting cut every month too," came a voice.

"… and getting threatened by the thugs in uniform, who seem to be multiplying, by the way!" called another, "How many people have licence to shoot people now? It's like bloody America!"

"There's barely any food, the woods are being cleared of dead branches for fuel!"

"My life ended when Starbucks had to close!"

Several laughed at this, but Brian wasn't finished yet. He replaced his glasses on his face.

"I don't think this is going to end soon," he sighed and his hands shook as he smoothed down the letter in his hands. The room hushed once more and he continued to read.

"Given the positive vote in the second legal Scottish Independence Referendum, where 81% of all Scottish residents voted to leave the UK or New Britain, as it is now, and the fact that this result has never been heeded or acknowledged by Westminster, and they have instigated court proceedings against us as a country which were recently upheld, we, as a nation have no choice but to take steps to secure our own future."

Brian's throat was dry but he pushed on. The silence was absolute.

"Public Notice is hereby given that the National Registration Regulations having the force of law, require - one, that all males and females having reached majority (16 years and three days) and being no more than 32 years and six months be registered for compulsory draft into the Scottish Armed Forces."

The whole room gasped. Voices rose, some stood up, a few began to cry.

"There's no such thing as the 'Scottish Armed Forces', Brian!" Don said.

Brian looked up at his old friend. "There is now," he said.

"Two …" he continued, more loudly to reach over the noise. Staff shushed others until the room was silent once more, "… All people in receipt of this notice must submit themselves for medical examination before a Medical Board at the nearest approved centre. You must bring formal ID in the form of passport or driver's licence.

"Three - you must comply within three days of this notice. Any attempt to avoid the draft will be punishable by imprisonment and the Security Units, under the Security Force Act 2023, have hereby been given licence to shoot anyone they think is impeding the rule of law in this matter."

Brian's voice began to waver.

"Four - exceptions will be made only for pregnant women or those who care for children under 12, the sole female head of a household, the officially physically disabled or incapacitated and their carers or those in basic public service or healthcare roles. No exceptions will be made for those accessing mental health services or addiction clinics."

"Yeah!" Lewis raised his fist to the air, "Public service role! That's us!" Lewis blew out a huge sigh of relief. Playing 'army' was not his thing. The room erupted into brief, confused cheers.

"No. It's not," Brian replied, firmly. The room quietened once more. "As of now, all schools are disbanded. All teachers under 32 years are to report for draft alongside everyone else. There's a list of reserve's but it's the usual. Doctors, nurses, sewage and water engineers, farmers."

"Did you say girls and women too? From *sixteen years old?*"

Brian nodded. "Looks like all the calls for equality have paid off." He paused, "After a fashion," he shrugged in disbelief.

The room was in uproar. Everyone spoke at once, each voice demanding answers. Brian fixed his eyes on his letter. It had been sent via courier that morning with strict instructions to be read at a certain time. He wasn't old enough to remember any kind of land war, only distant, faceless conflicts in far off lands. Now he was ordering his staff to lay down their pens and report for firearms. He fought the desperate urge to weep.

Through the noise, he heard his oldest colleague and friend speak. Don Jack was a quiet man who could keep a class of teenage boys in thrall with good humour, common sense, and a strict code of conduct.

"Brian," he began, and the room immediately began to quieten.

"Who exactly are we going to be fighting?"

The room returned to silence.

.oOo.

It had been snowing for hours that freezing November morning. In the weak light that appeared at dawn, the Scottish based troops, now ringfenced as the newly created Scottish Border Force could barely make out if they were standing in Scotland or England. It was a border that had only nominally existed before today so there were no walls or fences or access gates or checkpoints. It was just open fields, marshland, hills and back yards. But the orders were to secure it, whatever it was, and the hastily deployed battalion got to work. By the time Izzy switched on the TV in the hospital and Brian read the letter in school, and the First Minister delivered the address to the nation, there was a hard, impenetrable border between Scotland and England for the first time in the history of both nations.

CHAPTER 5

9th November (9.45am)

Fran MacDonald followed the Cabinet members back inside Bute House, the official residence of the First Minister, and a cacophony of noise followed them. Journalists shouted questions at their disappearing backs and protestors yelled their displeasure at the announcement. The group hurried through the building into the Cabinet Room with curtains drawn and all non-essential staff dismissed and the noise abated as they shut the door behind them.

The First Minister, the Right Honourable Andrea Taylor MSP, took her seat at the head of the long table in front of a roaring fire in the huge stone fireplace and her Cabinet Secretaries followed suit. Junior Ministers took seats and sat where they could, Fran MacDonald included. She looked around at all the people who joined them today; highly decorated uniformed officers, suited officials from the civil service, experts from the University. The room was heaving with people.

Andrea Taylor began with a gracious smile. "I want to point out, to those of you who still don't agree, that this is *not* a declaration of war ..."

The sound of breath being sucked in was followed by murmurs which grew into disagreements, opinions and finally a crescendo of noise.

"Then what is it, Andrea? What have we just done?" The voice of Todd Horton, Minister for Rural Affairs and the Environment, cut through the melee. He continued. "I never agreed to close the borders. We've been railroaded! You have made a unilateral decision! There was no democracy at work here. And as for a

Scottish draft, well that sounds like war to me!" his face quivered with anger.

Others around him nodded and awaited her reply.

Andrea held up her hands and made to speak once more but was drowned out by multiple others.

"Let her speak!" came a shout.

"We've done nothing but escalate tensions," Todd continued.

"It was necessary! We discussed this move at length and you lost, that's all!" came a shrill voice behind Andrea Taylor's chair. "We need to protect ourselves from the English grabbing that we *know* is going to start soon!"

"Yes, we discussed it, but we certainly didn't vote! You know how many of us vehemently still oppose the draft and the border moves! You can't just do this, Andrea!" Todd stood up and banged the table in front of him.

Andrea's smile froze to her lips. "We are protecting our resources, Todd," she said, through gritted teeth.

"Our resources are *their resources!* We are still one country!" he cried..

"We voted out last August. We are all but separate now, but they just won't let go!" another supporter behind Andrea Taylor's seat spoke.

"It's *illegal* Andrea! We have annexed a part of New Britain *illegally!* It's an act of terrorism, almost!" Todd cried, and the rest of the room erupted into shouts and argument..

Fran MacDonald watched the uproar from the back of the room and rubbed her throbbing head. When the noise died down a little, Andrea Taylor looked levelly at the angry faces around the table then turned and addressed Fran directly.

"Are the Scotland Office on their way home?" she asked her.

"As you requested, I gave the order to leave an hour ago," said Fran. "They're in the air now and will land in about 45 minutes at Edinburgh Airport." Other heads turned towards her.

"You evacuated the Scotland Office? All of them? From Westminster?" Todd asked.

Fran nodded. "We had to keep everything from them until the last minute. I couldn't tell them our plans because we know how the New Nationals like to keep tabs on all the phones. I've pulled out every Scottish official and representative in England."

"What about all the poor bastards who just work in England? Who gets them out?" Todd said, "They're targets now, every single one of them!"

Andrea Taylor answered smoothly, "We have seen Scottish people returning to their homeland, along with English spouses, children and friends. Anyone still in England, a year after the IndyRef success, clearly doesn't want to be here …"

"But you can't know that!" a loud voice cried.

"So anyone still the wrong side of the border is, I'm afraid, staying there. For now, anyway."

The room rumbled with mumbling voices. Fran's headache eased slightly as the shouts subsided but her hands still trembled. She eyed everyone in the room and wondered how many of them actually knew yesterday that this was going to happen. Fran knew. Taylor had very much kept her in the loop and Fran sat there now feeling more important and more central to events than ever before. She was ready for this challenge. She glanced at Andrea Taylor, who was already looking at her Junior Minister.

"Fran, get out of here. Go to the Airport and pick them up. Take three cars. I want to begin our bid to re-join the EU and you're an essential part of that." Andrea Taylor barked her orders, then turned back to the room.

"Me?" Fran asked. "You want me to actually go get them?"

Andrea Taylor turned her head to look at her junior minister and frowned. "Of course, you!"

"But, I," Fran stammered and looked towards the large, netted windows, "I'll … they'll …" she moved closer to the First Minister, "It's not safe."

"Of course it's not," Taylor stared at her. "But it's even less safe if they bloody well walk." She turned back to the room and smiled. Fran was duly dismissed. She left the room.

"Ladies and gentlemen." The First Minister began, "Please, take your seats. Todd, please give me a chance to explain." She gestured to his seat and he and others sat back down, murmurs subsiding.

"We are currently deploying all Scotland based troops at all strategic points along the border, making it all secure. I have taken steps to ensure that all water, food, energy resources and communications are kept running as normally as possible. They are all secure, manned and safe." She paused. "We have troops on the shores of Gare Loch. They will ensure that any attempts by the English Army to retain the … military hardware within, will be strongly rebuffed."

The room was now silent. No-one quite knew what to say.

"Now," she said with a beam, "Someone get Francois Janvier on the phone for me. Scotland and the EU have much to discuss."

She stood, lifted her hands in a gesture of finality and dismissed everyone from the room.

.oOo.

Five minutes later the room was empty and as the door closed on the last person leaving, Andrea Taylor stood and walked over to the window. The grey skies over Edinburgh were giving way to bursts of sunshine and she smiled at the sheer beauty of her beloved city. Since she was a small girl growing up in Stockbridge, Andrea Taylor knew she wanted to end up here, in this house, the official residence of the First Minister of Scotland. And thanks to her doctorate in politics from the university of Glasgow and a lifetime protesting every pro-Scottish cause up until her election as leader of the Scotland for All party, she could now shape the future any way she saw fit. Behind her, the door opened. It was her private secretary, Damian.

"First Minister," he began,

"Ah, do you have Commissioner Janvier for me?" she asked, beaming as she strode back towards the desk.

"No, First Minister, he was, uh, indisposed. But I do have the Home Secretary on the phone."

Taylor stared at him, her hand poised over the phone receiver. "Why did you call him? I said Janvier!" she hissed.

"He called here!" Damian protested, then added in a mutter, "Unsurprisingly,"

"What did you say?" she demanded, but he was gone.

Taylor cleared her throat and picked up the phone.

"Andrea Taylor," she said, her voice strong and unwavering.

"What the hell have I just seen, Andrea?" Marcus James, Home Secretary of New Britain shouted down the line.

"Don't pretend you're surprised, Marcus," she scoffed.

"You can't just leave the official political and legal process and amass an army, Andrea, for God's sake!"

"We warned you, Marcus! You deliberately held up our IndyRef result in the courts so that you could grab all our assets before we left. Don't think we didn't know what you were up to!"

"You forget yourself, Taylor," he growled, "All of your assets are our assets too. We have every right to hang on to them. Take down the border, or we will be forced to act. And you won't like it."

"I knew you lot were corrupt to the core, Marcus, and the carnage you invoked in Strasbourg just proves it. No-one in their right mind would want to be associated with your nasty little country or political system. Time to let us go. You lost Northern Ireland, and now us."

"Don't start a fight you can't win, Taylor."

"I don't recall starting anything." She paused. "Recognise our Independence result and let us go. Then we will take down the border. Not before."

"Any divorce takes time, Taylor. Never forget that all you have, you have because of us. Money, power, international influence, none of it is down to your prominent standing in the world. It's all from us. And we will do exactly as we please until you comply. Take down the border, disband that pathetic attempt at an army and wait your damn turn."

"You arrogant son of a bitch," she said through gritted teeth, "No deal, Marcus, the border stays until you let us go. We have legal and political right on our side."

"Have it your way, Taylor, but this will not end well for you. We own you. We have every right to take you and your barbarians down."

Despite all her political training and experience, Andrea Taylor slammed the phone down with a frustrated scream. How dare he! It was New Britain interfering with due process, not Scotland! She'd show him. She'd show all the detractors. Scotland can stand without New Britain hanging onto her coattails. What else did she have to do?

Andrea sat down with a thud.

"Damian!" she yelled. "Get me Janvier! Now! And if anyone else calls, ignore them!"

.o0o.

Izzy and Callie sat on the bed beside Steven, their beaten-up English patient. Callie had given him something for the pain and he lay in relative comfort as the bruises and swelling on his face turned purple. Other ambulant patients and staff joined them to watch the news, no-one wanted to miss a word. The announcement from the First Minister had exploded everything. There were pictures of the new Scotland-England border, a tangle of barbed wire and wooden structures, of patrolling troops with guns, of dogs and police horses at checkpoints. They watched films of traffic, backed up on all the major routes, as the soldiers asked for ID from every car.

"Are they just turning away everyone who's not Scottish?" Izzy asked, but no-one in the room really knew.

"I don't think anyone English in their right mind would try and get in," Steven mumbled through a swollen lip. Izzy looked at him.

"What are you going to do?" she asked.

Steven shrugged. "I live here, innit? My wife, she's from Glasgow. Our kids are both born here. What am I supposed to do?"

"Do you feel safe?"

"Of course I don't! Look at me!" he cried, "But what choice do I have?"

Callie looked at Izzy in despair. "What choice do any of us have?" the older woman asked then stood up. "I think I need to go," she said, and pulled open the door.

"Callie!" Izzy called, "What are you …?" she knocked into the overflowing bin and it slowed her down as she sidestepped the resultant mess.

Callie continued to her office, swept up her bag, dragged off her uniform and changed into her outdoor shoes and clothes.

"Callie, what do you mean?" Izzy appeared at the doorway.

Callie pushed past her into the ward. "You were right, Iz, I should've left with Rory and Josh. My boys will be drafted. I have to go. I have to find a way out."

"Where are you going? To Belgium? I'm no expert but I'd say the EU border patrols will be stepped up after this."

Callie shrugged. "If I were you, Iz, I'd get out too. You and Lewis need to leave. I don't know, but this can only end badly. There'll be bombs and guns and fighting and lots of death. I don't want any of that; to witness it or be a part of it, or have my boys be a part of it. The English, or what is it, New Britain Army is so much bigger than anything we could put together here. They're ten times the size of us. We're going to get slaughtered. If not by violence, then there'll be a massive Covid surge. Everything's changed so much and now this. There's no reason to believe it will get better any time soon. The EU wasn't perfect but look at what we've done to ourselves in the last 5 years. We're torn apart by hate and violence and small, nasty voices preaching destruction. If we stay, there's no telling where it will end. All I know is, Scotland doesn't stand much of a chance …"

Callie and Izzy used their key fobs to open the heavy ward doors. Outside, the long corridor had descended into chaos. People ran into and out of offices and wards, such staff as there were left reasoned with as many people as they could but were overwhelmed. There were screams and fights emanating from behind doors. Izzy stood with wide eyes, panic rising in her chest.

Callie slipped on her coat and shouldered her bag.

"But, Callie, what do I do?" Izzy cried, the tears strangling her throat.

"Whatever you need to," Callie replied with practiced, professional calm.

"But I'm not a nurse!" Izzy choked, "There's no nurses or doctors left! How do I take care of everyone!"

"Izzy, even though it goes against every nursing bone in my body, I'd say, at this point in the game, it's everyone for themselves. Get out and save yourself. If anyone in that ward has family, they'll come for them. Right now, I'm going to save mine, and you should go save yours."

Callie hugged her friend briefly, turned, and ran down the corridor towards the main doors. They were open and Callie ran through them, unlocked her bicycle and began the seven mile journey home to her boys to persuade them to leave everything they ever knew, pack only the essentials and throw themselves on the mercy of the country that only six months ago, they had voted so willingly to leave. There was no way Callie could afford to get them to Belgium. To save her sons, Callie had to go to England.

CHAPTER 6

9ᵗʰ November (10.40am)

Lewis hurried to his classroom and began to throw papers and stationery into boxes. He picked up his diary, a stack of unmarked exams and his pot of red pens. Then he stopped and straightened up. What on earth was he doing? The school had been disbanded, the staff dismissed and the children sent home for the last time for who knew how long? This was not another lockdown, there was no discernible end to it, this was for the foreseeable future. He wrung his hands and glanced around the room. Would the schools ever get back on track? Surely they would, he argued with himself, but maybe ... he bit a nail and fretted for a moment. What now? What next? He was lost. Teaching was all he knew. This school was all he knew.

"Alright, lad?" Don entered the room. He already had his coat on.

"Yeah, Don, no, actually, I don't know what to ..." his voice began to waver and he covered his face.

"Now, lad, come on," Don put his thick arms around Lewis' doughier frame and Lewis began to sob. Don patted his back and Lewis shuddered for a while, the tears coursing down his cheeks.

"When's it going to end, Don?" he sniffed as he finally pulled away.

Don sighed. "Not sure we're through the beginning yet, lad," he said, sadness etched on his face. "The whole world is hanging by a thread, economically and socially." He stopped again. "Like it was before." He looked at Lewis with tired eyes. "War is usually how all this ends."

"What do I do?" He wiped his nose on his sleeve.

"Not sure you have a choice, with the draft."

"But Izzy?"

"Her either."

"What do we do, Don? I mean, how do we live now? I don't know what we are supposed to do."

Don smiled, "None of your shoot 'em up video games prepare you for actual war and mayhem?" he chuckled.

Lewis laughed, "Surprisingly, no. All the zombies I've killed, all the bad guys I've blown away and here I am blubbing that I might need to do it in real life. You'd think I was prepared for this dystopia."

"No-one was prepared for this. None of us can fully understand the impact of our actions. We are very much on our own. The only person who can save you, is you. Good luck, son." He patted Lewis on the back, shouldered his backpack and strode from the room.

Lewis decided to walk home. He couldn't face the bus again and his leg was feeling ok enough to get him there. If not, he thought, I'll just sit and wait it out. Maybe one of his colleagues would drive past, he hoped, but wasn't holding his breath.

He walked into the near deserted streets. The kids had scattered with the news that big brothers and sisters or dads or even mums would have to leave and join the Army. *The Army, for God's sake,* he thought, and shook his head. It was surreal, surely, there'd be no fighting ... surely.

Lewis dug his hands into his pockets and quickened his pace. It was so cold and he couldn't wait to put on the bar heater at home. Or just stand over the water as it boiled for tea, or get into a frigid bed and wait for his own body heat to envelop him. As he walked, he became aware of a vehicle driving just off his right shoulder. He glanced around and saw a black Sec Unit van but continued on. He did not want to get into a conversation with them, especially not now.

The Sec Unit, however, had different ideas. The van pulled up just in front of him, on the path, blocking his way. Lewis stopped, his face wary.

"Alright, pal?" A Sec Unit guard opened the van door and jumped down in front of him. He leaned against the van and folded his arms, eyeing Lewis with a sneer.

Lewis returned his gaze. He didn't know what to say. He looked the guard up and down, who was dressed in black with a large belt at his ample middle, not unlike the belts the police used to wear. From it, hung a taser, a nightstick, a radio and a not insubstantial sidearm. He was joined by another man, then another. The three of them stood together in a line, dirty toothed grins on their jowly faces.

"Hi," Lewis managed. He wasn't sure what else to say.

"You, um ... you off to sign up for the draft?" asked the first one, kicking out at a stone. The other two grinned wider.

"I suppose I'll have to," Lewis replied, the sweat now forming on his neck. If he wasn't warm before, he most definitely was now.

"Oh, you suppose, do you?" the man nodded in imitation. He looked at his colleagues. "Then, I *suppose* I have no reason to go ahead and shoot you, do I?" he finished and they all guffawed at the joke, eyes still on their target.

"No, you don't," Lewis said, quietly, and eyed the handgun. He had never seen one up close before, not worn out in public like this. Only in American Cop shows. And once at the airport when he went to Heathrow and there was a policeman with a large automatic weapon over his arm at the security gates. That man had been smiling and friendly, his gun pointed down, and he gave the impression of a man who had been very well trained. The Sec Guard in front of him fiddled with the holster as he peered at Lewis, but his fingers seemed to search the gun as if it were unfamiliar; a new toy and he was itching to use it.

"On your way to the barracks now?" he asked.

"No, going home."

The Sec Guard tutted, shook his head.

"Looks like you've got three days to get out of here, pal," he said then advanced on Lewis. As he approached, he unholstered his gun and held it up, pointing at the sky. Lewis didn't move.

"I don't want to see you round here again, ken?" he said and slowly turned the gun so that the barrel grazed past Lewis' temple. Lewis held his breath, his eyes unblinking. For a moment, no-one moved.

Then a woman turned the corner with a toddler in tow. She stopped and sucked in her breath, gripping the child's hand. The Sec Guard slid his eyes from Lewis to the woman and dropped the gun. He grinned at her, re-holstered his weapon and leaned down to ruffle the boy's hair. The woman pulled back and lifted him onto her hip, turning on one foot to go back the way she came. The Sec Guard turned back to Lewis.

"Get tae fuck," he muttered and waved him away. Lewis obliged immediately and hurried on, hood back up, hands in pockets. Behind him, the Guards bellowed with laughter, then got in the van and drove off.

Izzy arrived home and parked the car in the garage. It was not something they used to do but when all the cars were being stolen, they decided it was for the best. It was old, but it was very useful. She walked into the kitchen, put on a pan of water and sat down with her palms turned to the welcome flames. The journey home had been slow and hazardous with abandoned cars on the road and protestors already throwing rocks and bricks at official buildings. She looked down at her hands, shaking, cracked and dry. No nails. It had been at least a year since she had had a proper set of good quality acrylics. She thought about all those sick people that she had left to their fate and began to cry. She cried a lot recently. She wasn't a nurse, but she knew that without doctors or family, some of them wouldn't make it through tonight.

She went in search of tissues and passed the living room door. Lewis sat, motionless, on the sofa, his cold breath blowing evenly into the air.

"Lewis? I didn't know you were home." She sat down beside him.

"What are we going to do?" he didn't look at her.

"There's a draft. You need to join the Army, Lewis. It's the law." He slumped forward and held his head in his hands. After a moment, Izzy heard him sob.

"It's ok, babes, everyone's in the same boat. It won't be that bad." She rubbed his back.

"It will!" he cried in a strangled voice, "It's fighting and a *war* out there! There's no guarantees I won't die! I'll be killed!"

"There's no guarantee you *will* be killed, either, babes. Come on, there's nothing you can do about it now."

"No! That's the problem isn't it! We have no say! It's like North Korea, we don't have a choice and if we don't do it, the Sec Units hunt you down! Did you know they have a shoot on sight policy for people who don't sign up? Like, the government have agreed to that rule! What the fuck?"

"Doesn't being a teacher mean anything? Get out of it that way?"

"The school has gone," he said, still sobbing. "I have to sign up within three days."

"I know."

"And so do you." His voice wavered.

Izzy paused for a moment, then said, "No, I don't."

"Yeah, you do, Brian read us this letter and it said …" he stopped and looked at her as she slowly shook her head. "What?"

"I'm pregnant."

"Holy shit! I mean great! I mean … um … oh crap, what have we done? Oh, this means … Izzy, how long?" Lewis stuttered through a multitude of feelings as he leapt from his seat and paced the room.

"I've known for about three months," she said levelly.

"But we always said kids were a really bad idea now, with everything that's ..." he waved his arm vaguely at the outside world beyond the window.

"I know! Don't you think I know that!!" she yelled. "I've been trying to get an appointment to get rid of it for weeks now!"

"Why didn't you tell me!?" he yelled back.

"I didn't want to burden you too. I don't want to bring a child into this godawful world right now, but I don't exactly feel like woman of the year either, deliberately destroying our innocent, blameless little 'mistake'!" She dissolved into tears, sniffed and continued more quietly, "The clinic is, like everywhere, overwhelmed and understaffed. It was supposed to be today. I was supposed to do it today. But there's no-one there now. After we heard the news, the whole place just disintegrated. No doctors, no midwives, no nurses, no-one at all. I left people dying, Lewis, starving, bleeding, oh god, and there was nothing I could do. I'm not a nurse ... there was nothing I could do. What could I do?" She sobbed into her dry hands and Lewis slipped his arm around her.

"I wonder if Don knows someone?" Lewis said, quietly.

"Why the hell should Don sort this out? Poor guy has enough to worry about with Maggie being sick and the farm! You think of something for a change!"

Lewis sniffed loudly as he held her tightly.

"Don did say something," he said.

"What?" She looked up at him.

"*Just save you*," he whispered. "The only one who can save you, is you."

CHAPTER 7

9ᵗʰ November (12.30pm)

Fran sat in the arrivals hall and waited, just like everyone else. She could've sat in her car but it was chilly and the coffee from the small cart inside the Terminal was hot, if a little bitter. Every now and again, she felt someone's eyes burrow into the back of her neck. She kept her head down to avoid eye contact. Why on earth she had to pick up Steve and his two colleagues personally was a mystery to Fran - usually, members of the Scotland Office were scooped up by official cars. The drive out west from Bute House had been strange, more cars on the road than usual, piled high with belongings, all headed for the bridge, she presumed, and the relative safety and obscurity of the Highlands.

At least, that's where she'd be going, given the choice. A country girl she wasn't, but she had an idea that it might get tricky in the capital. After that little power display from Taylor, the airport was an incredibly dangerous and exposed place to be for an elected official and she felt the heat rising under her jacket.

Across the large concourse, people scurried around at speed. Some were crying, others rushed to the tv screens to watch the news, over and over. Everywhere she heard the words, "War, we're at war." Crowds of people hurried for the exits and the ones left held small radios or, if they still had them, phones up to their ears. The check-in desks and car hire booths were in chaos, as people abandoned their jobs to go home to ask their loved ones, "What now?"

Fran approached the Air New Britain desk and joined a small group of people who all seemed to be waiting for the same flight. They all spoke at once and the two young men behind the desk struggled to keep them quiet long enough to answer their questions.

One held up his hands, "Look, only flights currently in the air are authorised to land, and anything which originated outside of Scotland has to be turned away."

"So they're still coming?" asked a voice.

"The London flight AN3006 was the last one out of England. After that, every flight will be refused." The young man sounded at the end of his tether.

"Is it going to be on time?" Fran asked them.

"As far as we know yes. Please, people, keep an eye on the arrivals board. They are updated just as often as we are. We have nothing else to tell you. I'm sorry." They both turned back to their screens. Requests were rebuffed with silence and people turned away, but no-one was in a mood to go quietly. The noise rose and Fran watched as police and Security Units moved towards the loudest complaints. She side stepped the crowds and sat in a far corner. At least he was still coming.

Her phone rang.

"Fran!" the distant voice of Steve Lister crackled.

"Steve? You are on the flight, right?"

"Of course I am!" he hissed. "Fran, listen, there's something else. It's in the pack I sent, but I don't know for sure, and I couldn't tell you over the office phone."

"What are you talking about?"

"Andrea Taylor, she sent me to Strasbourg. Before the bombings."

Fran's hand clamped over her mouth. "Steve," she whispered, "You didn't ...."

"No! Of course not! But she sent another man with me, and we ..." The phone crackled and died.

"Steve! Steve! What did you do?" Fran listened for a few more seconds before hearing the message '*The other caller has cleared*'. She looked at the phone and punched his number. '*Number not*

42

available', came the reply. Fran sighed. She'd ask him when he got there. Fran looked at her watch and took a sip of coffee.

Over at the IrishAir desk, a man lay face down on the cold floor and a Sec Guard had a chubby knee in his back. The man swore and spat at the guards surrounding him and in one movement, they hoisted him up and marched him away. She watched them go and then looked back at the arrivals board. It still said, *'On time'.*

Fran sighed and looked at her watch. She had so much to do. Time was running out to get to a safe place. The shit was hitting the fan as she stood there, and she was dangerously exposed to the ire and violence of a disgruntled public. Couldn't Andrea Taylor have sent someone else? Was it really necessary for her to be put at such risk?

Suddenly, the arrivals board blinked into life. It went off momentarily and for a second Fran thought they were going to experience a common but very inconvenient power cut. It flickered on again and Fran saw that every Scotland flight was now delayed. Then she noticed, the flight in the top line, *AN3006 : London City Airport : cancelled.*

Fran frowned. "What the ...?" She stood up and walked to another board. It said the same thing. The London flight, mid-air, right now somewhere over the Lake District, had been cancelled. It didn't make sense. She swiped at her phone and called Steve once more but got the same answer, *"Number not available".* She watched the screen blink then turned to the desks. Everywhere, staff were taking calls and speaking into walkie talkies. The armed police hurried towards the security gates and manned the exits. She swivelled her head and looked through the large glass windows onto the car park. Every vehicle with a siren or flashing lights suddenly burst into life and moved off. The hairs on the back of her neck stood up as she turned back to the urgent, confused noises around her.

Finally, the news hit. On the TV screens dotted around the airport, the New Britain news channel broadcast the breaking story. The flight was lost, presumed shot down over New Britain airspace somewhere near the Scottish border. *Shot down.*

Fran watched, slack jawed, at the screen. Shot down by whom? Why? What did …?

Fran shook her head, started to dial into Bute House, then stopped. Behind her, a group of distressed families wept and shouted, pointed at the staff with menace and screamed for information. One or two people looked in her direction. She knew that at least two people suspected who she was. She had to get out of here. She slipped her phone into her pocket and started for the door. A red-faced man in a football shirt pointed in her direction. Fran looked away, pretended not to notice but quickened her pace. The shouts got louder - seeming to follow her. Fran hurried out of the doors and across the road. She wrestled her keys from her bag and her hands shook as she found the door lock. Behind her, a small mob followed. Fran began to sweat; breathing hard she pulled open the car door and threw herself into the driver's seat. The group reached the door just as she pushed the lock button.

"Aren't you that politician?"

"You're that MacDonald woman!"

"What the hell did you do?"

"Are we at war? With England? Did they shoot down our plane? What the actual fuck …?"

The thumps on the roof and window came thick and fast. Fran started the engine and put her foot down. She had to get through the barriers and that required winding down the window, and she did not relish the idea of a face-to-face confrontation. She screeched around the car park and launched the car over the mini roundabout. She rummaged for her card before realising that the exit barriers were already open for the emergency services to get through.

"Stay up, stay up!" she muttered to the machine as she flew past. The automatic sensor wished her a good day and a safe journey, but Fran had already gone. Behind her, several cars swerved into her lane to follow.

Fran drove out to the main road and joined the carriageway. The cars followed.

"Oh, crap." She sped up. They kept up.

Her breathing quickened and she spent more time glancing in the rear-view mirror than at the road ahead. She hunched over the wheel and gripped it tightly. "Now, what now. What now, what?"

She swerved into a small lane and gunned the large executive government car through small, overgrown roads. There were so few cars on the roads these days that she took more risks than she would have normally, and threw the car around tight, skinny corners, bludgeoning the speed limit. The car flew over a humpback bridge, she screeched to the left. Her entourage followed.

"Leave me alone. *Leave me ALONE!*" she shouted in terror at the rear-view mirror but put her foot down once more, careering right onto the road towards the west.

A few miles later, with superior power and speed in one of the few well-maintained cars still on the road, Fran MacDonald was sure she had lost them. Every check in the rear-view mirror confirmed that she was no longer being followed. She clicked a button on the steering wheel and connected to Andrea Taylors private line.

"Andrea, it's Fran," she spoke loudly over the engine. She was not inclined to stop right now, not even for a phone call.

"Fran, have you heard the news? Where are you?" Taylor's smooth voice did not serve to make Fran feel any more comfortable.

"West Lothian, I think. Heading into the Pentlands"

"Well, what on earth are you doing there?" Taylor's voice raised a notch.

"Escaping a braying mob who wanted my blood! They chased me from the airport."

"I presume you lost them?" Taylor seemed to relax.

"At the moment, I'm very much alone, thank God, on a high moor. Is it true? Was it shot down?"

"Yes, it was shot down. All the remaining members of the Scottish office were on that plane, including your old friend Steve Lister, poor chap. We moved to close the border and it would seem that they retaliated immediately."

"There are questions, Andrea, about Steve. I think we need to talk. I think there was something going on that doesn't sit right. Do you think they wanted him silenced?"

"Oh, most certainly, Fran, how clever are you? Steve was clearly up to no good." Taylor spoke with rounded politician's tones once more.

"What now? What should I do now? Can I get an escort? People are not happy out here, Andrea."

"Well, if I were you, I think I'd stay lost, Fran. For your own safety."

Fran paused. Something in Taylor's tone gave her chills.

"What the hell do you mean?" Fran asked.

"Well, you gave the go ahead for the evacuation. You chose their escape route, and *you* organised their travel. Within a couple of hours of the border closure, we have lost senior officials in a massive act of aggression against the Scottish people. Fran, either you are massively incompetent, or you have a leak in your office."

Fran's jaw dropped. "Are you laying the blame for this plane crash at MY door?"

"Do you want to admit to a leak?"

"No!" Fran squeaked, "I ... I don't actually have a staff left now, I ..."

"So, I think we have our answer."

"Andrea, why would I want to harm anyone in the Scotland Office? Steve was my friend! Why would I, how could I possibly organise for someone to shoot down a plane!!"

"You were snooping around, Fran, you said it yourself. You and Steve were asking awkward questions, and no-one seemed have any answers. Steve was sneaking around in Europe. If anyone got wind of that, well, there are a lot of violent and disaffected people in the world today. Fran, my dear, any one of them could've done it."

There was a pause as Fran momentarily stopped breathing. She blinked back tears.

Then finally, Fran understood. "Am I being set up as the patsy here?" she swallowed.

"Not set up. You are to blame. I need to have my cabinet and country behind me and a dangerous individual such as yourself who cannot keep Scottish citizens safe is not needed."

"… but … I am needed to set up the bid for the EU," Fran groped for reasons to be rescued, to continue to be relevant.

"Not needed. That unfortunate incident over English Airspace has brought them running to us, it's amazing the attention we gathered just from that one perceived act of aggression by an unhinged government which already has blood on its hands after Strasbourg …"

Fran pulled off the road and coasted to a halt. One thought crushed all others.

"Andrea, what did you do?" she asked.

"Just what was necessary."

"Did *you* order the plane shot down?" Fran could barely get the words out through dry lips.

"Of course not," Andrea bristled. There was a pause. "All is fair in love and war and all that, Fran. If we are going to finally get our independence from that broken and evil country, we need to take whatever actions are necessary. This was necessary. In the long run, you'll thank me."

"I doubt that."

"In the long run, Scotland will thank me," Andrea Taylor took a deep breath and sighed.

"I supported you. I supported independence above all else. I can help. Don't do this to me, Andrea. Don't do this to Scotland. There has to be another way. Please." Fran spoke quietly as tears rolled down her cheeks.

There was a pause.

"Goodbye, Fran, and thanks for everything. Take care." She was gone.

Fran switched off the engine and looked around her at the bleak winter brushed farmland of the Pentland Hills. A copse of trees and an abandoned house, Fran knew there was little going on here now, since the sanctions hit. People had moved into towns to get access to food and supplies. No petrol meant no deliveries this far out. Only the hardiest of people remained.

She knew vaguely where she was, but she was a city girl. She'd been born and raised in Edinburgh, holidayed in St Tropez and New York, and worked in Zurich, Brussels and Munich. Farms were foreign to her. When her own government had urged the population to keep chickens and goats to supplement reducing diets after the euro-blockades were enforced, Fran was forced to have her photo taken with a large, bad tempered hen called Cheryl who didn't like being held and wouldn't stop flapping noisily every time the farmer handed the creature to her. Fran had hated it and the disgust was evident on her face in every photo taken. For a while she was trending on twitter as #oldmacdonald and #karmafranchickenKFC and became a meme for a while.

But here she was, alone, hunted by all sides; the English, her own government and the people she served, even though she had done nothing wrong. She was the fall guy. The patsy. She had to hide, and amongst the chickens, sheep and horses of the hills seemed to be her only option.

But who did she know out here? No-one. Except ... she pulled out her blue leather book and opened it up. Letters and notes fell into her lap and she searched through them. She opened the pack from Steve Lister and sifted through the pages. Then she slapped the book shut and sat for a long moment staring into the distance. She started the engine and pulled onto the road once more.

Half an hour later, in the remotest southern reaches of the Pentland Hills, she pulled into an old farm track and stopped, out of sight of the road. This was as far as her car would take her, she would get stuck if she pushed it further. A copse of gnarled trees and an old sheep barn flanked the track ahead but it didn't look like anyone had come through here in weeks. She grimaced and wiped her face dry. Sweat had formed on her cheeks alongside the tears and now dried, making her face cold. She pulled her phone, purse and a bottle of water into her handbag then looked around for other things to take with her. She had a gym bag and a brief full of documents as well as her blue book. She changed into her gym shoes, they were almost unused, and threw her suit jacket into the bag. She pulled on a sweater and got out of the car. With no clue which track to take, Fran headed into the hills with only the vaguest sense of which way to go to find the house, and as she tramped along the muddy path, she began to cry once more.

CHAPTER 8

15th February (8.20pm)
Three Months Later

Sophie McCall finally lost them. She squeezed through a broken window and fell in a heap on the floor of the boys cloakroom. Breathing hard, she still had to fight the urge to retch at the lingering male toilet smell, despite the school being empty for weeks. She opened the door to the corridor and looked out. The lights were off and the school was deserted, just as she suspected it would be. The security units were all usually too old, fat, unfit and stupid to catch a teenager so she was confident she was alone.

Another day, another draft dodge. She wondered how much longer she could stay hidden. The Sec Units were quite happy to shoot on sight so she kept her little trips to the dark hours of the night. She wasn't a coward, she just had a family to look after, with mum getting sick again when they could no longer get medication. She couldn't leave her little brother and sister with mum's unstable moods and outbursts. Despite this, Sophie was still not recognised as an official carer, so her draft call remained active.

Sophie crept stealthily through the cold corridors, her breath piercing the cold air, the steam rising from her oversized jacket. It was her dad's coat but after he left and her puffa zip broke, she claimed it. It had deep pockets; especially useful when you were 'collecting' for the family. She turned a corner and peered into the darkness. So far so good. She tried the door handle, it was freezing on her already cold hands, and it opened easily. She slipped into the Home Economics room and flicked on her torch. It was warmer in here. Some shelves had been cleared but what Sophie was looking for was right there in front of her. Salt. *Thank God,* she mouthed. She gathered up all three packets and shoved them in her pockets.

Sophie closed the door and scanned the room for anything else she might need. A pair of scissors flashed in her torch light and she picked them up, along with a sewing kit.

"String!" she exclaimed out loud and grabbed it. Immediately she froze in fear. She knew there was something not quite right when she walked in and now she realised what it was. It wasn't cold. It was almost pleasantly warm, not normal at all. Suddenly, she knew she wasn't alone.

She swung her torch around the room until it illuminated a bundle of bedding on the floor. On top of the blankets, a baby grimaced a little at the light, then snuffled and wriggled in the makeshift bed falling quickly back to sleep. Sophie was astounded, who would leave a baby here alone?

"Hello?" she called softly, stepping closer.

"Hi Soph," came a voice from behind her and Sophie let out a surprised squeal as she turned around.

"Aaron! What are you doing here?" she squeaked, and lit up his face with the torch, "Why is Amy here?"

"Warm. Warmer than home. Besides ..." he sat down next to his baby sister, "If I'm here, they can't find me. My next-door neighbour said they raided my house one day when I was away, so I know they're still coming for me." He had hung wet underwear on the oil radiator beside him.

"The draft?" Sophie snapped off her torch as Aaron switched on a small lamp.

He nodded and looked unhappily at his fingers, twisting at his socks.

"If you're not presenting for the draft, they'll put you in jail. They'll *shoot* you!"

He shrugged. "What would they do with Amy? Where would she go? I wouldn't see her again; dad can't get back from Jamaica and Mum's been gone months ..."

"But the Sec units, they'll find you, they'll …"

"I know what they'll do. Remember when I was arrested at school? Useless bastards left the door unlocked, so I escaped. I've been dodging them ever since and now I'm here. So now I'm a wanted man but I just can't leave her. Anyway, what are you doing here? You're over 16 too."

Suddenly they both heard the bang of a door closing nearby. Sophie sucked in her breath and Aaron gathered up his sister, preparing to hide in the store cupboard behind him. They both stared at the door. Sophie switched off the lamp.

A torch light swayed in the corridor beyond. Footsteps creaked on the linoleum floor. The door handle moved slowly. Aaron silently moved to the store cupboard, dragging Amy with him on her blanket. He closed the wooden door with a practiced tug and held it shut as they sat in the darkness with the sleeping baby between them. Sophie hugged her knees and stared at Aaron through the gloom, her terror-widened eyes unblinking. He placed his spare hand onto her arm to calm her and she gripped at his fingers.

The classroom door opened and a man entered. On his shoulder was a large bag, already half full of stolen equipment; a laptop, jars of chemicals and powders, seeds, a first aid kit, bottles of water and old lab coats. He moved quickly around the room, opened another bag and began to fill it with paper, pens, fabric … suddenly he stopped and mumbled to himself. He strode to the cupboard and threw open the doors, then jumped backwards and fell onto his bag in shock. The cupboard flooded with light and Sophie and Aaron squinted at the change.

"What the hell …!" Lewis exclaimed, "What are you both doing here?" he cried, "You almost killed me!" He stood up and brushed off his trousers.

"Shh! Keep your voice down!" Aaron hissed, and indicated the baby.

"Sorry, but … why are you in the cupboard?" Lewis stood back.

"Why do you think?!" Sophie rolled out of her hiding place and stood up.

"Draft?" he asked, although he knew already. Both of his ex-pupils were old enough to be called up.

"Why aren't you drafted?" Aaron asked. "You're not that old, are you? Is it your bad leg?"

"I have been called." Lewis pulled a crumpled piece of paper form his pocket. "Went for my medical back in November. *Pending review*, it said, so I had to wait. Until now. Got the all clear today. Have to turn up tomorrow in Edinburgh. Which is why ..." he stopped.

They had all heard the noise. The sharp sound of shattering window glass muffled by the heavy closed door.

Shouts. Male voices. Police. Sophie gripped her coat.

No. Worse. Sec Units.

.oOo.

Lewis opened the door and peered out. It was still dark. The corridor looked deserted. He had to get out of here. There was still a chance to escape. He slipped from the room and the students stared wide eyed as he left without a word.

Lewis crept as fast as he could along the corridor, ducking at windows and listening at corners. He reached the front office and slipped inside. On the wall was a small metal box, where the master keys were held. It was open as Lewis knew it always was. He hooked some keys and slipped them in his pocket then withdrew back towards the classroom. He relaxed a little, that was the easy part. Around the last corner, Lewis exhaled and ran for the door.

Just then, torch beams swept around the corner behind him and briefly illuminated his face. He heard one of the men shout.

"Up here!" Footsteps, turning to run.

"Oh shit," Lewis squeaked and took off at top speed. The adrenaline kept the pain in his leg at bay as he sprinted (boy, it had been years since he had sprinted anywhere) along the corridor, past the home economics room door and through the library.

They followed him, three, maybe four pairs of stomping feet. Lewis darted through the shelves and launched himself down the back stairs which led to the kitchens. The torches followed. There were three doors he could choose from there and he made a quick decision to take the boiler room exit. He had his school key fob and he pressed it to the plate. The door opened and closed swiftly behind him. There was no way they could follow without an official key. Lewis crouched down behind the huge heating pipes, breathing hard. The torch beams shone in a confused jumble in the kitchens beyond as the men ran and disappeared through the door to the refectory. Their shouts subsided; the footsteps grew fainter. Lewis continued to breathe hard although he was no longer out of breath. His heart thumped audibly.

After a minute, Lewis opened the door and listened. He couldn't afford to sit there for long, he had to get out of here. Neither the draft nor the jail alternative appealed to him. Everyone else he knew had been swept up in the initial push for draftees and two of his colleagues reluctantly left for Dreghorn Barracks only two days after Brian read out the notice in school. Lewis said he would meet them there and they'd all do it together, but when it came to it …

Scores of his kids disappeared off the streets and he presumed they had all left to join up. He often felt conspicuous as the only one left, but he had his 'letter' which he waved at grumpy old ladies or disgruntled veterans when they asked why he was still hanging around here when his country needed him.

He was grateful Izzy didn't have to go, despite the growing problems she would face with a new-born. She would be alright without him; her pregnancy had been smooth so far. There were government appointed doctors in those new … centres – Lewis couldn't bring himself to say the word 'refugee' - and other women in their neighbourhood who'd had kids before, so she'd be fine giving birth, at least, that's what he kept telling himself.

He didn't know what to do, or how to raise a baby, so he was much better off out of the way. She didn't need him. They always argued. They barely had enough food for themselves so if he left … The very idea of being a father filled him with sheer terror. So here he was … Lewis swallowed a sob and began to tiptoe out of the boiler room.

He closed the door quickly and headed through the refectory. He gripped the van keys stashed in his pocket and crept along the gym corridor towards the back car park where all the school vans were parked. They weren't used often but Lewis knew Don had been keeping them serviced. He stopped, heard voices. No, they were upstairs. He ran on, still on tiptoe, as quietly as possible. More shouts and footsteps. Lewis stopped at the external fire door and checked to see if the alarm was set. It looked clear and he grabbed the cold steel fire door rail.

No. He stopped himself. They might be out there parked alongside his only escape.

He gripped the rail again and made to push it outwards but his subconscious spoke more loudly this time. He had brought the Sec Units to the door. They must've followed him. Now he could escape but Sophie and Aaron would be caught. Thrown to the wolves. All because of him.

His hands squeezed the rail tighter. "Shit. Just save you, just save you." He grimaced, trembling, and pushed the door open to creep out into the darkness. He saw the three school vans parked neatly together and held up the keys to press the unlock button. This was the last gamble. One of the vans twitched and blinked for a split second, but it was enough.

"Over here!" a man's voice yelled. "They're taking the vans!"

Lewis sucked in his breath in terror and had no choice but to run back into the school. He didn't stop to close the door behind him which would have slowed down his pursuers, but instead he whimpered and sobbed as he ran towards the library. Then he slowed. He heard shouts but they seemed confused, and he was sure they took a wrong turning.

He moved silently back through the library and tiptoed along the corridor to the home economics room. He heard nothing now except the rumble of the occasional car outside. The heating was off, the pipes were cold and still.

Had the Sec Units gone? As he opened the door to home economics, he heard a faint rustle before he whispered, "It's only me."

The room rustled again as Sophie and Aaron emerged from the shadows.

"We thought you'd left us!" Sophie hissed.

"No, I, uh, no, they chased me. I got a van key, but when I tried to unlock it …" Lewis sat on the floor and breathed heavily. He hadn't had this much exercise since he was forced to run on sports day last year.

"Unlock it?" Sophie whispered. Realisation crossed her face. "Unlock it? So you *were* going to leave us behind?" she squeaked as quietly as her growing anger would allow.

"Of course not! I was …" he breathed hard and the question remained unanswered.

"Come on," Aaron beckoned, "Bring as much as you can carry. We're getting out of here. If they're at the back, we'll try the front."

"I'm not going with him!" Sophie growled, "He was going to leave us! Bring the Sec Units here then leaves! Fucking coward!"

"Soph, we don't have a choice," Aaron warned, "… and he's the only one who can drive."

Sophie rolled her eyes and tutted. "Whatever," she mumbled and picked up her bag.

Lewis hoisted himself up with a groan, shouldered his bags and grabbed as many things as he could within reach. With Aaron leading, they cautiously tiptoed down the corridor to the main front doors. Lewis was about to press his fob to the pad when Sophie stopped him.

"No! Look! There they are!" Outside, yellow lights on top of blue Sec Unit vans flashed and blinked. The three ducked down to consider options.

"So they're surrounding the school! Shit." Aaron whispered.

"They might not be near the vans now," Sophie spoke.

"Maybe. Ok, let's go. Try the vans," Aaron gestured the way.

"Through the gym?" Sophie suggested.

"No, there's a lock and chain on the outside," Lewis murmured, chewing at his nail. Sweat trickled down his trembling cheeks. "But the Science fire doors," Lewis said. "They're open, and not alarmed ... I was there a few ..." he stopped as Sophie stared at him.

"Damn, that's miles away!" Aaron sighed.

They skirted the corridors as fast and quietly as they could. They could hear muffled shouts and footsteps upstairs in Home Economics and knew that Aaron's hideout had been found.

"Fuck, let's get out of here!" Sophie hissed and began to sprint towards the science department. She barrelled through several heavy doors and left them open for the men to follow. Aaron ran gingerly, his sister was awake now and he didn't want to jolt or hurt her. And he definitely did not want her to start crying. In the last long corridor, Sophie sped up.

"Careful, Sophie!" Lewis called, "We don't know if the Sec Units ..." but it was too late and as Sophie shoulder charged her way through the fire door into the back carpark, as the boom of the flung door filled the air.

"Shit!" Lewis threw himself down the steps to the vans once more as he tried to read the registration number on the keys in his hand.

"Which one is it!" Aaron called, eyeing three dormant minibuses. New shouts behind them. "Which one?! Quick!"

Lewis pressed the locking button on the key fob and a van winked at them once more. "Middle one!" Lewis cried between heaving breaths. He slid along the side of the minibus and tried the driver's side door. It was open. He threw himself into the seat and stabbed the keys into the ignition. Meanwhile, Sophie yanked open the back doors and Aaron stepped in, clutching his sister to his chest. They both held big bags on their shoulders, and Aaron held the oil radiator under one arm. Sophie pulled the doors shut as Lewis turned the key. The ageing minibus had not been started in at least four months and possibly a lot longer, and it fussed and groaned. He tried again and the starter motor sounded optimistic but refused to catch. "Come on!" he said through gritted teeth and bounced in his seat. Sophie and Aaron arranged themselves into seats.

The windows in the science department glowed with approaching torches. They were definitely being pursued now.

"What is the problem?" Sophie hissed. "Let's go!"

"It won't start!" Lewis said and tried again.

The Sec Guards emerged from the fire doors and ran towards them.

"Shit," Sophie said through gritted teeth and frantically felt for the seatbelt. She flung it off, opened the door and threw herself out of the van.

"Sophie!" Lewis yelled, "Get back here!" The engine finally sputtered to life and coughed and hitched.

The Sec Guard yelled and raced towards the van, sidearm drawn and waving around in the night. He was an older, puffy looking man and was out of breath from his evening's shift. He reached the van and was about to open the back doors when a hammer blow slammed down on his outstretched hand. Sophie drew the baseball bat back again and this time, with a primeval yell from the bottom of her stomach, she swiped it sideways, connecting with his face with a crunching blow. The Guard fell to the ground and lay motionless. She stood above him, breathing hard. Nope, he wasn't getting up in a hurry. She looked around for others, but they were still inside. Closer now, but not upon them. Sophie held the bat, almost disappointed there weren't more people to take her anger out on.

The van popped and coughed until it maintained a regular rhythm. Lewis clenched his fists in triumph and began to back out of the parking spot.

"Sophie!" he cried, "Get in!"

Aaron echoed Lewis' shouts and opened the door for her to jump in.

She dived back into the van and Aaron shut the door.

They drove out of the parking lot and out onto the streets without checking the road. Cars were a rare sight, especially after curfew, and Lewis crossed his fingers for luck. He threw the van around corner after corner until he finally screeched onto the main road.

"Uh-oh," Aaron muttered, squinting out of the back window.

Lewis looked in the rear-view mirror. There were lights following them. It must be the blue vans of the Sec Units. He pressed the accelerator, and the van speeded up but protested. The lights behind them crept closer. Lewis' pulse began to race. If they were caught, it was the draft. Or jail. Oh shit, thought Lewis, this night has not turned out how I expected. Escape had sounded easy until he actually tried it.

He went as fast as the van was able. The following Sec Unit remained behind them, despite being a younger, faster machine. After a while, Lewis frowned and loosened his grip on the wheel. Was it following or chasing? Suddenly, the vehicle behind them exploded in a burst of light and sound, as its sirens blared and yellow lights blinked on and off.

"Holy shit," he wailed and pressed his foot to the floor with force, although it made little difference. The Unit was gaining on them.

"Go faster!" shouted Aaron, twisting in his seat. Sophie curled into a ball and buried her head.

"It's as fast at it'll go!" Lewis cried and looked again in the mirror. The van began to shake. It was right behind them. Then it pulled out, overtook and sailed past. It didn't stop in front of them, but carried on, speeding away. So it wasn't following them, Lewis gaped. He loosened his grip on the steering wheel and pulled his foot up slightly. In the distance, they could now see three, four cars all wailing and flashing, going in the same direction. They were passed by another and another; vans, cars, troop carriers, lorries, all screaming with light and sound. They appeared, as if from nowhere and then were gone.

"What the hell is going on?" Sophie said quietly.

Lewis switched on the radio and tried to find a station. Eventually, on the AM channel, they found Radio Four, the only thing really left on the airwaves this time of night. It wavered and crackled but behind the static they heard the news. For weeks it had been a roundup of minor skirmishes and troubles along the border, between English troops and the Scottish draft army. There were stories of multiple shootings of draft dodgers and refugee boats sinking or being intercepted by EU warships. There were reports of meetings between nations to try to calm the waters, with the United Nations overseeing and refugee and aid agencies assisting. Andrea Taylor was usually on, with her unique brand of propaganda.

Tonight, however, it was something new. Tonight, New Britain wanted it to be over. They wanted to crush the insurgent Scots. Tonight, there was talk of invasion.

CHAPTER 9

15th February (10.05pm)

The alarm in Don's pocket sounded. He reached in and switched it off then pulled out his phone and viewed the live footage. A van slid sideways across the muddy track by the bottom field and he could see black smoke puffing from the exhaust. He didn't need audio, he could hear the van revving hard from the farmhouse. Quickly, Don shut down the perimeter lights and switched off the generator.

"Maggie," he called, candle in hand, "I think we've got visitors, love."

Don's wife sat up in bed with her crochet in her lap. She smiled at him as he entered the room and sat on the duvet.

"Good visitors or bad visitors?" she asked. "Is it Eva? Has she come back?"

"No, my darling, I don't think Eva will be back soon. One day, maybe." He patted her frail leg.

"Do I need to do anything?" she asked and reached over to the bedside drawer.

Don held out his hand to stop her. "No, love, not that. We're ok," he said quickly, "I think I know who it is, and it'll be fine."

"Are we safe?"

"Yes, love, we're all safe." he replied.

Maggie withdrew her hand and Don let go his breath.

"Is it that funny woman?"

"No, my love, she's still upstairs."

"I don't like her, Don."

Don looked at his wife of many years. She may have had a stroke and lost some of her memory and her reasoning and her balance was not great, but in some ways, she remained as sharp as a tack.

"Me neither, Mags."

"So why is she still here?"

"Because she ... thinks she knows something. She's trying to stop the fighting. In her own way. She needs somewhere to stay and ... she knows she'll be safe here." Don struggled to explain. Fran didn't just stumble across the farm, he knew that. She came to find him.

"Well, of course," Maggie beamed and grasped his hands, "Everyone is safe with you, my darling," she said.

Don held his wife's hands and marvelled at her trust in him. At one time, that was true. Everyone was safe. Now, as the whole world destabilised around him, he wasn't so sure.

He left the room and went out into the entrance hall. He slipped his feet into large boots and grabbed his gun. He walked from the house out towards the yard gates and crossed over into the lower paddock. The air was cold and the night a perfect black. With the lights off, the valley was as black as pitch and Don took up a seat on a stone from a tumbledown wall. Crouching, he felt his younger dog, Pip, slide in beside him. She is a clever girl, he thought, she knows when to be quiet. With one hand on the rifle and one on the dog's head, Don waited.

The last thing he wanted was a visit from, well, anyone. When he left the school for the last time, Don knew this was the right place to be. Nestled in the glacial valley between two steep hillsides, under the rocky outcrops that gave the farm its name, Wolf Craigs Farm was the safest house in the Pentlands. There was no tarmac road, only a dirt track which ran from a cinder trail along the length of the bottom field to the small stone bridge over the burn outside the yard. Don had sheep in the Upper Paddock over the hill, chickens in the barn and a small dairy herd. He grew fruit trees, vegetables and potatoes and he filtered water from the burn for irrigation. When his wife, Maggie gave up her nursing career, before the cruelly early stroke which robbed her of most of her mobility, she ran the farm, spun the wool, made ice cream and fruit pies and ran a small flower nursery. Now Maggie knitted and crocheted but couldn't manage much else. They sold the milk instead and stored and sold the excess seeds.

Don only taught at the school because it brought them an income in uncertain times. Now it was closed, he concentrated on the farm, where they were safe and out of the way. Most people did not know it was there and according to Don, that was just fine. When Fran MacDonald turned up way back in November, he was wary. When she refused to leave, he became suspicious. When she started talking about taking down the government, he doubted her sanity and when she said that he was involved, whether he liked it or not, he stopped asking questions. She did cook from time to time, she could bake well and was happy to help out with laundry, but mostly, she sat in her room and scribbled away in her book. They lived, side by side, in a wide berthed truce.

Usually, visitors announced themselves in a similar way to the van stuck in the mud halfway up the field. Don chuckled to himself now. Only he and his two sons, currently safely overseas working in the middle east, could negotiate their way up the bottom field, avoiding hidden boulders and sinkholes. Whoever it was, it was not a good time. Whoever it was, he was ready.

Don and Pip waited in the dark by the gate. As he listened to the commotion and the note of the engine, he knew it was a school vehicle. Only one person at school knew where he lived. Don was not surprised; he'd been expecting Lewis for a month or so now and was amazed it had taken him so long. He smiled ruefully. He liked his young co-worker but knew that he wasn't really cut out for farm life. If Lewis and Izzy had turned up here, they must be desperate.

.oOo.

"We're stuck!" Sophie cried. "We have to get out!"

Lewis revved harder but the wheels just spun and the van did not move.

"Sir, just leave it," Aaron spoke quietly, now cradling a crying Amy on his shoulder.

Lewis stopped but blood pounded in his ears with the frustration and stress. It was a little further, he knew they could make it. He desperately wanted to scream at the bloody kid, who had been wailing for about twenty minutes, but he stopped himself, closed his eyes.

"Ok," he began, "It's not much further, we can walk from here, and only carry what we can. I'm sure we can come back for it later."

"Where are we going?" Sophie asked.

"It's not far," Lewis replied as he shouldered a bag and slammed the side door shut.

They tramped through the icy mud up the hill. Amy continued to cry but less so now, and she began to take in the new surroundings as she bounced against her big brother's chest. Sophie gritted her teeth, pushed herself on. She had long since stopped asking herself why her life was like this. Now, with grim acceptance, she just plodded on, day to day, trying to make sure she was warm, fed and most of all, not caught. Now, it was even more important not to get caught. Was the Sec Guard dead? She hoped not. Except ... she somehow hoped he was, too. She had to take her anger out on someone, and he just happened to be in the way.

Sophie blinked at the blackness and tried to make out shadows and shapes. She desperately needed to get back to town, her mum was waiting for the salt for her legs and her little sister and brother were too young to feed themselves. How could she go back? She'd dodged the draft and was already wanted for breaking and entering, theft and trespassing. And now, possibly attempted murder as well. If she returned to help the family, she'd be taken away within days. Her mind raged on but she knew, right now, she had little choice.

Lewis led the way. He limped slightly, his leg aching. Good enough for the draft, though, he thought. He headed for the tall poplars which surrounded the farm buildings but as he reached the gate, he paused. He knew Don would be watching, he knew about the CCTV.

"Why have we stopped," Sophie asked, whispering.

"Wait," Lewis said and they all stood at the gate, breathing out clouds of warm air into the cold night.

The farmhouse was completely still, no wind rustled the trees and all the animals were shut in for the night.

"I see you boy," a voice growled, close enough to make them all jump.

Aaron clutched at his sister and prepared to run.

"No," Lewis caught his jacket, "It's ok," he said. "It's Mr Jack."

.oOo.

Izzy sat with her hands to the fire, trying to remember what Callie had taught her all those months ago. She mumbled as she knitted, *in, round, over, off* ... but it never really looked like anything Callie knitted. She sighed and persevered. After all, where else was she going to get baby clothes?

She was now six months pregnant and dangerously undernourished. Winter brought new challenges to Scotland shores, with no imported vegetables (who could afford them anyway?) and the reduction in cattle because of the shortage of vets. Of *Vets!* No vets meant no slaughterhouses and there were precious few people willing to do it themselves. Lewis had proven himself adept at trapping rabbits but neither of them had the stomach for the skinning part, until, one day, the hunger had outweighed the disgust and Izzy took a cleaver to the steaming carcass.

They both had rations but Lewis' would now stop because he was reporting for duty. At least he'd be well fed there and would send back his first wages in months, she shrugged, wondering if he had managed to get into Edinburgh on time before curfew to start his draft. Izzy went back to her knitting, one ear on the radio. The music was nice, but the news was all she waited for.

She couldn't contact her mum or brothers; they were all up north and no-one had a mobile. Her gran was in England in her nursing home, and she hadn't heard from Callie since she left the hospital. The houses in their estate were mostly empty now, as people moved back with parents or left the country. So many of her friends had gone. She and Lewis might have had their differences, but he had been gone less than a day and already she was lonely.

The phone rang and Izzy jumped. It was such an unusual sound now. They had only plugged the house phone back in when the mobile system went down, but as so many people no longer had phones, who were they going to ring?

"Hello," she said, tentatively.

"Izzy, it's me!" Lewis' voice rang with relief. "Are you ok?"

"Lewis, sure I'm fine. Did you make it?"

"Ah, well, no...not exactly. I...well, I got into a situation and now I'm at Don's house."

Izzy frowned at the receiver. "Don's house? You mean Wolf Craigs Farm? In the Pentlands? What are you doing there? How did you even get there?"

"I had to come, I … I'm with a couple of students. We … they …. We can't go back. They … well, I suppose we are all wanted."

"What, so you dodged the draft and ran away? You left here to join up and you end up *there*? What the hell, Lewis? I'm bloody pregnant! There's no doctors or midwives left! I can't reach my mum and I'm all alone and you decide to dodge the draft!?"

"I'll be back as soon as I can," he replied, but his tone was unconvincing. "I need to...I dunno, ditch the van and walk I guess. But I had to make sure the kids were safe."

Izzy scoffed. Since when did he walk? Since when did he care about any of his students? About anyone?

"Izzy?" Lewis said in a small voice.

She was silent.

"Izzy?" he said, a little louder. He was met with more silence. "Iz …"

"What? Lewis, what?" She was furious.

"Iz, can you come get me?" he whined. "You've got the car."

"Are you out of your mind?" she screamed into the phone, "You want me to waste my precious petrol on getting you back here just so the Sec Units can arrest you?"

"Well, I mean, we could go away together, I mean, you could …"

"*I could do nothing!!*" Izzy shouted, "It's a draft, Lewis! You have to go! *They* have to go! You'll go to jail! What the hell am I supposed to do now?" Izzy shouted, "What good are you in the hills, or in jail? Bloody hell Lewis, my mum was right, you're a selfish prick and you never ever put me first! Well, goodbye, Lewis, I'm leaving. You've left me absolutely no choice but to go find a refugee service. Fucking refugee service! That's if I want to eat ever again! Thanks a lot, Lewis! Thanks a sodding lot!" Izzy put the phone down and burst into tears.

She sat and sobbed into the quiet cold air for a few minutes. But after a while, there seemed little point in carrying on. There was no-one to hear her or comfort her and crying was getting her nowhere. Izzy wiped her face, stuffed a few warm clothes and her baby supplies into bags and hefted them all out to the car. She thought for a second, then turned back to the kitchen where she packed up all the food that was left, blankets and their emergency bag. If he returned, tough. He could starve, just like he'd left her to starve.

Izzy backed out of the garage and into the street. It was late, way after curfew, but if she was stopped by the Sec Units, she was pregnant, distressed and obviously in need of medical attention.

And if it weren't obvious enough, thanks to high school drama lessons, Izzy could cry on cue and make herself look pathetic. Worked every time.

CHAPTER 10

16th February

Sophie sat at Don's kitchen table and clutched at her hot coffee. She glanced around at the skinny, po-faced woman in the corner curled into an easy chair by the stove but she hadn't spoken at all since they arrived and Don didn't introduce her. She turned back to Aaron.

"He was going to ditch us," Sophie growled, "Like, totally leave us to get caught. He's a bastard, and I hate him. He was always fucking useless as a tutor too. Only liked the kids he could do gaming with or pretend he was one of the boys' gang," she scoffed, "Like anyone wants him in *their* gang."

She thought for a second. "Loser," she concluded.

"Don't be too hard on him," Aaron fed Amy with creamy, farm produced milk and rocked her gently from side to side. "He didn't expect to see us there. He's not responsible for us."

"No, and now we're stuck in the middle of nowhere because he led the Sec Units right to us and we have no choice!" Sophie drank her coffee. "My mum will be going spare. She can't take care of herself and she expected me back hours ago!"

"So leave," Aaron hoisted his sister for a burp.

"We are miles from town. Mr Jack's farm is off all the tracks and roads. He always told us that he likes it like that. And unless you noticed, the reason we got away back there was because I …" she swallowed, "I killed a Guard." She twisted her fingers in obvious distress.

"Don't you think that's why Mr Sinclair came here?"

69

"He came here because he's a fucking coward who wants Mr Jack to sort it all out for him," Sophie hissed, angrily biting into a biscuit.

At the door, Lewis' face flushed but he entered the room, head down. "I'm sorry I got you guys into this mess," he mumbled as he began to wash out a cup at the sink.

"Don't be," Aaron said graciously. "Me and Amy are definitely better off. Thanks."

Lewis smiled wanly but Sophie rolled her eyes. "Why are you dodging the draft?" she asked, pointedly. "I mean, I have mum to look after and Aaron has Amy and we're both pretty stuck, but *you* ... you dodged the draft *and* you deserted your pregnant girlfriend." Sophie stopped and pierced him with a look of pure hatred.

Lewis continued at the sink with his back to all of them despite the cup in his hands being clean and dry. He had no answer to her claim. He opened his mouth to say something, but she was right. He didn't want to fight, and he didn't want to be a father, not under these circumstances. Maybe if everything was ok again, and there was no draft or sanctions or Brexit or IndyRef and his mum and her mum were around to help, and he basically didn't have to do anything. He shuddered at his own selfishness.

He turned to face them and wiped his wet eyes. "I am scared," he said, barely a whisper.

Sophie stared at him a little longer then shook her head and returned her focus to her coffee cup. Aaron rubbed at his sister's back as she slept, dribbling on his shoulder.

Lewis sniffed and wiped his face.

"None of you know what it means to be scared ..." came a voice from the corner of the room.

Sophie barely looked up, "Oh yeah?" she mumbled.

Lewis eyed the woman. "You're that politician, aren't you?" he asked cryptically. "Wanted for war crimes or something? From the government?"

70

"She's a fucking drama queen, sitting there all 'boat captain from Jaws' being mysterious and old," Sophie grumbled.

"Do you remember Jaws?" Aaron asked her, suddenly, "Brilliant, wasn't it? Remember, Soph, we studied it in English and there was the bit where that head fell out the bottom of that boat and ..."

"I was betrayed, thrown to the wolves ..." Fran cut across.

"Yeah, well join the club," Sophie muttered.

"Sometimes life isn't all about you, young lady," Fran spoke louder now, archly.

Sophie slammed down her coffee cup and turned to Fran MacDonald.

"My name is Sophie," she spat through gritted teeth. "And yes, actually it is all about me, and Aaron, and Mr Sinclair, and Mr and Mrs Jack, and how we're all fucked because of your stupid government fighting with England. We've all been thrown to the wolves. By you!"

"And now you're all at Wolf Craigs Farm, people," Don entered the kitchen and threw several pairs of gloves onto the table. "And whilst you're here, you all have to help. Dogs, chickens, cows, sheep and cats all need fed. Sheep need to be penned for the night. My wife needs a carer, and the perimeter needs securing. You all need to learn how to use a gun, and milk the cows, then set the alarms and ride a quad. Aaron, there are two rooms upstairs, you can take one with Amy. There's my boys' old crib in the attic. Sophie, you can take the other one, but it's small and cramped. There's linens and blankets in the upstairs cupboard. Lewis, you're in the conservatory."

He paused. "There's a basement," he continued. "No-one is allowed down there. Ever. Understand?" He stopped and looked at their faces. Fran buried her head in her knees. Aaron looked hopefully up at him, Sophie wide eyed and Lewis tearful.

"Lewis. You're with me lad," he said and turned and left the room.

Sophie followed. "Mr Jack! I can't stay! You have to take me back! My ... my mum!"

"Sorry, Sophie, love, no-one leaves right now. Too dangerous. You heard the radio reports, the English and Scottish are fighting at the border more and more. They're threatening to invade."

"But they've been threatening that for weeks! Please Mr Jack!"

"Sophie," he stopped to shrug on his coat. "You are running from both sides right now. The radio says the Sec Patrols have picked up everywhere because so many people are dodging the draft. New Scottish troops are all around, and the English knocking at the door. You're safer here. Your mum will get picked up by the aid agencies very soon, I'm sure. You're no good to anyone in jail, or dead,"

Sophie inhaled sharply.

"... but you are very useful here and now, to me. I'll make sure you're safe, love, but I can't take you back. Sorry."

Sophie looked at him, and nodded. Mr Jack always won them round.

He grabbed a gun and strode to the door, "Lewis!" he called, "Now, lad, please! We need to make sure you weren't followed and secure the fences."

Sophie flattened herself against the wall as Lewis pushed past. She scowled at him but he lowered his head, unwilling to catch her eye.

CHAPTER 11

17th February (pre-dawn)

Izzy nursed a pounding headache and looked at both packets of painkillers in front of her. Which one was she *not* supposed to take? She couldn't remember. She shrugged and popped out two paracetamol which she swilled down with some flat cola she had found in the door of the car. Outside the night was completely black. She looked up from the driver's seat and saw no moon anywhere. Even the nearby motorway had no streetlamps illuminated. No spare electricity and no point if there were no cars on the road after curfew. She sighed and shifted position. It was already uncomfortable to sit for long periods. She couldn't imagine what it would be like three months from now when she was a beached whale and had veins everywhere and huge boobs and a bad back. Yuk. Izzy balked at the idea of birth. Then she whimpered. She felt desperately alone.

Outside, the air was so cold Izzy was convinced it would snow again soon. There had been lying snow for about three weeks now and the arctic wind was relentless. She reached for and rattled the map once more to reassure herself that she had been going in the right direction. She squinted at it, but the lettering was tiny. Bloody sat nav was often useless but it was better than this, she thought. She couldn't follow the main roads because she would be stopped so the slow back roads had to do, even if it was all the way to the coast. If Lewis had deserted her and mum couldn't help, Izzy's last option was going to find Callie. At least, Izzy was going to the place that she knew Callie had crossed the border. From there, Izzy wasn't sure what was next. Claim asylum in England? No. That just sounded weird.

She started the car once more and immediately the fan began to blow warm air at her face. She sighed with relief and pulled onto the rutted road, trying to avoid pothole after pothole. Izzy estimated she would be at the centre around midnight at this rate, if she found it at all. She knew there were big hills and moorland in the way and would need to go around and she was not sure how much petrol she would need. It was a journey of delicate balances; towards England, but not over the border, fast roads but not visible roads, populated enough to need petrol stations but rural enough to be unfrequented. Izzy pushed on.

Eventually, the snow began to fall once more. Izzy was certain she was on the right road, but the petrol situation had become dire. She had such a small allowance to go to work on, but with no work it had sat in the car, unused. But it had been so long since Izzy had ventured out of the town to go anywhere - after all, where was there to go these days - that she underestimated how far away she was from the border towns. The small car pushed on, the petrol light blinking just in Izzy's line of sight.

A few miles later, the car finally died. Izzy turned the engine over a few times, but she knew it wasn't going to start up again. She switched off the lights and sat for a few moments listening to the wind as she contemplated her next move with a grimace on her face. The road was deserted, there wasn't a house in sight. Talking to herself, she silently listed her choices in her head. "One. Stay here and walk when the sun comes up, providing you haven't frozen to bloody death. Two. Get out and walk now and hope that a patrol picks you up or you, by some miracle, stumble upon the Borders refugee centre just outside of the town."

Izzy closed her eyes and sighed. Some choice. She really wanted a cup of coffee. A hot, strong cup of real coffee like the ones in The Edinburgh Coffee Co where she and all her girlfriends went back in 2022 after lockdown was lifted . It was the best coffee she had ever tasted, especially as everyone had been cooped up for most of the year before. After the coffee, she remembered cocktails, shopping, dinner then a club but damned if she could remember which one. Orchids? The Amphitheatre? No. Couldn't remember. Both of them closed, now, anyway. Izzy sighed and opened her eyes to her immediate future. Best to stay here, she thought and turned to grab a blanket.

Suddenly the gloomy grey sky lit up with a white blast of light. It lingered for a second before a huge boom deafened her and shook the car. Izzy shrieked in shock and pulled the blanket on top of herself. A split second later, soil and debris rained down on top of the car roof and a large metal pole crashed onto her bonnet. She screamed once again and began to cry. Where the hell was she? What the hell was that?

Out of the back window, Izzy saw lights. With both hands still clutching the blanket, she held her breath, terrified. The big black Land Rover came to a stop and both doors opened. She heard the now familiar click of a gun being readied and remained still so whoever held it had no reason to use it. Both doors slammed and two sets of boots charged towards her. A young man dressed in black with a balaclava over his face yanked open her car door and pulled Izzy outside.

Izzy screamed.

"Identify yourself," he yelled.

Izzy swallowed. "Isabelle Atwood," she managed.

"Are you armed?"

"No."

"Are you alone?"

"Yes."

"Are you pregnant?" another male voice from behind the first.

"Yes."

"Why are you here?"

"I'm looking for the Refugee centre," she said as boldly as she could. It was freezing out of the car and she shivered with cold and shock.

"On what grounds do you seek refugee status?"

Izzy stood for a second, she didn't quite know how to answer that question.

"I ... I ... don't know," she managed. It wasn't a question she had ever considered.

"Ok, come with us, now," he pushed her.

Izzy paused.

"NOW!" he repeated, louder this time and grabbed her elbow.

"I just need to get my bag and there's loads of ..."

"Just the bag. We can come back for the rest when it's safe."

"Safe?" she asked vacantly, as she half fell and was half dragged from the car.

"Skirmishes, fighting, you just saw that missile, it barely missed you and us!"

They threw Izzy into the back of the vehicle and sped off. The sky lit up once more and another boom rocked the air. The car bounced along the road, trying to avoid debris.

"What is going on?" she asked, terrified now.

"They call them border 'disputes'," the driver said, and the other man scoffed as they bumped through a particularly rough patch of road.

"Is it the English?" she asked.

"English troops push forwards, then the Scots troops push back. The Sec Units are usually involved too," said the second man. He was adorned with a patchy ginger beard.

"With lots of sniper fire and guerrilla tactics thrown in for good measure," relayed the driver, slim with curly dark hair bursting from under a black hat. Neither man was much older than twenty.

"It wasn't on the news, bombs, I mean," Izzy said.

"Course it wasn't," said ginger beard. "Old slimeball Andrea Taylor doesn't want poor innocent Scottish folk being upset at the thought of their sons and daughters being blown to pieces on the border, does she?"

"You mean the English have *invaded*?" Izzy cried.

"Not yet," ginger beard reassured her, "But it's only a matter of time. They could take us easily, no problem. Besides, did you know you were just a mile or so from the border?" Curly driver nodded agreement.

"Then what is happening?" she asked.

"It's a mess. Houses are burned down, farms raided. But it's the Sec Units that are the worst. They decide to fire on the English for a bit then - when they hit someone - the English come through the weak spots and give them what for then leave. The English mostly just sit there. I think they're just waiting for the politicians to sort it out. The 'disputes' are almost a game, a way of passing the time. They're playing with us. Probably think it's funny," ginger beard explained.

"Waiting for the politicians to sort out what?"

They both shrugged. "Who owns Scotland, I guess. Who gets to be in charge? It's all about power at the end of the day. Bastard English. Arrogant twats."

Curly driver chuckled. "We were both born there!" he laughed.

"Fuck off, Elliot, don't fucking tell everyone!" ginger beard complained, and the driver chuckled once more. Izzy couldn't help feeling his prolonged laughter was only just shy of deranged. She sat back and closed her eyes, relieved at least to be warm once more.

They drove on with the lights off and the heavy fire receded behind them.

Izzy opened her eyes after a few minutes, as realisation dawned. "Did you say 'missile'?"

The driver just looked at her in the mirror.

"Jesus," she breathed and stared out at the grey morning. "Sounds like a proper war already."

"We are at war," Elliot said, looking at her in the mirror. "With the English, and with ourselves. So we're never going to win. It's a real mess."

She watched the bleakness outside for a while as they rushed past hedges and pylons. Izzy could almost imagine it was the summer of 2022 again, in a car with no lights packed with friends driving to an illegal party in the hills, to dance and drink and stick two fingers up to the Infection Control Bill that prevented gatherings over 30 people.

"So, who are you, then? I mean, officially," she asked.

"Scottish Army," the drivers expression softened, "I'm Elliot. Me and my brother Matthew here were drafted."

Ginger bearded Matthew mumbled, "Only reason I agreed to get drafted was so I could kick the shit out of those Sec Unit bastards. Don't really care about the English."

They continued for about ten minutes before Izzy could see a dimly lit building ahead. They pulled up and got out. Elliot helped her down and they went inside. The snow swirled and drifted by the walls, driven now by a stiff breeze from the North Sea.

Inside the refugee centre, which was once a leisure centre, given its modern curves and motivational quotes on frosted windows, Izzy lifted her eyes to the ceiling. Every second light had been removed - so that they could preserve electricity she presumed - and the walls, once a jaunty yellow, were dulled and peeling. People sat around in small clumps, around ceramic cups of coffee. The smell of stale cooking permeated the air and reminded Izzy of the meal rounds in the ward. She grimaced and turned to the two men.

"Go over there," Elliot told her and pointed to a desk manned by two older women. They were busy scribbling away in dun-coloured files. Then the two soldiers turned and went back outside. No-one batted an eyelid at their guns or their uniforms.

Izzy approached the desk and smiled.

"Where are you from, hen?" The woman continued to write.

"Muirbridge."

The woman looked up sharply. "Muirbridge? Why are you here? There is a centre closer to you just south of Edinburgh. You should have gone there." Her tone was irritated and matter of fact. She looked back down at her work and continued making notes.

"I was trying to cross the border," Izzy replied quietly.

Both women looked up now, with wide eyes and rueful chuckles.

"Oh, I don't *think* so, doll, not unless you want to die." They exchanged looks.

"You do *know* that we are just about at war, don't you?"

"But *just about* isn't war, is it? Why can't I cross the border?"

"Look, hen, are you English?"

"No."

"Then unless you're on a suicide mission, you're staying. Name?"

Izzy sighed and gave her name. She was issued with blankets and a pillow and a few meagre items for cleaning and eating. They showed her to an army cot in a room with ten others. She felt wretched and kicked herself for even attempting to leave the house. There may not have been much food or anyone to help, but at least it was her own bed. Oh well, she thought as she tried out the cot for size, I will get petrol and drive back home tomorrow. It can't be more than a few miles.

She lay down on the cot, which surprised her with its comfort, and pulled up her covers. The dim lights made her drowsy and she was soon asleep.

Izzy slept for days. For the first time in months, she was warm, fed and safe. It was a refugee centre but it felt more like home than anywhere else had in the last few months. Every day a Sec Unit appeared, shouting and waving guns, and dragged away a young man or woman, and the rumble of gunfire and shelling permeated the coastal peace, but apart from that, it was as calm as it had been in Izzy's life for years.

A Red Cross doctor looked her over and declared her fit and well and gave her a few basics for when the baby came. There were even movie nights and little clubs, crafting circles and art classes. It almost felt civilised. Her initial quest for petrol was thwarted with laughter and shaken heads. There was no way on God's green earth that anyone was giving her petrol to drive her car either back towards Edinburgh or onwards to England, they said. It was far too precious a resource. She was stuck there, there was no doubt, but after a while, this sense of "stuck" started to feel quite pleasant.

For weeks, she knitted and sewed for the baby and herself and kept a record of things she wanted to say or do or tell her mum or shout at Lewis when it was all over. In the small leisure centre crammed with people displaced from their homes, she was lonely, but never alone.

"How far along are you, hen?" a voice asked from two cots over. A new family had arrived the day before.

Izzy looked up from her sewing and saw an older woman sitting on a cot, flanked by two teenage children, a defeated, angry look on her lined face.

"About seven and a half months, maybe eight, I think," she said and returned to the Babygro she was creating.

"Bit shit being pregnant right now, I should imagine," the woman mused.

Izzy looked up again, "Yes, not great," she replied and hoped that was the end of the conversation. For a moment, it was.

Then, "Radio says the latest talks with New Britain failed." the woman began again, conversationally. "The UN says we have to get rid of the army. Scum."

Izzy looked up. "Scum? Who's scum?"

"Fucking EU scum."

"I thought you said it was the UN?"

"UN, EU, they're all fucking scum at the end of the day, trying to tell us how to live."

Izzy looked at her levelly for a moment, thought about replying, but stopped herself. The woman went on, "Best thing that ever happened to us, that Andrea Taylor. Really brought discipline and order back to the streets. Do you remember how it was before, hen? When there was looting and violence all over the place, and people just went and took whatever they wanted. Shocking. Wouldn't catch my kids doing that."

Izzy didn't reply. Her current situation was hardly 'the best thing that had ever happened to her'.

"Sec Units saved my Tony's life, they did. One night, when we was broken into and some scumbags took all the cash I had stashed. My Tony went after them with his bat and kicked shit out of one of them when he was jumped by at least five of them."

Izzy raised her eyebrows. She couldn't guess how this story was going to end.

"He took out three when he was caught unlucky on the back of the head. The Sec Unit turned up just in time, and boom, boom!" she simulated the sound of gunshot, "Wee shits got what was coming to them."

Izzy looked away but felt nothing. It was amazing how far removed from basic humanity they had come when the random shooting of desperate looters caused not a flicker of either sadness or remorse in either woman.

"Course, mine will be signing up for the army, once they're old enough," she went on, smiling at the grubby teen to her left. He sat, vacant faced and stared at Izzy. She thought he was about to drool.

"Where's your husband now?" Izzy asked.

"Joined the local Unit." She said, proudly, then inclined towards Izzy and said in a lower tone, "Got five kills to his name already - all New Britain soldiers trying it on at the border." Her eyes twinkled in delight and pride, "Scum English," she sneered. "One of them was shot in the arm. He was trying to drag his mate back behind the border as he'd taken one in the leg so couldn't walk. My Tony shot them both. One in the back, one right behind the ear. What a shot." She chuckled and shook her head in wonder.

"You must be so proud," Izzy sighed, tired of this bloodthirsty chat.

"Definitely," she beamed. "They was trying to lure the kiddies to the border with sweets and stuff. Probably a couple of paedo scum."

Izzy got up and left. She desperately needed a glass of wine, but water from the distant fountain would have to do. She followed this with a walk around where the swimming pool and spa once was and sucked in the faint smell of chlorine and hot tubs, still lingering in the air. It was enough to make her feel almost normal for a moment. She missed normal so much it hurt. She missed her family, who hadn't heard from in months. She stared through the frosted glass to the snow in the shrubs and flowerbeds.

"Fuck it," she said, pushed the glass doors open and walked outside. It was bitterly cold and the wind bit straight through her sweater and jacket. Her trainers were old but warm, coupled with a new pair of socks she had managed to create on her first attempt at knitting.

She walked past the grey and green army vehicles, parked here and there, and the cars which had either brought refugees to the centre or had once brought gym goers who had just never left, such was the bad timing of their visit. They were all old and worn, dirty and unloved and Izzy wondered if she would ever drive again. She really liked her old V-dub; it was comfortable and familiar and smelled like home. She wondered if she could reach it on foot, then remembered the gunfire and shelling the night she was picked up and decided it was not a good idea. Besides, there was no traffic except army vehicles on the A1. She could just walk.

That's what she was going to do, walk.

Walk to England. To her gran's home, miles and miles away from any border, in peaceful, rural England.

England, where there were still sanctions, EU threats, blockades and shortages of everything, but they had sweeties. The soldiers would give her sweeties and everything would be all back to normal.

Izzy made her way out of the car park and onto the main road.

CHAPTER 12

March

There wasn't much space in front of the fire and most of that was taken up by Pip and Mol, the mother and daughter Border Collie working sheepdogs. They lay on the thick rug, legs outstretched as Sophie stroked their fur. She didn't mind being pushed away from the warmth; she loved the dogs. She had never owned a dog, mostly because mum was too unstable to keep one, and she relished this evening time when she got to watch them snore peacefully by the fire. With no TV and no internet, sleeping dogs were the only entertainment in the dim light. Even book reading, Sophie's other new hobby, was not possible when the lights were low. She never thought of herself as a reader when she was younger. It had never appealed when the delights of fast paced social media held so much brightly coloured flickering promise. But now, a good book - she especially liked whodunnit crime novels - and a warm dog were her comforts.

Sophie looked at her fingers. After a month of farm work, her hands were cracked and sore and her nails remained short. She fantasised about long, fiery red acrylics with jewels and decals. And strappy heels. And the feel of a hairdresser blow drying her long hair. She sighed. Of all the jobs she thought she would end up in, farm hand never featured on the list. She wanted to be a beautician, or work in a nice modern office up in town. Maybe a receptionist in a posh hotel or bank. But she knew that kind of job just didn't exist anymore. It was either producing food or fuel, sewing clothes and sheets, building shelters, working in food banks or joining the Sec Units. And now, joining the new Scottish Army.

She didn't mean to break the law and dodge the draft; it was just never a convenient time to go. She didn't mean to kill the Guard either. It was the only way though, she kept telling herself.

At least on the farm they were fed. She was sick of carrots and turnips, and eggs with everything but at least she didn't starve. The farm hands that Don once employed had been forced to leave with the draft and when Lewis and the kids showed up, Sophie could see some relief in Don's eyes. She and Aaron had filled the gaps naturally, taking care of Maggie, the animals and the land.

Sophie thought about her mother and brother and sister and wondered how they were. It had been months since she had seen them, and she hoped the Red Cross or the '*Médecins*' people had found them. She looked around the room. Amy slept in her bassinet on the sofa, full of milk and Sophie saw that Fran had tucked herself into a ball next to her, staring at the flames in the grate. Sophie shook her head. Bloody woman did very little and Don never seemed to make her. Right now, Aaron was on watch up near the paddock in the freezing cold and Lewis and Don were still out checking the perimeter. The room was warm and the lights low and Sophie willed herself to be grateful for everything Mr Jack had given them. However, she couldn't help but think that sometimes, even now, adults were taking the bloody piss.

"Eva!" a weak voice called from the next room. Sophie got up. Eva and Lynette had been Maggie's carers before they left to go home to Poland last year, along with almost every other EU national, and now every time Maggie called for someone it was the same name. If Sophie turned up, it didn't matter, she was now Eva to Maggie. She struggled to name everyone except Don; there was a special area of her brain that clung onto his memory through everything else.

"What is it Maggie?" Sophie replied softly, as she entered Maggie's room. It was brighter in here, cleaner, furnished solely for Maggie's disability with a hospital bed, hoists and clinical equipment.

"I think I'm leaking, Eva dear, sorry." Maggie continued.

"It's ok, I'll sort it," Sophie smiled. "Fran, would you fetch me a new sheet from the laundry?" she called. Fran didn't move.

"Fran? I need to change Maggie's bed. Please?" Sophie asked again. Fran remained motionless.

Sophie looked at Maggie and rolled her eyes and Maggie grimaced in sympathy. "Sorry, Eva dear," she said again.

"Back in a minute, Maggie," she said and closed the door.

Sophie strode up to Fran and stood in front of her. Fran continued to stare into the flames. She didn't even acknowledge Sophie's presence, but she did put a finger in her mouth and begin chewing at a nail.

"Fran!" Sophie hissed. "I know you aren't bloody deaf, so listen to this." She leaned closer, hands upon hips. Pip and Mol sat up, sensing the tension in the air. "I am sick of you doing absolutely bloody nothing around here. We all work really hard to keep it all going. There's a load of utter shit coming down outside this farm and you should be bloody grateful we haven't given you up to the Sec Units. For God's sake, pull yourself together!"

Fran smiled at her sardonically. "Don wouldn't let you give me up," she said, her voice dripping with ire.

Sophie's face reddened with rage.

"You all do what Don says," she continued, "And Don does what *I* say." Fran chuckled at her and looking away she reached a hand into Amy's makeshift crib and began to coo a quiet lullaby to her.

Sophie threw up her hands. "For fuck's sake ..." she muttered and went to fetch the linen for Maggie.

Fran watched out of the corner of her eye as Sophie left the room. She had always hated teenagers, along with children, animals and anything dirty - but teenagers were the worst. "Little upstart," she muttered to herself, "You know all about grateful, don't you? Dodging the draft, stealing, breaking and entering ... murder." Fran smiled. "Little schemie scrubber benefits cheat.

85

Now pretending like you're living a virtuous life on the farm. Like you've done nothing wrong. And they let these undereducated morons actually *vote!* Oh, you'll get yours little girl, just you wait, once law and order is properly reinstated and I'm in charge ..." Fran stopped and stared into the fire, although she was already too hot. She caught sight of herself in the glass of a picture frame beside the grate and saw that she wore a furious frown. She backed up slightly and realised that she was also gripping the side of Amy's cot with white knuckled fingers. She let go and stretched both hands. They were creaky and stiff from all the writing.

There was no laptop or computer of any sort in the house. There was no wi-fi here and all the farm accounts were kept in old fashioned ledgers. When the entire online system went down finally after years of partial shut downs and loss of coverage, Don managed to retain accounts and invoices on paper going back years in filing cabinets and drawers. Fran, however, living in a digital world in Holyrood and Bute House and other sumptuous government buildings, and who had managed to retain limited access to the internet until the day she left for the airport to meet the plane that never arrived, lost everything. All the emails and memos that would have cleared her name. All the waves of shit that would implicate bloody Andrea Taylor in the push for war and isolation. All gone.

Fran wasn't going to lie down and let everyone take advantage of her though. She had a bloody good memory and a paper diary; post it notes and memos in her bag and even an old fashioned address book. She had Steve Lister's letters. Most importantly of all, Fran had her thick, blue, leatherbound note pad with a ribbon to tie it shut. Every meeting, every phone call, every letter, every note-to-self from the last six months was written in this book.

Fran was going to clear her name and everyone in this house was going to help her, like it or not. Sophie was right, she didn't do much of the manual work. Why should she? She was a busy and bloody important woman. She had pages and pages of evidence to take that bitch Taylor out for good. She spent every day putting together a coherent and watertight argument for removing her from power. How *dare* Andrea use her like that? How dare she wipe her feet on Fran MacDonald?

Fran was nearly finished with her tome. Soon, it would be Taylor's day of reckoning. Fran smiled into the flames. She was not beaten, not by a long way. When the time was right, she'd need to borrow that Land Rover of Dons. "... just for a day or two, just to pop into town for a couple of errands, I'll try and put petrol in it for you but it will probably get confiscated or blown to pieces, you don't mind, do you?" she whispered.

Fran looked down at baby Amy sleeping in her crib. "Maybe I'll take her with me when I go," she said. "Just as a little insurance, just in case anyone in this damp, corrupt little hole wants to make a big fuss. Just in case anyone at Bute House has decided she's fair game to shoot on sight."

Amy awoke with a snuffle and began to chew on a fist, her brown eyes wide.

"Hello, little girl," Fran cooed and put a hand to Amy's chest. "You're going to help Auntie Fran out of a little sticky situation, aren't you? Yes, you are."

Amy burbled and fussed, then flashed Fran her biggest, gummiest smile.

.oOo.

Lewis sat down opposite Don at the kitchen table and put a mug of steaming tea in front of them both. They had been out walking the perimeter all day and Don had finally let him take out a quad bike on his own. Lewis had quite gotten out of the habit of driving. A walkie talkie sat between them on the table but it was silent. Just a small green light glowed on its top edge.

"Any news?" Lewis asked. He was exhausted unlike anything he had felt before but felt fitter and clearer headed. He picked at the blisters on his palms and grimaced. Farm work was not his forte but it might, as his mother might have said, be the making of him.

"Aaron hasn't reported anything in the last hour."

"Not the best night for it," Lewis shook his head.

"He's got big boots, a rifle and a flask of tea. What more could a soldier want?" Don smiled wanly.

Lewis sighed, "He didn't want to be a soldier."

"None of them do," Don replied, "Scottish and English alike. None of them should be out there."

They sat silently for a while. Lewis wondered where Izzy had ended up. He had tried to call again several times but there was never any reply. She must've followed through with the threat to leave.

"We need to send Sophie down to town to get supplies tomorrow. Take the baby, it's good cover so she won't get stopped."

"It's too dangerous. Too much violence out there. Send that woman instead."

"We can't. You know we can't, Lewis, she'd be recognised. You heard the news, she's a missing person."

"So?" Lewis grimaced, "Who cares?"

"Fran said she's been set up."

"Do you really believe that?"

Don looked down at his cup, "Yes, I'm afraid I do."

"She's a liability! She barely does anything else. In a week I think I've seen her bake once and she never looks after Maggie. Sophie might get stopped. I ... don't want that. It's my fault she's here."

"Ok, then you go ..." Don began.

"I ..." Lewis couldn't reply. The thought of capture, even by his own side, terrified him.

"We might have no choice, lad."

"I could just go and sign up," he said with resignation. "We all could. Leave Amy with you and Maggie." This was the last thing he wanted and he was praying that Don would say no.

"Son, I have people to feed, a sick wife and a ... a politician to keep safe. I couldn't do a baby as well."

Lewis breathed a sigh of relief. At least he'd offered. "Don, I am so sorry we came here. You don't deserve this."

"Don't be sorry. The whole country is in crisis. Wolf Craigs Farm is probably the safest place this side of the Highlands. I am grateful to share the work. But …"

Lewis looked up at Don, "But what?"

"Lad, listen to me. Sooner or later someone is coming to that door. It might be the new Scottish army looking for you three, Sec Units looking for Fran, someone looking for me. Who knows how any of them will react to a farmhouse full of dodgers and a notorious wanted woman? We have to be prepared to fight or…"

Tears began to form in Lewis' eyes and spill down his cheeks. He began to tremble.

Don looked at him with sympathy and patted his hand but he was tired of Lewis' tears. "Come on lad, you've got to be bigger than this," he said, "All men cry these days - I get that - but at some point you have to accept the situation and get on with it."

Lewis stopped crying and wiped his face but the emotion still showed in his eyes. He nodded; his look stoic but wobbly.

"I was supposed to show up at the barracks in Edinburgh weeks ago," Lewis began through the sniffs. "So I left home with every intention of going straight there. I did. I didn't want any trouble and I needed the money to keep Izzy. Our savings are long gone and with no salary …" he wiped his face with his hand. "I got scared. I mean really petrified. I couldn't do it. I've never done anything like army stuff in my life. You know how I felt about the Duke of Edinburgh stuff, I gave that a massive wide berth. The closest I got to war is on the Xbox. I hate the outdoors unless it's a beer garden." He paused and Don chuckled.

"So instead of going into Edinburgh to sign up, I went to the school and picked up loads of stuff. I didn't know what I was going to do, and I don't know where I was headed, but Izzy had told me that her friend Callie headed to the border to England. So I thought I might head south and cross the border, I dunno, into

Northumberland. Then I saw the kids, at the school. When I saw the Sec Units I panicked. I'm a coward and a crap boyfriend. This was my fault and there was only one way to sort it out. You were the only person I could think of to help us. I didn't know what else to do."

Don sighed, stood up and poured more tea.

"I … I just need it all to, you know, pause. Stop, just stop so we can all catch our breath, you know?" Lewis sniffed. "It's crazy. All of it for years now nothing has made sense. Brexit, Indyref, United Ireland, New Britain, it's all so … unstable."

"You forgot Covid …"

"At least Covid made sense! Slap on a mask, keep away from one another and we won't pass it on. Simple rules. Not that people did follow the rules. Now look at us. A hundred thousand dead and then a million more because the NHS fell apart." He stopped. He knew Don had heard it all before. He sighed. "Do you remember 2016" he asked.

"I do, yes."

"All those celebrities died, you know, and we all said what a terrible year it was and then the Brexit vote and then America lost it's mind and voted for Trump. We thought we had it bad but it was just the beginning, wasn't it?" He looked at Don who held his gaze.

"It all comes from that one year when everything went wrong. Like a switch that's stuck and we can't turn it off, and even if we did there's been so much … damage." Lewis struggled with his rising tears. "And now Izzy is pregnant and because of all this she couldn't … so we've brought someone new into this shit show and it's so unfair. And what are the government doing? Closing us in and cutting us off. I wanted independence, Don, but not like this."

Don reached up and picked a bottle off the top shelf and poured two glasses of whisky. "I think you need it."

"I need one too," came a voice form the doorway. Fran stood with her arms folded, her clothes hanging off her now skinny frame.

"Sit down, lass," Don poured another.

Lewis eyed the ex-politician across the table. She strutted around like she owned the place and Lewis didn't understand why Don allowed it. Why the hell didn't Don hand her over to the Sec Units?

She saw him staring at her. "What?" she snapped at him.

"What are you even doing here?" Lewis asked. "Don't you have some corrupt government to help run?" he mumbled into his drink.

"What are *you* doing here? Aren't you dodging the draft?" she spat.

"Illegal draft into an illegal army!" he growled.

"Bull! We had every right! We were being held to ransom by a bigger power!" she slapped her hands onto the table.

"So instead of talking to each other you pick a fight? A big, massive, illegal fight?"

"It's not illegal! Westminster were holding our country at ransom after a legitimate referendum!" Fran shouted.

"So why are you here? What do you hope to achieve sitting in Don's kitchen? Why aren't you and Andrea Taylor directing troop movements from some underground bunker?" Lewis' voice raised alongside hers.

"And what do *you* hope to achieve leaving your girlfriend alone, cold, starving and with no medical care when she's pregnant? You're hiding as much as I am! We all are!"

"You know why I'm here! I had to bring the kids. They had nowhere to go! I wasn't just saving my own sorry ass!"

"Of course you were!" Fran laughed hysterically, "You were running away, and they just happened to get in the way! Don't give me that bull, Lewis! You didn't want to go in the army so you ran off, didn't tell your girlfriend and came running to Don to take care of it all. Just like everyone always runs to Don to sort it out," she looked at him intensely and Don held her gaze.

"It wasn't like that!" Lewis cried, "It wasn't … I never meant to abandon Izzy …" he stood up abruptly, "And you're twisting everything I told you!"

Fran scoffed, "Of course I am!" she shouted, "I'm a bloody politician!"

Don sat and watched as they both stood and stared at one another. Then he rose and turned on the stove. He placed a pan of water on to simmer.

"Pass the milk," he said mildly.

"What?" Lewis turned to him.

"The milk. I think she'll need some, don't you?" he asked.

"Who?" Fran asked.

Just then, they heard the baby hitch and begin to wail. Sophie walked into the kitchen, with the crying bundle in her arms, scowling at the both of them, and sat down.

Don placed the bottle into the water and sipped his whisky. He drew breath and they all turned to him. "I've been farming a long time, but I've been teaching longer and been a chemist even longer than that," he said. "I've learned a lot from many different people, but I think one thing rings true in everything I do and everyone I meet. People are fundamentally good. They all want to connect with others. They all want what is best for themselves and those around them. The difference between us is *what* we all think is best and *how* we go about achieving it. That's the problem here." He sighed, rose and checked the temperature of the milk. He decided to leave it a little longer.

Everyone took a seat at the table as he turned back to them and picked up his whisky. "The IndyRef showed that 81% of people wanted independence. I wanted independence. So this result should've come as no surprise to anyone, and neither should the fact that Westminster cannot let us go. Some people want to fight this through the courts. Others want to appeal to Europe to set us free but the First Minister wants us to stand up and take our independence forcibly, by creating an army and a draft. You see?" he looked at the faces around the table, "Same goal, different tactics."

Sophie nodded, looking at him eagerly, Lewis sheared a corner off the baking paper in front of him and began to rip it into tiny pieces.

Don continued. "Andrea Taylor is looking at the bigger picture. She thinks the end will justify the means. That the death of a few young people will be worth it to liberate Scotland. A show of force to an aggressive neighbour that could bomb innocent people in Europe and shoot down civilian planes will at the least bring international support and potentially give us the freedom we voted for. Most of us want the same thing, but very few of us would've chosen this path."

Don took the bottle from the water and handed it to Sophie who still held the baby. "But the bigger picture rarely affects normal people on a day to day basis," he continued, "we are all busy trying to make our own lives the best they can be." He pointed towards Amy, eating happily on Sophie's knee. "Taylor thinks she's creating a just and equal Scotland by drafting men and women with no exceptions. But Aaron is Amy's only caregiver. If he's forced to join up, she will be essentially orphaned." He looked at Sophie, "Sophie runs her home, because her mum can't. But her contribution is not recognised. So she also has to go. Do you see? There may be equality there, but no equity.

"None of us chose this path deliberately. It came about because we trusted Andrea Taylor to do a good job. But our lives have become almost impossible and we all have to do things that are unpleasant. Things we would never have done if circumstances were better." He paused and sipped his whisky, reaching for the bottle to pour himself another glass. "And why do we do these things?" he asked rhetorically, "Because we are trying to keep our loved ones safe. The smaller picture. The things that matter only to us. That's how we all ended up hiding out here, oh yes, I'm hiding too, I want no part of the world out there, believe me!" he slugged more whisky.

The room remained silent for a while, only the sound of the stove crackled in the background.

"We might have to get up and fight," Don said finally. "One day. We might need to get up and defend what little we have left. And I'm sorry," he stifled a sob, "I am so, so sorry."

"Well," Fran said, finally, picking a dog hair from her sweater with a look of disgust, "I think we are *all* responsible for the mess we are in." She sipped her whisky primly.

Sophie turned to look at her, a sneer on her face. "So do something. You're a politician. Go and do something. You're hiding just like us. Or are you all talk, like the rest of them?"

Fran's face returned to a scowl and she downed her whiskey.

Just then, the radio crackled. "Don? You there?" Aaron's metallic voice pierced the quiet with a frantic air.

Don picked it up, "Here, boy. What's going on?"

"They're here. I think they're here. I think the English finally came. I see lights in the hills to the south, on the Drovers Track."

"How many lights?"

"Uh … not sure, lots, I think there are vehicles as well as … oh shit!"

"What is it?" Don asked urgently.

"Lights from the other way too! I … I mean two lots of lights, moving towards each other. Holy shit. I think …" there was a static pause and the whole kitchen was stilled as they waited for him to return.

"Aaron?" Don asked.

Static.

"Aaron, are you there?" he asked again, his tone more worried than before.

"It's Security!" Aaron's voice returned in a harsh whisper, "Sec Units! The Sec Units are coming! There's hundreds of them!

They're … I think they're going to fight with the English! What the actual …?"

The radio returned to static. Don and Lewis stood up and stared at the walkie talkie. Before either of them could move, the air pressure pulsed and the boom of an explosion ripped through the valley.

CHAPTER 13

March
Bute House

Andrea Taylor awoke to a knock at the door.

"What is it?" she asked, dragging herself to a sitting position. A glance at the clock told her it was just after midnight. The door opened and Damian, her senior secretary, entered.

"First Minister, we have a problem."

"Don't we always," she mumbled and rose from the bed to grab a dressing gown.

She followed her secretary down to her office along thick carpeted halls and pushed open the door. The phone was off the hook.

"It's Commissioner Janvier for you," Damian said and closed the door behind him as he left the room.

Andrea Taylor took a deep breath, raked her hands through her hair and exhaled noisily. She sat in her seat and picked up the phone.

"Monsieur Janvier, comment ca va?" she beamed in her best politician's French.

"Je vais bien, merci, mais vous n'aimerez pas ce que je vais dire," a voice replied.

Andrea Taylor knew just enough French to understand, but it was his tone that she didn't like.

"What's the problem?" she asked in English.

"I'll not waste your time. But I did want to give you the news before it arrives in official channels. The initial EU bid failed. Scotland is still not recognised as a separate country."

Andrea sat up more alert, "But you told me …" she cried.

"Principally," he continued, "You have raised an illegal army against your elected government."

"You barely recognise that government yourself after the Strasbourg bombing!" Andreas usual political tone evaporated as she increased in volume.

"And you have created an illegal draft, erected an unrecognised border and attacked official UK troops. You have requisitioned nuclear arms from New Britain in a move contrary to the Treaty on the Prohibition of Nuclear Weapons Act 2021."

"You know full well that the UK did not sign that treaty!" Andrea stood, her voice sharp. Her fist sat curled on the desk.

"No … but New Britain did, about an hour ago," he replied calmly, "… and the nuclear subs are in Scotland, in Gare Loch, as you well know. And we also know you have taken steps to secure the weapons for yourself. Now that those weapons are in the hands of, as New Britain describes, 'domestic terrorists', we shall be forced to act. Andrea, you have forced our hand."

Andrea Taylor sat down. She twisted both fists in her temples and grimaced. The scum English signed the treaty! Deliberately, the minute they lost control of Scotland they signed the treaty so they could get hold of the nuclear subs! So they could invade! So that Europe would move against them! Bastard, bastard scum! Andrea opened her mouth and screamed silently into the darkness of her office, then she quickly gathered herself and smiled.

"Francois, look," she began smoothly, "We are *not* the bad guys here, and you know it. Domestic terrorists? Of course not! Francios, it's me! Andrea! New Britain have only signed the treaty so that we look bad and they will garner international assistance. And look, my friend, it's worked. A few months ago the sanctions came thick and fast. Now you're assisting them in their … their …" she groped for the best word, "… their genocide and … and … illegal invasion of a foreign nation,"

"You're not foreign, though Andrea. Your country harbours what looks like thousands of insurgents and guerrilla combatants, willing to fight dirty."

"It's just the Security Force, the police, I mean, they're nothing to worry about, they keep the place crime free and the food shipments moving. They're a welcome addition …" she dismissed his concerns with a wave of her hand and a chortle down the line.

Commissioner Janvier was not deterred. "The Geneva Convention is not on your side in this, Mrs Taylor. We cannot allow this situation to continue on the EU's doorstep. Call off your troops. Open the border and stand down. There is no need for the pointless loss of life."

"What do you think I'm doing here?" she cried, "I'm trying to get Scotland out of this situation! We voted out of New Britain! We voted to stay in the EU! We wanted *none* of this, Francois, and yet here we are under sanctions and restrictions that leave my people starving and jobless! What else could I do? They did the Strasbourg bombing! We voted to get away from them! We knew the corruption and murder they were capable of! And you left us here to rot under their corrupt government! We didn't vote in the right-wing Nazis that are in power in Westminster! But Scotland is paying *all* the consequences!" Andrea felt herself begin to seethe with anger and the phone trembled in her hand.

She heard him shift and sigh on the other end of the phone.

There was a pause.

"Go back to the table, Andrea."

"They don't have anything I want."

"If you open the border, we can help broker a deal." Francois said.

"And if I don't?"

Andrea stopped as a deep rumble crawled through her office. The door opened immediately and Damian stood there, ashen and shocked.

"Bombs," he said simply. "They've started dropping bombs."

CHAPTER 14

March

Don, Lewis and the two dogs ran down the farm track to the burn. They crossed it in three jumps, rock to rock, and ran up the other side as they followed the fence to the upper paddock where Aaron was doing his lookout shift. It was a steep, boggy hillside and water seeped through their boots and soaked their trouser legs. The dogs ran to heel with Don up ahead but Lewis laboured quickly, still unfit and aching at his injured hip. Don bounded up the slope, gun in hand, and reached the top with ease. He was greeted with a cacophony of noise and devastation.

From the top he could see the distant lights on the Drover's Road but they were weak in comparison to the towering flames licking at his feed shed. In his paddock, all the summer hay silage was on fire, along with several trees and at least an acre of bushland, stretching out down the other side of the hill. A bomb had hit the side of the hill and gouged a huge hole; soil and debris landed everywhere. Birds flapped and flew away, leaving nests and youngsters; in the pen beside the feed store, his sheep brayed and called, terrified of the fire and the noise. He pulled at the heavy aluminium gate and let them all out. They fled into the darkness, as far away from the fire as they could get. Some hid in darkened corners and he whistled smartly to Mol, his most experienced sheepdog and she raced in to flush them out. She returned in a few minutes and lay at his feet. Don praised her and then whistled again and both dogs ran off to clear the last of the remaining sheep from the Drover's Road. Lewis eventually arrived and helped re-close the gate.

"Where is Aaron?" he asked through hacking breaths.

"Not found him yet," Don replied as he picked up a bucket and filled it with water from the open trough. He splashed in onto the base of the shed and went back for more.

Lewis stood rooted to the spot and watched the chaos in front of him. Swirling animals, fire, a huge gaping hole in the landscape where a rocky gorse filled field once was, lights getting closer …

"Lewis!" Don called sharply. "Walkie talkie! Find Aaron!"

"Oh shit, yes, of course," Lewis fumbled it out of his pocket and pressed the button.

"Aaron! Are you there?" Static. "Aaron!" More static. "Shit. Where is he?" Lewis swept the ground with his torch around the area they knew Aaron would have sat on his lookout shift. But he was not there. His flask sat open and empty, upended on the dirt.

The dark bushes and gorse illuminated in the firelight. The Drover's Road lights got brighter and Don stopped dousing the flames to look. There were troops, he didn't know which troops, tramping towards them over the blasted ground. The ruts and holes in the hillside slowed them down but Don estimated they would be on them in less than ten minutes. He put the bucket down and retreated to where Lewis searched the bushes for Aaron.

Suddenly the night air was peppered with the sound of gunshots and both men threw themselves to the ground. Quick fire rounds followed by the sound of handguns. The noise rose and fell as the English troops and the Sec Units exchanged fire not 250 yards from where they lay in the gorse. Don and Lewis looked at one another, breathing hard. Lewis' eyes were wide and terrified.

"Aaron?" he managed. Don shook his head, then stood up so that he could see the fighting. The troops had taken cover in bushes and behind crags but he could still see the tiny blasts as each one fired. He waited for a lull in the noise, then Don put a finger to his mouth and whistled sharply.

"Come on, we have to go." Don said with urgency.

"But he has to be here somewhere!"

"I've taken care of that."

"What do you mean? We can't leave! No, Aaron will be killed!"

"Lewis, lad, look! If we don't leave now then you are either captured by the English, killed by the Sec Units or drafted by the Scots. Aaron is being taken care of. Now *come on!*" Don began to crawl away in the direction of the fence line.

Lewis whimpered slightly as he rose and caught sight of some of the advancing soldiers. They were coming directly for them. He crouched down even lower.

"Wait, Don! Don't leave me! Don! Don't go! If we go back, we'll lead them to Maggie, and Sophie!" Lewis croaked in a stuttered whisper, out of breath once more.

"And if we don't, they'll find them. Sophie is armed. They might kill her. Do you want that?"

"Shit." Lewis whimpered once more and scurried to catch up to Don as he now strode over the crest of the hill. He was so confused, had no idea which way to turn. There were shouts, more gunfire, multiple voices. Orders barked. Then the walkie talkie crackled and Lewis grabbed it.

"Aaron!" he whispered, "*Aaron!*"

More shouts, more orders, more shots. They heard a vehicle, moving slowly.

"Aaron!" Lewis was getting desperate.

The walkie talkie crackled and Aaron sounded stoic, "I didn't want to get drafted because of Amy. But here I am. I can see the bastards. I'll make her proud."

"Aaron! Please come back!" Lewis listened, still staring into the darkness, one hand now on the fence, his safety net connection to the farm. Over the radio he heard a faint giggle.

"Watch this, sir!" Aaron said.

The air exploded once more, this time with rapid gunfire.

Shouts, howls, shrieks, mayhem, more rifle shots. Orders yelled at screaming pitch. A brief return of fire. More rifle shots. Orders to retreat.

Lewis listened in horror. He had never heard such noise. He fought a desperate urge to run as far away and as fast as possible. Then, the voices receded into the distance. The crackle of the barn fire continued and he became aware of the burn trickling over the top of one boot. Don stood behind him, listening.

"Aaron!" Lewis whispered shakily into the walkie talkie.

Silence.

"Aaron!" he said louder and looked back up the hill. He trembled in fear, rooted to the spot. Just then, a figure threw himself out of a bush at the top of the hill and down the slope towards them at breakneck speed. It was followed by two smaller, faster figures as Mol and Pip chased the boy towards them. Don's last whistle was an order to find the boy. Aaron slid over the damp peat and slithered towards the fence line.

"Fucking got one," Aaron breathed as he ran, "Bastard English, bastard Sec Units, they can all get tae fuck."

CHAPTER 15

March

The road was, at least, smooth. The A1, as it was always called before Andrea Taylor built the border and went to war, had been resurfaced for a stretch just north of the border, where Izzy now walked. It was now called the, now what was it? Freedom Trail, that was it. After that road in Boston where that guy said '*The British are coming, the British are coming!*' in the American Revolution. Izzy frowned. She thought that was right, they had had a big thing on it on the NBBC, where they explained all the changes they wanted to implement. Suddenly she chuckled as she remembered they wanted to change the name of Yorkshire Puddings to '*Saltire Puddings*'. She sniffed and wiped her cold nose. Saltire Puds. Didn't sound very nice. Her gran made great Sunday roast dinners, Izzy recalled.

The snow continued as the sun began to dip down in the sky. Izzy caught a glimpse of it behind the clouds here and there, it wouldn't be up much longer because it would sink behind the hills to the west. But that was ok, she was sure she could reach the border by dark. It wasn't far from the Refugee centre, '*The first and last refugee centre in Scotland*' she giggled to herself, then thought of the pub with the same name and was reminded how much she wanted a glass of wine. She sighed. The pub had closed months ago. She walked on.

Izzy's hair whipped about in the wind and she coaxed it back behind her ears and into her hat. It was so cold this winter and being so close to the coast meant gale force winds that cut to the soul. She shivered as she walked, now stepping over rocks and dirt strewn over the road from what she could only presume were bombs or gunfire as she got closer to the border. There were no moving vehicles but she saw a series of green army trucks in the distance, parked. As she continued, she saw figures milling about in the dusk, army personnel and civilians, lit up by small fires and torches. It was then that she saw the scale of the hard border first hand.

She had crossed this border many times in her youth, with mum and dad and her brothers going to Lincolnshire to visit gran, and then with friends on her way to Newcastle Airport and foreign holidays or camping in the Cotswolds. It was a 'blink and miss it' moment in every journey which came and went with the minimum of fuss and herald. If you weren't paying attention, as she usually wasn't when she wasn't driving, you'd never know you were suddenly in another country all together.

What was once a collection of tall, fluttering flags and low, stone walls with understated lettering saying simply, 'England' or 'Scotland', was now a jagged and shiny arrangement which loomed large over the four laned road. It was at least four metres tall, a series of wooden and metal X structures which disappeared over the parking lot, into the trees and down towards the sea to the east and up into the hills to the west. At the roadside was a tower, like the ones she remembered seeing from the war films, with two people on top with guns and helmets on. A saltire flew from the top, flapping and rippling in the wind.

Izzy walked on, unnoticed by all until she reached a bench in the parking lot by the border lookout. Through the barbed wire, she could make out another border, this one lower but denser about 50 metres into New Britain territory. It must be New Britain's checkpoint. There were no towers along its length, but smaller huts and temporary buildings, made of shipping containers. People in green moved about there too, and she could see silhouettes of guns and armoured vehicles. Between the two fences was a pock marked wasteland. Holes and piles of rubble were strewn along the road and fields. Izzy viewed it all as she sat shivering, the wind now at her back.

"How did you get here?" a voice spoke behind her. Izzy didn't respond.

"Are you ok?" it spoke again then Izzy felt a person approach her shoulder.

"Careful, Brookes, remember your training," another voice said quietly.

Izzy looked up to see two guns pointed at her, held by two startlingly young people, a boy and a girl, both of whom looked like they should still be at school. They approached with efficient caution, their stance crouched, knees bent, eyes up to the gun sights.

"State your name," the girl said. Izzy looked at her and continued to shiver.

"What's your name," the boy said.

Izzy frowned. "How old are you?" she asked them both, the sight of the gun a half-regarded trifling. Guns were of little consequence nowadays, when everyone had one.

They paused. They weren't sure if that was a question they were supposed to answer. Their training had been quick and not terribly in depth.

Izzy tried again. "My name is Isabelle Atwood. How old are you?"

They both relaxed slightly at the sound of Izzy's obvious Scottish accent and the now obvious sight of her pregnancy bump.

"What are you doing here?"

"I want to go to England."

"Why?"

"I want to be safe."

"You're no safer there than here."

"Where is safe then? I want to go where it's safe."

The squaddies looked at each other, the woman in front of them was obviously slightly unhinged. They saw this kind of thing a lot with weirdos storming the fence dressed like extras from films; blue faces, axes and rippling tartan. Not to mention the large groups of peace demonstrators setting up camp right next to where they had parked their artillery, shouting slogans and planting huge flags.

"Listen, ma'am," the girl sat beside her, the gun now pointed at the ground. "You do know there's been fighting between New Britain and Scotland, right?"

Izzy nodded.

"And this is the border, right here," the girl indicated the fence.

Izzy looked where she pointed and nodded again.

"And the English troops are just the other side. Every now and again, we have to fire on them and they fire back. We're at war, sort of, do you understand?" She took a breath. "So I can't let you into enemy territory because they'd arrest you or maybe shoot you or send you back. Either way, your route to England is blocked."

"But I want to go and see my gran."

"I'm sorry."

"I miss my gran." Izzy sniffed as tears trickled down her cheeks.

The young soldier's face crumpled as Izzy cried and she wiped her own tears away with heavy gloves.

"I miss my mum, too," she said, her voice wavering. "My name's Rianne. I'm from Inverurie."

"We've both come a long way from home," Izzy said.

"Too far. But we have to keep going. What choice do we have?" Rianne smiled. "Let's get you inside, it's too cold here." Izzy rose and went with her, without protest. She walked her to a green truck, got in, and drove her north once more.

Izzy wordlessly stepped down from the truck, and - without a backwards glance at the soldiers who brought her - entered the refugee centre once more. In the gym studio, she moved her cot over to a corner behind the stowed trampolines and set about creating a homely space around it. It was as close to a room as she was going to get and suitably far away from anyone who wanted to make her life worse by their mere presence. She was sick of people. Sick of all of it. She wanted to disappear and this was a good start.

She balanced one of her art class paintings on the chair stack beside her bed to cheer herself up as she settled down once more to knit clothes for the baby. As the needles clicked, her mind wandered. What she wouldn't do for a magazine with lots of lovely free sample sachets in it. Or a phone with loads of her favourite music on it. She longed for the taste of chocolate and strawberries and really good coffee. Izzy sighed and went back to her knitting-picking up a dropped stitch as her life continued, under bombs and weak tea and thin blankets.

.oOo.

The evening drew on slowly. It was snowing heavily and even inside; she could feel the weight of the snow deadening the noises outside and in. It was March, she knew that, but as she drowsed, her knitting abandoned in her lap, she realised that she had begun to lose track of the days. Must write that down, she told herself. She finally fell asleep late in the evening, after all the general noise died down and stayed there, and all was peaceful for a while, with no evacuation into the basements and boiler rooms below. Bombs had only dropped twice this week but it was terrifying each time.

Later, at some undetermined hour, Izzy awoke. She felt a hand on her shoulder, felt shaking.

"Izzy!" the voice said, softly. "Izzy!" it said again. "Wake up!"

.oOo.

Izzy sat in a plastic chair at a Formica table in a basement corridor of the refugee centre. It was just about dawn, she thought, about 7am, but she was still groggy from her fitful sleep and the small matter of almost being blown into a hundred pieces then dragged from her bed to be evacuated down here at about 3am. The bombs had been dropping ever since. About two an hour? Three? Izzy wasn't sure. Each time one fell, the whole corridor

107

shook. Or was it missiles? Gunfire? Izzy wasn't sure she knew the difference yet. It was just loud and scary and she had no idea what was going on.

There were people on the floor lying on bundles of linens or in small family groups. The corridor had a low ceiling, criss-crossed with old pipes, lagged here and there with wool. It smelled warm, like a massive furnace roared in the next room, but also dusty and stale. The rising smell of fear and sweat crept up the walls. Callie walked over and sat across from Izzy. Between them she placed two cups of strong tea and then fiddled with the small wind-up radio. It whistled and crackled and occasionally broadcast a voice.

"I knew it was you, the moment they told me," Callie whispered and the sound echoed around them. Izzy peered at Callie's tear-streaked face through tired eyes. How was she here at a refugee centre? Didn't she make it across the border?

"I thought you were taking your boys over the border?" Izzy asked in a croaky voice. She was coming round but was still exhausted. Being pregnant was hard work, even when you didn't do anything.

"Too late," Callie shook her head. "The border was closed from the moment Andrea Taylor made that speech. We were caught just before the fence. I convinced them to let me help, because I'm a nurse, you know, and they let me stay with the border forces. The boys were drafted, both of them."

Izzy woke up slightly at this news and grimaced. "Callie, I'm so sorry. Where did they go? Do you know?"

"They were the ones who brought you in, when you first arrived. That was my Matthew and Elliot. Then last night, the girl who brought you back, she's in their squad, they worked it out. Worked out who you were," Callie said.

Izzy thought about the two young men who rescued her from the explosions weeks ago. They were only in their teens. She frowned. The bombing was now relentless. If their squad was on the border, did that mean ...

"Callie, where are your boys now?" she asked but didn't want to know the answer.

Callie swallowed her sob and covered her face. "I don't know!" she wailed, "They went off last night and they haven't been in touch since."

Izzy crumpled her face in concern. "I'm so sorry, Callie, but I'm sure they'll …" she stopped. She couldn't make a promise like that. She wasn't sure of anything anymore. After all, she wasn't sure where any of her family were.

Callie sniffed. "It's entirely my fault. I shouldn't have tried to get across the border. Stupid idea. I should've paid for them all to go to Belgium with their dad. I thought I could protect them. But I can't. No-one can." Callie stared at her tea cup.

Izzy considered for a moment. "Are we officially having a war, then?" she asked. "Like, with England?" She stopped and bit a nail. "I have loads of cousins in England and my gran. Why are we fighting? I don't get it. I don't want to fight them."

Just then, the radio found a small voice backed up by static. Callie turned up the volume.

"…with the return of all citizens to the EU until further notice.

"In Scotland, the recent skirmishes along the newly erected border with England developed into full scale fighting last night as New Britain's troops pushed into the Scottish Borders in some places as far up as Lanarkshire and Ayrshire in what has been described as guerrilla warfare. As many as 500 civilian casualties have been recorded so far by the Red Cross, already present in Scotland since the Illegal Scottish draft was declared five months ago by First Minister Andrea Taylor and the locally run refugee centres are filling up fast with people displaced from their homes by the fighting. EU and NATO sanctions placed on New Britain for terrorist activities in Europe has ensured the attack is muted by modern standards, but both sides have been urged to call a ceasefire and return to the negotiating table once more. The UN High Commissioner for Refugees are deploying and should be establishing and supporting local refugee centres within a few days.

"Asked to comment on the ongoing conflict, First Minister Andrea Taylor had this to say:

"We are a free and independent nation! We voted out of New Britain and out we shall go! This incursion into our border counties is a violation of our sovereign nation! We are being invaded by a larger power and where is the EU? Who is lifting a finger to help? Scotland stands alone against the aggression of Westminster. We fight to the end!"

"When we contacted the office of the New Nationalist Party in Westminster, no-one was available for comment."

Callie turned the volume down. "Fight to the end," she said, and burst into tears.

CHAPTER 16

March

Don and Sophie sat at the upstairs window. The sun was up but it would take another hour to crest the ridge and reach the farmhouse. They could see the sky blazing bright blue above the hilltops. There were no clouds yet but they usually turned up by lunchtime. Sophie leaned on her rifle, eyes half shut and Don noted the time from the news on the radio. "Fight to the end," he repeated and shook his head.

Since the upper paddock burned down, they had counted twenty-two blasts which sounded like bombs but could be missile or heavy artillery or anything. The gunfire had moved away for the most part, but they could still hear shots fired around neighbouring valleys. None of them were that familiar with the noises of war. Although they saw flashes and lights in the sky, nothing fell near the farmhouse and it became clear that no-one had followed Aaron over the hill last night. The last big sound was over an hour ago and it sounded further away, like thunder receding into the distance as a storm rolls away.

They were silent for a long time and watched the brightening sky. Then Sophie spoke.

"Mr Jack, I mean, Don," Sophie corrected herself, "Why … um, why, I mean, what are they doing here? Why are they trying to invade?"

Don sighed. "I wish I could tell you, Sophie, love, but I don't altogether know. I think that Holyrood has been waiting for independence for so long, they just couldn't wait any longer. New Britain are trying to take their land back, I suppose."

"Is that why they needed an army?" she asked.

"Yes, love."

"So they had to make one out of all the young people? Because there isn't really a Scottish army, is there?" she searched his face for clarity.

"No, love."

"And the army is supposed to stop England getting in? Is that it? So that Scotland can be by themselves, like a different country to New Britain?"

"That's the idea, I think, yes."

Sophie was quiet for a moment. Don glanced at her. How on earth could a country take such innocent young lives and expect them to fight? Poor kids didn't even know what the fighting was all about.

"Why don't New Britain use their, like, warships to sort of surround us?"

"They're not allowed, in a manner of speaking. New Britain's government did a terrible bombing in Strasbourg, remember? So the EU and NATO must make sure New Britain don't get in their warships and start fighting with them. So that means if they want to get to northern Scotland, they must go over land."

"They won't like that!" Sophie laughed. "I remember when you took us to that big mountain by Inverness and we all camped. It was *freezing!*"

Don chuckled and they both looked back out of the window.

"Don?"

"Yes, Sophie, love?"

"Would you go out and join the army?"

"Too old, doll!" he chortled. "They wouldn't want me!"

"But you're good at all this stuff, you know, guns and being a lookout and being sort of good at taking care of people. You know, like, *everything,* and that's got to be useful."

Don thought for a moment. "Most likely that's the reason they don't want me. I know enough to be dangerous."

Sophie sighed, "I miss my mum," she stated simply, but the words pierced Don's heart like a knife.

"I know you do, sweetheart," he said, patted her shoulder, stood up and went for the door. "Tea?" he asked, and she nodded.

Don shut the bedroom door and Sophie looked back out the window, her head on her hands, and sighed. She considered for a moment. She was sixteen years, seven months and five days old. She was born on 12th of July, Cancer, although she didn't like that word because it took both her grandmas away. Her mum liked all that astrology stuff but Sophie was less convinced. You just are what you are, she thought and surely the stars have nothing to do with it. After all, if it were all true, there would be one three-hundred-and-fifty-sixth of the population walking around who were just like her. She frowned. But there weren't. So it was stupid.

Sophie sighed again and sat back in the chair. In the bedroom behind her was a double bed with a crocheted throw on it and cool blue flowers on the duvet cover. The walls were also blue and the furniture looked old and a bit fancy. The light was off so the room was dull and dim. Sophie had a day bed at home; it was white metal with white duvet and pillows, strewn with teddy bears. When she was allowed, she put on the heated blanket and snuggled down with her favourite, Jingle Bear, who had little bells in his ears. Her little sister, Abbie, didn't have a heated mat, so sometimes she would sneak in too. Since there was no internet, she would read to her; Sophie's current favourites were Rebus and Agatha Christie but Abbie didn't really understand them so she read about dinosaurs and talking dolphins and fairies. Sophie smiled. She missed them all so much. It had been more than a month since she had left and Sophie still had the salt in her bag that her mum needed for her sore legs. Her smile evaporated. "I'm sorry, mum, really I am," she said to herself, "I would have come straight back but the Sec Units were on to me. Then Mr Stupid Sinclair turns up and leads them to us. Then I did something that I might never forgive myself for."

Sophie held the rifle upright, the butt on the floor and leaned against it, her eyes closed. She sniffed and a tear trickled down her nose. She wiped it away but another one took its place.

Sophie McCall sat for a few moments and let the tears flow. She wanted to go home so badly but knew that couldn't be, not now at least. She wanted to argue with her mum over going out or clothes or make-up. She wanted to make a fuss about who got the TV remote. She wanted to sleep til noon. Without her help, mum would need to be in hospital. Her little brother and sister were too small to look after themselves so where were they? If she went back, she'd be drafted anyway or sent to prison. There was no real way out this mess. And what a mess. Even Mr Jack wasn't sure what to do sometimes and he knew everything.

Sophie just wanted someone to tell her everything was back to normal and she could just go home and finish her Highers and go out with her friends and apply to college and eat pizza and get a McDonalds, "Ooh, that's so unfair, brain, you know there are no McDonalds left in Scotland." Sophie had a strong recall of fries and vanilla milkshakes and mucking about outside the shops with their little brown baggies of food and she closed her eyes to savour the memory. "Oh shit," she said quietly, "just don't think about it, Sophie," as her memories turned to pain and longing.

The bedroom door opened and Lewis entered with two cups of tea and a plate of home-made toasted bread. He sat in Don's chair and placed the toast on the windowsill between them and they each took a mug.

"Thanks, Lewis," Sophie sipped her tea. "Where's Don?"

"In the basement."

"Again? He's always in there. What's down there?"

"Dunno. It's a man-cave. He closes the door after him," He made a rueful face. Sophie chuckled.

.oOo.

Don closed the basement door and slumped down the stone steps to his workbench. He fell into his chair and held his head in

114

his hands. He could feel the roughness of his palms against his cheeks and then the warm trickle of tears as they fell from his eyes into his growing beard. He took a deep breath and rubbed his face, wiping tears onto his sleeve.

How had it come to this, he thought, children forced to bear arms and families ripped apart, and for what? Was it worth it? Was any of this worth it?

He looked up and scanned the scruffy, overloaded notice board in front of him. It was filled with scraps of paper, formulae, academic papers, jokes, notes and letters. He lifted the corner of a yellowing scrap of paper and viewed the photograph below. It was old and dog-eared, the colours draining after all these years.

Don smiled as he recalled the day it was taken. Maggie and the boys were fossil hunting on the shore at Stonehaven Harbour and they stopped to pose for him. Their old dog, Bess scampered in and out of the water behind them and the camera captured her as a blur. Right after Don clicked the shutter, a wave covered their shoes and they danced and tiptoed their way onto the dry sand, squeals of laughter and joy filling the sea air. It was a precious memory of them together as a family. He missed his boys, but he missed this Maggie more. He would hold onto his darling wife for as long as he could. For her, it was worth it.

.o0o.

Upstairs, Sophie took a slice of toast.

"Is Aaron ok?" she asked.

Lewis looked out of the window at the hill and the trickling burn. "He'll be fine. I don't think it's sunk in yet. How are you doing? I'm really impressed with the way you've mucked in to help run the house. You're a credit to yourself."

Sophie rolled her eyes. "I don't want to hear any of that guidance teacher speak, please, I had enough of it before."

"I mean it."

Sophie looked straight at him. "No, you don't," she said with a shake of her head. "That's teacher talk," she continued, "... and there's actually no such thing as a teacher anymore. Not in Scotland. I don't care if anyone is impressed with me or thinks I'm doing a great job. *I'm* unhappy and I want to go home to my mum. There's people invading who used to be our friends."

"It'll be ok,"

"Ok? When?" Sophie cried, "Nothing's ok and the worst thing is I can do nothing to change any of it. I'm stuck. And that feels worse than anything at all." She returned to stare out of the window and wiped her tears away angrily. "I'm stuck," she mumbled and gritted her teeth in a frown to stop more tears.

Lewis backed off. He had no idea how to respond to her. She was right.

"Eat your toast, Sophie," Lewis urged and picked up a piece for himself. He ripped off a corner and began to chew but stopped suddenly and inclined towards the window, squinting.

Sophie reacted to his movement and turned sharply to follow his gaze. She stood up and gripped her rifle. Her eyes finally fell onto the spot that he peered at and she gasped quietly.

There, halfway down the hill, curled up and drinking from the burn, was a soldier. A wounded, English soldier.

CHAPTER 17

March

Izzy sat on her cot and rummaged through her bag. It would seem this was all she had left in the world and she was bloody furious. After the soldiers left for the fighting after the invasion began properly, the Sec Units came in to take their place to help 'secure' the refugee centre. From that point on, nothing else got through. They said the Red Cross was busy elsewhere and would likely be back soon but in the meantime the food was running short and all medical check ups and assistance were suspended.

Just like the centre staff and the soldiers, none of the Sec Units was prepared to go back to Izzy's car to get the rest of her stuff.

"Bloody Sec Units, think they own the bloody place, come in here and take over but never bloody help," she grumbled, grabbed her hairbrush and began pulling it through the mop on her head. And when, for that matter, was she going to be allowed in the showers today? It was definitely her time slot but the last few days had been a free for all, all the rules out the window and everyone for themselves. She turned in her seat but all she saw was the grumpy woman from reception hurrying through the room and Izzy didn't want to speak to her again. Where was Callie?

Izzy stood up and stretched her back. Night after night of broken sleep in a plastic chair listening to the roar of bombs did nothing for her mood or her posture. She grimaced and thought again about how she was going to manage a baby. Around her, the dim gym room was now filled with extra cots, unmade and rumpled. Under each cot were bags of unwashed clothes and rotting leftover food, plastic water bottles and rubbish. The smell was becoming unbearable and her chin began to wobble.

Just like before, when Izzy had cried into cold, silent air at home, she stopped. She could not afford to fall apart. She took a deep breath and considered her next move. She didn't want to stay here but she had no way of getting out. The border was clearly closed to everyone and there was no way of getting anywhere. The Sec Units were as dangerous as they were unhelpful and the centre was run by local volunteers who had no power and even less information. Even the Red Cross overseers refused to move people because of some law or other. None of them really knew what they were doing.

Izzy considered. What should she do? Walk to the car? No, too dangerous, too far. Get to Lewis at Don's house? She thought about this for a moment. It was tempting, after all. Don and Maggie were self sufficient for the most part and they had dogs and a wood stove and Izzy could help do everything around the farm … Izzy shook her head. Maggie must find it hard to cope after the stroke and besides they probably still had three wanted criminals under their roof. They didn't need an expectant mother too. And there was a small matter of it being miles away. Plus, Izzy scowled, she never wanted to see that selfish bastard Lewis Sinclair ever again.

Izzy needed medical supplies, a safe place to give birth and baby stuff. She didn't even know what she needed. Izzy brushed her hair in longer, more thoughtful strokes. Staying here was the obvious answer. But … surely the Red Cross would understand her position and find someone to take her home or to her mum's house or … Izzy shook her head. Why would they care? If they agreed to let her go home, they'd have to take everyone. Besides, she reminded herself, there was no food, no resources, no power. Home was a shell. Where was home now? She remembered the young soldier, Rianne's words, *still a long way to go*, and stopped to think. Where was home now?

"Iz, pick up your bag, let's go," a voice behind her whispered. Izzy turned, startled out of her thoughts. It was Callie.

"What are we …?"

"Shh. Just pick up your bag in a moment, then follow me out the front doors. There's a black Land Rover out there. Get in it," Callie hissed.

"What are you …" Izzy started but Callie turned and stiffly walked away.

Izzy looked around herself at the dozen other people in the old gym studio but they all seemed involved in their own little world. One rocked back and forwards. One lay with the covers over her head, and one stared into space, chewing on her nails. At least 300 more people arrived last night during the bombings and they were sleeping in corridors and corners now. Izzy was lucky to be in a smaller, safer room, even, if it did smell like sweat and onions.

She picked up her tote and walked to the doors. She went down the long corridor towards the main entrance past several Sec Unit goons who stood and brandished their guns at every opportunity. Some of them had an audience of young fluttering women but most were too flabby or unpleasant looking for even the thinnest of attention spans. Izzy walked on through the murmuring crowds which lined the corridor. They all looked haunted, shocked and shaken. The smell of unwashed bodies and sewage had begun to permeate every corridor and it was all she could do not to throw up. Izzy tried to compose herself.

Outside the plate glass windows, Izzy could see a black Land Rover. She saw Callie in the front seat and swallowed hard. Where were they going? She hesitated. Then she went to the café hatch and asked for a coffee. It seemed like the thing to do but Izzy wasn't sure why. A cover, maybe? She took her weak drink and pushed open the front door. The sun was up now and she felt some warmth. The vernal equinox was near and the days were a little longer. Izzy smelled the damp leaves in the air, mingled with fire or scorched earth, or possibly both. There was no snow now, they were too close to the coast and it melted quickly. With a small backwards glance, Izzy slipped into the passenger seat and the Land Rover pulled away immediately.

"Where are we going?" Izzy asked.

"Europe," Callie replied.

"How the hell are we going to get to Europe?" Izzy cried, incredulous. "Have you lost your mind?"

"Nope. Remember, I sent my husband and youngest to Belgium. I know how this works."

"Surely, now, there's no chance of getting there, Callie, we'll be killed! I don't understand, it's pointless! You've just stolen an army vehicle, they'll be on us in no time!"

"No they won't," she replied, her eyes firmly on the road. "Recognise this car? Elliot and Matthew picked you up in it. They left me with the keys when they went to the front. And they left their army overcoats."

"So we are going to pretend we're army?"

"If we need to."

Izzy pointed to her middle. "I don't think we'll get away with that."

"Any better ideas?"

"Don't you want the boys to come?" Izzy asked quietly.

Callie gripped the steering wheel but said nothing.

"Where are we going?"

"There's a harbour a few miles up. We'll buy passage there."

"Buy? What with?"

Callie took her eyes from the road for a split second and grabbed Izzy's hand.

"With this!" she cried triumphantly and held up Izzy's finger upon which sat the modest engagement ring Lewis gave her all those years ago.

CHAPTER 18

March

His name was William Paul, Pauly to his mates. Aaron's – or someone else's - shot had grazed his temple and as Pauly fell, he had broken his ankle in one of the holes gouged out by the bomb blast. He had fallen unconscious into gorse and disappeared. It was no surprise that his unit had thought he was dead. As both sides fired more shots, Pauly slipped from view. No doubt someone would be back for him soon, but in the meantime, he had regained consciousness, crawled to the burn and collapsed.

Don realised his ankle was broken when they picked him up onto a quad. He created a makeshift splint to move the young soldier and they hauled him back to the farmhouse.

Sophie, Aaron and Lewis watched over him as he lay on the sofa, although it was clear he wasn't getting up any time soon. They had closed the curtains when they brought him in just in case anyone else decided to drop in and the room was in constant murky shade. The fire burned in the grate and the lights were on, but dim.

The door to the hallway opened and Fran entered the room. She looked from Pauly to Don and the others.

"What the hell is going on here?" she asked.

"We picked him up from the hillside. He's hurt," Aaron said.

"He's English," she stated, her tone cold.

"That's right, lass," Don said as he rummaged in the large first aid kit.

"Get him out of here."

Aaron turned to her, "That's really unkind. He needs help."

"Don," she rounded on him. "We have to get him out of here. He'll lead them all to us, to me, to *you!* He has to go!"

121

"He's not going anywhere, Fran," Don replied.

"He'll ruin everything!"

"Fran, just calm down," Sophie sighed.

"Don't you dare speak to me!" Fran screeched and fled from the room.

"This will hurt, lad," Don apologised before he set about binding Pauly's ankle as best he could. He gave Pauly a shot for the pain before he began to manipulate the ankle into a roughly straight line and applied the splints and bandages. The soldier gritted his teeth and tears sprang to his eyes, but he breathed through it until Don finished his final knot. Then Don gave him one last shot and Pauly slowly sank back into unconsciousness.

Don stood up, "I don't think he's going anywhere in a hurry. We can leave him. There's still a farm to run, people, let's get on it."

Sophie, Aaron and Lewis filed out of the room and Pip and Mol followed. Don heard them leaving the house, the familiar sound of quad bikes starting and gates opening.

Don walked into Maggie's room and sat down in an easy chair.

"Everything ok, love?" Maggie asked.

Don dropped his face into his hands and sighed. He was quiet for a moment before he emerged. "It's getting closer, love."

"Is that anEnglish boy, Don? You did the right thing helping him. He needs it."

"I know. You'd look after everyone, if you could, Mags." He stood up and held her hand. "And that's why I love you."

They smiled at one another for a moment.

"We're so lucky, with everything we have," she said. "And everything we've had."

"That's what I hold on to, Mags, what we both have to hold on to."

"Are we safe, Don?" she asked.

"We're all safe, my love." he replied.

He left the room and walked through to the outer hallway, unlocked the basement, switched on the light and closed the door behind him.

By the next day, Pauly began to look more alert. He tried to sit up with regained composure. Lewis handed him a washcloth for his sweaty, dirty face and he took it with thanks. He looked around the room at the armed teenagers, dogs and older men, all bearded and unkempt, and nodded his thanks. Don inspected his leg carefully.

"We'll have to keep an eye on that ankle. I'm not sure it's a clean break," he said.

"Are you a doctor?" Pauly asked Don. His accent was Mancunian.

"No, lad, I'm a farmer, but I've had to set bones in sheep before. It's not that different. How are you feeling?"

Pauly nodded, "Better," he said. "Thanks."

Aaron sat down, "Are you a proper soldier?" he asked. "I mean, like a soldier who signed up, like, before it all started?"

"Yes," Pauly nodded. "I've been in the army for two years. Stationed in Catterick."

"So, aren't you supposed to just give us your name, rank and serial number? Or is that just the movies?" Aaron asked.

Pauly thought for a moment. "I guess so," he shrugged. "It's just …"

They waited for him to continue and he looked at each of them. Sophie leaned on her rifle. Aaron had a tea cup, Lewis held another wash cloth and Don pulled off his blue surgical gloves.

"It's just, none of us think this is real."

"Us?" Aaron asked.

"Yeah, the lads, my unit. When they said we were going to the Scottish border, we just thought we were going on manoeuvres. Doing some moorland training, camping, that kind of thing. Then they said we should be battle ready and we thought, 'Yeah, right, fighting with Scotland just because they had that referendum', and we thought it was a big joke." Pauly shifted in his seat and gasped in pain.

Don prepared to give him another shot.

"But we got to the border and there was barbed wire and lookout towers and all the things you see in bases but with Scottish boys patrolling, like a totally new army. Then we find out you've had a draft and we started to get scared. Loads of lads said they didn't want to fight with the Scots. At least four lads in my platoon are from Scotland."

"What did they do?" Lewis asked.

Pauly shrugged, "They were all reminded that they pledged to the Queen and that comes before where they were born, and that. They had no choice."

"What was your remit?" came a voice from the door as it opened. Fran McDonald growled at the boy, hardly able to contain her mistrust.

Pauly looked up, "My what?"

"Your orders. What were you supposed to do? Why are you here?" she spat through gritted teeth.

"Look, Missus, I'm just a regular army bloke, I don't ..." Pauly shook his head.

"I said, why are you here?" Fran repeated and emerged through the door with Aaron's gun on her arm. She then lowered it and pointed it straight at Pauly, who reflexively put his hands up.

"Whoa, Rambo, chill out," Sophie cried and tried to take the rifle from her.

"No!" Fran shouted and now pointed it at Sophie. "No! No-one tells me what to do!" Sophie raised her hands with a "Fucking hell ..." under her breath but she backed off. The look in Fran's eyes was enough of a warning.

"I have had enough of this! I've had enough of all of you!" She swung the rifle around to point at Lewis who put his hands up, turned away and squeezed his eyes shut. Aaron, next to him, continued to sip his tea. She avoided Don's stare, however, as he sat next to the wounded boy.

"What were your orders?" she asked Pauly again. She pointed the rifle at him once more. "Where were you going?"

"Ok, we were headed north. We were to take back the country from the illegitimate Scottish force with as few casualties as possible. We were to secure civilians with food and supplies and only engage with enemy combatants. We were headed to Edinburgh to stop the people in charge."

"Liar!" she snarled. "You just want to hold onto Scotland! And you need to subdue us to do that! You want the nukes, and the power and the oil and the land! You just want to invade and never leave!"

Pauly looked at her, the scepticism clear on his face.

"I dunno what they've been telling you but we don't want to hold on to Scotland if you lot don't want to be a part of New Britain. Why would we?"

"Your government need our resources. It's the old story," she spat.

"Well, I dunno about that," he shook his head. "I think you might need to look a bit closer to what's around you. Your government is as mad as ours."

"What do you mean?" Despite herself, Fran was curious to hear his English perspective. It had been many months since she had listened and spoken to anyone outside her small circle of Scottish politicians and now the farm dwellers and she hadn't been in touch with anyone English since she was chased into the hills.

"Well the way I see it," he continued. "These people in uniform everywhere. Different uniforms. Turns out, you've sent two armies to fight. One made of people who were drafted and don't really want to fight, and the other in black uniforms with vans with sirens like the cops, the Security Force."

"The Sec Units," Sophie rolled her eyes.

"Yeah, them. They're the nasty bastards, that lot. Itching for a fight, spoiling. No training. They were a crap shot, the lot of them, and easy sitting targets, but sneaky bastards. Mean. They were the ones that set fire to the barn. Sorry about that, Don, that wasn't us, I swear. We don't want to fight anyone who's been drafted who doesn't want to fight. Nothing is ever as clear cut as politicians tell you it is. But I'm just a soldier. I do as I'm told. And my orders were make as few casualties as possible, only engage armed opposition and secure the capital."

"That's a lie!" Fran screamed and came a step closer to the sofa. Don stiffened, Pauly put his hands up higher.

"No lie, Missus, that's the orders I got. We all got. Your First Minister has done something illegal and we have to stop it.. Nothing more."

"What about the nukes?" she snarled.

"We haven't got any nukes," he shook his head with a confused frown.

"No, but we do," she replied with a crooked smile, "and you want them, don't you?"

"Damn, Fran, you sound like a fruitcake," Aaron shook his head.

Sophie giggled. "Fucking mental," she chortled.

"Come on, Fran, now that's taking it a little far, hmm?" Don stood up and held out his hand for the rifle. She scowled at him but didn't move.

"The rifle, please," he said. He took another step.

"Get away from me, Don, I swear to God!"

"Come on Fran, you don't want to do this. This lad is not your enemy."

"Yes he is!" she screeched.

"No, Fran, he isn't. He's just said he was sent by the army to protect people like us. Like the kids and Lewis, from the draft and the stupid border dispute. He's just a lad. He doesn't want to kill anyone, any more than they do." Don stepped close enough to grab the rifle but he just stood there with his hand outstretched.

His eyes drilled into hers. She shook her head wildly and whimpered.

"Please give me the rifle, Fran," he repeated and moved his hand towards the barrel.

"No! Don, you can't believe him! He's English! We, the government, Holyrood, *we* are the ones trying to protect Scotland!" Fran trembled.

"Fran, we all want independence but the government have gone too far to try to get it. We ... we all have gone too far. Even me. Andrea Taylor has gone too far. Lost perspective. But you can use your knowledge and your influence to stop it. You have evidence. Use it."

"I want to stop her!" Fran cried, "Stop her blaming me!"

"You can stop it all, Fran. The war, the sanctions, the draft." He moved closer to her.

Fran stared at him.

"Everything you could possibly need to stop the killing is under this roof." He looked back at her, his old, crinkled eyes piercing hers. "Now, please, let me help. Give me the gun."

Don reached for the barrel and suddenly grasped it.

As he did, Fran screamed, turned the weapon towards him, thrust it against his chest and fired.

CHAPTER 19

March Bute House

Andrea Taylor sat behind her desk, a cold cup of coffee untouched in front of her. She stared into the middle of the room, although she didn't see the dust specks that danced in the filtered light, her mind was on something much bigger. Her birthday. She and her husband usually spent birthdays at the family seat in Inverness but she couldn't join him this year. He had left shortly after the border closed in November and taken the cats with him. Andrea Taylor wasn't sure who she missed more, him or the cats. She raised her eyebrows at this thought. Definitely the cats.

Damian slipped in through the open door but she ignored him.

"First Minister?" he prompted. He sat down and waited patiently on an easy chair for her to start, his pen poised over a blank page in his notebook, his memos and messages in a pile beside him.

Andrea took a deep breath and mentally returned to the room.

"Ok," she began, "So what's going on out there?"

"What do you want first? I have the …"

"Just tell me what's happening!" she snarled, her anger rising fast along with her stress. "How many are dead? Where are they? Why aren't the EU knocking my door down to talk to me?"

He smiled nervously and picked up a memo. "Um … well, the casualties are quite … we've lost about 50 personnel and 50 civilians in actual fighting with New Britain. But the casualties from street fighting are way higher. It's …" He paused.

She waved at him to hurry up, "It's what?" she said.

"It's the Sec Units, shooting people. People who haven't shown up for the draft, or who break curfew or other minor offences. Then other people come out and attack the Sec Guards and every major town and city has reported running street battles with Sec Units in the streets, you know, like guerrilla warfare, throughout the tower blocks and tenements."

She stared at him, hard, but didn't reply. This was not supposed to happen.

He continued, "From what I've been told, the New Britain troops have been moving north. The border breaches happened along the more remote sections. We've tried to shore up defences in other places, but there doesn't seem much point, so most of our troops are in the cities. Which leaves Sec Units, or people with guns and uniforms who say that they're Sec Units running the show out there with no co-ordination and no accountability." He paused and peered at her but she tilted her head back and frowned at the ceiling, so he continued. "The reports are coming in from the Borders and southern counties. The New Britain forces show up and instead of finding our troops, they're fired on by the Sec Units, so they then fire back, so ... it's a mess out there. No-one knows who to hide from or who to trust. What makes it more confusing is that The New Britain troops have brought and are distributing food and supplies and since we closed the border and nothing gets through, people are really grateful." He swallowed, nervously eyeing the growing fury on her face, but pressed on.

"But, um, they have taken Cruachan. A hydro-electric power station."

"I knew it!" she cried. "They just want our power!" Taylor sat, lips pursed, breathing through her nose. Damien eyed her. English troops were also in Pinkston and Chapelcross Power Stations. He thought it best to keep that to himself for now. He continued.

"Our drafted troops, the new Scottish Army, well," he stammered, "I think it might have been a mistake to draft people. No-one wants to fight. They all know the New Britain army is miles bigger and better equipped. They're deserting in their hundreds, going home, going into hiding. This then creates more targets for the Sec Units who are shooting at everyone and everything, no questions asked. I don't know what else to tell you, except it's possibly time to stand down?"

"Stand down?!" she screeched and thumped the desk, "How *dare* you presume to tell me my job!"

Andrea took a deep breath and turned her chair away from him. She closed her eyes and exhaled for a long time. This was bullshit! Eighty one percent of her people voted for Independence! Why were they not prepared to put their money where their mouth was? Why were they fighting the very people who kept them safe and *why the hell* did they not want to fight to get away from that evil, corrupt, murdering Westminster government? She didn't understand but they would all pay the price, if it killed her.

"First Minister," Damian began again, "The New Britain army are swarming all over Glasgow," he began, "And they will be knocking at your door any day now. The Prime Minister is just waiting for them to secure the city but I don't think they're in a big hurry. I think they want us to go back to the table and negotiate before they, you know, do the ultimate thing and," he swallowed, "… arrest you … us all."

She pierced him with a stare. "How can you know that?" she barked reaching an accusing finger across the wide table.

Her secretary squirmed in his seat. She continued to stare.

"My … my cousin works in the Home Office in Westminster," he said, finally. "He's an economist." He paused. "That's the problem, First Minister. Scottish, English, we can split the country physically, but we can't split the people quite as easily. There are so many of 'us' down …"

She sat back, her face lined with scorn and spoke over him.

"How many of them have we killed?" she asked.

He grimaced. "First Minister, we have no data on that. Sorry."

"What about the refugee centres I keep hearing about? Bloody over reaction if you ask me."

"Ok, refugee centres. There's about ten of them, and the Red Cross are in some, St John's ambulance on others and there are smaller hospitals accepting people who are displaced. The numbers are general but we have about 65,000 displaced people who came to centres after they lost homes or just because our supply lines are so … weak. With every border through land and sea blocked, and all the roads and distribution disrupted, the result is as you'd expect. My Great Uncle lives just outside Fort William and he says it's like the clearances, people abandoning their homes in the Highlands because there's just nothing getting through."

"Whose fault is that?" she sneered.

He fidgeted nervously in his seat. "We don't have full data on who we have … um … left in the country after so many people left in the last year," he stammered. Andrea made everyone nervous, and Damian was no exception. "So we aren't sure how many are left in their homes. Or what they're doing."

Andrea sat back in her easy chair and it squeaked underneath her. She drew a deep breath and looked at the ceiling, a pronounced frown on her face. The English had stepped over her hard border to engage her people. *They* were in the wrong. Just because her troops were too chickenshit to fight …

She turned back to her desk. "What else have you got?" she asked.

"The EU have offered again to sit around the table with us and Westminster to broker peace. However, we must have a ceasefire before they'll make any deal. And stop the draft."

"They know what we want."

"Some of your Ministers want to talk to Fran MacDonald."

"What for?"

"Because you said she was responsible for the plane crash."

Andrea waved the request away, "She was working for the English. She leaked the evacuation plans. She's a war criminal, gone to ground. I've no idea where she is. The plane didn't crash, they shot it down, acting on her information. An act of terror." She shook her head and repeated the lie. "An act of aggression because we closed the border."

"But I don't think …"

"Please don't think, just take my messages and keep me up to date. Can you do that?"

"Yes, First Minister."

There was a pause as she sat back again and looked at the ceiling.

"Ok, here's the thing. We need to secure the city."

"It's too late, there are English troops surrounding Edinburgh. They are approaching from the south and the west."

She held up a hand and shushed him.

"We need to secure the most *important* part of the city. Have the troops set up a ring blockade, from Charlotte Square, along Queen Street, York Place, along London Road. Secure Calton Hill, Holyrood Palace and the Parliament then up the High Street to the Castle. Keep them out until the EU see what atrocities they're laying at our door. We'll see how much *bigger and better equipped* they are."

"What about the rest of the city, I mean the outer suburbs?" he asked, quietly.

She stared into the distance.

"Let the Security Units deal with that," she said, at length. "Tell them to bring in as many draft dodgers as they can. If the Sec Units can get them to agree to joining up, we invite them in. After all, it'll be much safer in here when we are blockaded."

Damian felt he could almost weep. He couldn't believe what he was hearing. "But …" he began, "It's only safer once you join up because the Sec Units stop firing at you! It's nothing to do with New Britain troops. We're just fighting with ourselves!"

"So it's a win-win situation, then, isn't it?" she smiled.

"What about everyone else? I mean the rest of the country?"

"We'll secure our independent future from the official seat in Holyrood. Then we'll worry about who's left." She turned away from her desk and closed her eyes. It was the price of freedom, she thought.

Damian cleared his throat. "First Minister?" he asked quietly.

She didn't respond.

"One last thing."

"What?" she snarled, eyes now open, irritation etched into her face.

"The English. They've taken control of Faslane. We've lost our biggest bargaining chip."

CHAPTER 20

March
Eyemouth Harbour

Callie drove into the small town of Eyemouth and parked on a side street not far from the harbour. It was drizzling and a cold wind whipped the grassy verges and trees around them. It was not an ideal day to put to sea if you were at all nervous about it. Izzy picked up her bag and the huge army great coat and struggled out of the passenger seat. Callie slammed her door behind her and started to walk away but turned back again, opened the door and placed the keys on the seat.

"We won't need it anymore, no point denying someone else," she said, "I can tell the boys where we left it."

Izzy shouldered the coat, it really was way too big for her but she was grateful for its warmth, and they both walked through the streets towards the front. It was a small place, now deserted and the harbourside buildings were shuttered and dark. The large stone fortifications stood watch on the hill above and the seagulls kept their sentry positions on the edge of the harbour wall. It smelled strongly of the fishing fleet, although Izzy wasn't sure if they even went out now. The salt air tugged at her hair and the sea spray spritzed her face. She could hear a buoy just beyond the entrance to the North Sea as it let out the occasional 'bong' from the bell which sat on top of it. The waves were not insubstantial as she looked beyond the safety of the harbour.

"There he is," Callie said and pointed towards a fishing boat, its engines chugging. Smoke puffed from the stack and the water beneath it rumbled and churned. Izzy eyed it with dismay. She really wasn't keen on boats, even less keen on the wide-open sea and spray and the frigid water. The boat looked rusty and worn, like an old bath that needed a new coat of enamel. It looked cold and leaky and as they drew closer, Izzy could see the captain was old and bristly. She took a deep breath. She was most definitely *not* looking forward to the next few hours.

"We need a ride," Callie said as they approached the boat. "You took my husband and child. Are you able to take us?"

He looked up. "No," he said, gruffly, "No pregnant ladies."

Izzy and Callie exchanged looks. "She's only seven months."

"No."

"Look, I'm a nurse, I'll take care of everything. It'll be no trouble. I promise."

The old man eyed her and then thrust out his hand. He wanted payment up front. Callie elbowed Izzy who began to tug at the ring on her finger. As much as she hated Lewis at this moment, the thought of handing over the ring he gave her made her pause. Lewis wasn't all bad. He wasn't mean or rude, he was just a bit thoughtless, a bit lazy, selfish. A scaredy cat. Work shy, always looking for the easiest path. She stopped herself. She realised she was talking herself back into hating him afresh. She pulled off the ring and gave it to Callie who handed it over.

The old man peered at it for a few moments and turned it over in his palm. Izzy rolled her eyes. Like he *knew* all about jewellery.

"Ok, ladies. Tomorrow. Or the next day. If it's safe. We're full today."

"Wait, where do we wait?"

The captain shrugged. "Where did you come from?" He turned back to his chores.

Callie and Izzy looked at one another.

"Did you know we had to wait?" Izzy asked. The wind whipped her hair up into a tangled mess.

"No idea. But it doesn't surprise me. Do you want to go back to the centre?"

"Did you see it back there? It was horrible."

The two women looked around the deserted harbour and out over the grey waves.

"We could always," Izzy began. "Take the truck back home. Like, Muirbridge home."

"Is that what you want to do?"

"Well, yes, but no. I'm not sure. There was no-one left in town when I came out here. There was no food, nothing. That's why I came. But now the Refugee Centre has been taken over, I'm wondering ..."

Callie caught her next thought immediately. "Do you want to go and find Lewis?"

Izzy rubbed her hands together and then pulled her coat closer around her bump.

"I think I probably should, don't you? Now I have transport and some petrol. Don't you think I owe it to him?"

"Frankly, no, but I see your reasoning. Should we take back your ring and head for the hills?"

"Ok. Let's do it. He might prove himself for the first time ever. Besides," she looked back at the boat, "It's homeward. It makes me feel, sort of safer going back that way." Izzy said hopefully. "Besides, I'm ... scared," she finished.

"Come on, let's get the ring," Callie put her arms around Izzy's growing frame and they walked back towards the dock. Just ahead of them, the boat rumbled in the water but they could hear raised voices from inside the cabin.

Just then, an older woman in an oversized parka tumbled out onto the dock, her shoulder bag thumping along behind her.

"... I said I couldn't leave them, Alan, and I won't! I don't care about being safe, I want my kids back!" She hauled herself up from her knees and picked up her bag. "You can't make me go!" she yelled behind her as a man, hatted and bespectacled, leapt from the boat and followed her.

"Helen!" he called, as the woman thundered past Izzy and Callie, "Helen! It cost me a fortune to get us on there! Come back! They'll catch us both! I'll be drafted too! Helen! Wait!"

Izzy and Callie watched the couple as they stormed up the small hill, obviously still arguing.

The captain stood on the deck and scratched his head as he also watched them disappearing. Then he shrugged and looked at the two women in front of him.

"We've changed our minds, too," Callie said to the captain. "Could we have the ring back?"

He looked at them levelly, pulled out the ring and held it out to them.

"You sure?" he said. Izzy nodded.

He looked beyond their shoulder towards the car park.

"Are you sure you're sure?" he asked again and nodded towards the black land rover which now contained the bickering couple as it backed out and roared off out of town.

"Oh ... bugger." Callie managed.

They both watched the Land Rover disappear as the sound of the engine was swallowed up in the wind. This is pretty much as far as you can go, Izzy thought. From a house to a refugee centre, to a dock on the far east coast of Scotland with no way of turning around and retracing steps. If she felt stuck before, she was most definitely completely stuck now. The only way was into that boat and on to Europe.

Izzy closed her eyes, "Let's do it," she said.

"Ok, ladies, jump aboard. Put on a life jacket, sit down and if you get sick, sit by the door. I can't tell you how long it'll take or what the in-voyage movie is. There's a war on and I would not like to get stopped by any warships, if you don't mind. So I am going to make it up as I go along and I don't need anyone to question me." He turned away again.

Callie jumped onto the deck and took Izzy's hand so that she could step down. Jumping wasn't a thing in the third trimester.

They both pulled yellow life jackets over their heads and clipped them closed. Izzy put the great coat back on top. She was freezing and knew it would only get worse. They ducked their heads as they entered the boat's cabin and in the dim light Izzy could see that they were not the only ones desperate to leave the country. The cabin wasn't designed for the dozens of bodies it now held. They stood and sat, leaned against walls and windows. Three sat on the table, a dozen sat on the wooden floor. Every set of eyes turned to them as they entered and a few murmured and shuffled. They were making room for Izzy on the padded bench. She sat gratefully and pulled her coat closer.

The boat tipped and rolled gently in the harbour waters, as the wind blew them around and Izzy felt an urge to vomit, except it would mean she'd lose her seat. She swallowed. It was going to be a long journey.

The engine noise deepened and Izzy felt the rumble beneath her feet. The boat moved backwards and turned to face the harbour entrance. This was it. They were going to Europe.

Money, tickets, passport! Izzy giggled at her mildly hysterical thoughts. She always worried that she would forget something crucial back when they went on holiday years ago. She frowned. Her passport wasn't even in date, was it? Will the Belgian refugee people ask for passports? Wait, Belgian? Dutch? She wasn't sure. She didn't know. Even after the uncertainty of the last few years, she still couldn't quite believe that it had come to this; she was a refugee, that old man was a people smuggler, she had paid in gold, she had only the bag at her side and the clothes she stood up in. Lewis was a wanted man and Izzy might never see him again. She was escaping from the country she loved even though she never, ever wanted to live anywhere else. Scotland was home and she was leaving behind her brothers and mum. She looked out of the small window and saw the broad sandy beach beside the harbour. It was cold and dreary now, but the beauty of Scotland's rugged coastline was indisputable.

It was *them* that had made her life unbearable. Civil war, armies, bombs, warships, blockades, sanctions; these were all words that didn't belong in her little life. She never voted for Brexit, never voted for the people in charge in Westminster. She didn't bomb Strasbourg or make the deal with Northern Ireland. She didn't have anything to do with the army either side of the border, or the austerity or the hatred or the curfews or the Sec Units.

Izzy didn't ask much of life. A pretty garden, a holiday every year, nice new cushions on the bed, prosecco with friends. She was a secretary in a hospital ward with a small house and a mediocre boyfriend. She didn't smoke or spit or drop litter. She recycled and didn't use a lot of plastic if she could avoid it. She was a good girl, as her mother used to say. However, it seemed that now Izzy was dressed in ragged clothes with unwashed hair on a smelly boat headed into the darkness of the North Sea and none of this was her choice. She had made good choices and yet she was the one forced to leave her home. All of this was not her fault but she and all these other people paid the price.

"Callie," she whispered to her friend who sat on the floor beside her.

"What?"

"Where are we going? Exactly, I mean."

"Holland."

"How long will it take?" Izzy already felt sick.

"You heard him. It could be two days, more. Well into tomorrow, at least. He's got to avoid the blockade ships and any movement from the English. He's going south first, into the fishing areas. If the Europeans catch us," she shrugged, "We may have a chance. Most likely we'll be turned around and sent back. I don't really know."

"I'm scared."

"Me too."

"What if we never come back?"

"That's the risk we run," Callie held out her hand and Izzy squeezed it tightly.

"I don't want to go," Izzy sniffed.

"Me neither."

The boat hit the open sea and immediately began to toss and pitch. The waves sluiced them from side to side and she felt the bodies beside her press against her. Izzy lay her head on her arm and seriously contemplated staying there for the whole trip. In fact, right now, Izzy would have been happy never to wake up again but as long as she still had Callie's hand to cling to, there was a little piece of Scotland, and family and home left in her heart.

CHAPTER 21

March

The ear piercing bang of gunshot exploded in the low ceilinged room. The flash illuminated Fran as she was thrown backwards with the force of the rifle's kick and she landed in the grate on her back. She touched the scorching hot fire surround with an outstretched arm and screamed in pain as the skin on her right palm burned away. The small puff of smoke from the gun seemed larger in the confined airspace and the noise ripped through eardrums and rattled the windows.

In a widening pool of black liquid, Don lay face up, his arms thrown at strange angles across his body. His chest was a mess of blood and tissue, held together by strips of thick cotton shirt. The bullet had pierced his heart with unintentional clinical precision then scattered bone and flesh around his abdomen before exiting through his ribs at the back.

Lewis held his breath. His ears rang and the thick metallic smell in the air invaded his nostrils. He couldn't believe he had just seen a man get shot. Don was dead! What the fuck? Actually shot in the chest and *died*. Really, just, *died*. Lewis couldn't move, his legs wouldn't work and his brain didn't engage. Don was dead. What the fuck?

"Don!" Sophie cried, the first to move, "Aaron! Help me!" Aaron jumped up at her request. Sophie put a hand to Don's head and spoke his name softly.

"Don?" she whispered. "Don? Please don't die," she pleaded, "We need you, please don't go!" She began to sob.

Aaron knelt down and felt for a pulse. Years ago, when the school had a pool, they had lifesaving classes, and he had never

141

forgotten the lessons. He wanted to be a lifeguard for years afterwards, but eventually all the pools closed and such lifeguards as there were retrained into other positions. So he knew to look for signs of life. He moved his fingers along Don's arm but felt nothing. He thought there might have been a faint pulse here and there but he couldn't be sure. He leaned over and put his ear to Don's mouth, listening and feeling for breaths, but there was nothing there either. His chest didn't rise and fall, his neck didn't pulsate, his eyes didn't flicker. The black stain beneath him grew until it was evident there was too little blood left in the body to sustain it. Don was dead.

"Soph, he's gone, mate," Aaron said gently.

She looked at him with big eyes shimmering with tears. "No," was all she said, "No." She sat and sobbed quietly on the carpet, Don's blood soaking into her socks. Aaron sat beside her. The room was silent for a moment until a wail filled the air from the other room. It was Maggie.

Lewis swallowed and scanned the room expectantly but no-one moved. He looked at Maggie's door then at Pauly, then Aaron and finally at the whimpering Fran.

Pauly looked frozen in shock – woozy from the painkilling shots Don had given him. He lay with his mouth open, his eyes wide.

Aaron had a hand on Sophie's back as she sobbed. He covered his eyes with the other hand, dirty and grimy from hard farm work. Tears streaked his cheeks.

Fran sat in the grate, holding onto her burned hand. Her whole body trembled with shock. The rifle, now silent and cold, sat next to her on the floor. She stared at the carnage she had created.

Lewis blinked a few times, took a deep breath, turned and pushed open the door to Maggie's bedroom.

Maggie held out a thin hand to him, tears flowing into a tissue which she held at her mouth.

"Maggie, I'm sorry, but …" Lewis stopped as his lip began to tremble and words caught in his throat.

"Don, my Don!" she cried as she looked beyond him to Don's body lying on the floor.

Lewis quickly shut the door behind him and grasped her hand.

"I'm sorry Maggie, but Don's ..." he sobbed, "Don's dead," he whispered and burst into tears.

From under the bed, two furry heads emerged and Don's faithful dogs looked up at him, their whole bodies trembling with the shock of the noise and smell of the gun in the house. They were used to noises in the fields, but not inside. He felt a wet nose in his hand and a warm body by his leg. Lewis sat down beside Maggie and they both wept.

Fran picked herself off the floor and dusted off her trousers. Her hand throbbed where she had fallen against the grate and she sucked in her breath with pain. She looked at Sophie and Aaron on the floor, then at Pauly, and then at the closed door to Maggie's room. She heard Amy distantly begin to fuss and immediately rolled her eyes in irritation. Then she checked herself.

"You weren't a murderer before, Fran, even though they accused you of it. Now you are. You were an elected official, a woman of the people who touted for votes and approval ratings for years to build political status almost as high as First Minister. You were Minister for Europe, an exalted position at the forefront of Scotland's bright, shining Independent European future. People were going to remember you for ever for all the good things you were going to bring. You *cared* about people. You deliberately worked *for* the people. Now look at you.

"A good man is dead on the floor at your hands, his wife sick and in extreme distress, teenagers lost with no future except one of destruction and pain and you, *you*, Fran think that a baby's cry is the worst thing about this single moment in time. Shame on you, Fran MacDonald," she said quietly, "*shame on you.*"

Fran picked up the rifle and bolted from the room into the kitchen. She dragged open the first aid kit and found a bandage for her hand. She sprayed it with cooling disinfectant and wrapped it up. She was going to need this hand to drive. Then she stopped, her eyes darting around the kitchen for one more thing. It wasn't there. She scanned the hallway, then the outer kitchen and pantry, scattering pans and crockery as she searched. She gathered up her bag and shoved her feet into her trainers. She selected a coat at random from the hooks and pushed her arms into it as she walked. A form appeared at the kitchen door.

"What are you doing? Where are you going?" It was Aaron. He had heard the smash of plates.

"Where is it?" she asked.

"Where's what?" he asked.

"The hammer, the big one, the sledge thingy," she replied, distracted, now emptying umbrellas onto the floor from their stand with one hand, the rifle firmly gripped in the other.

Aaron looked at her warily. He might not have been the brightest kid in school, but no way was he stupid enough to give the murdering bitch another opportunity to kill.

"Don't do it, Fran," he said, but as he spoke, Fran spied the sledgehammer behind the yard brushes in the corner. She grabbed the handle and hoisted it. It was way heavier than it looked and she stumbled slightly as her weight shifted.

"Fran, put it down," he warned but Aaron could see she wouldn't be able to handle the weight and his immediate concern abated.

"No, Aaron, I've got to do this," she said steadily as she put down the rifle and turned to the basement door, the one they were never allowed to enter. The padlock was large and heavy, slightly rusted. Don never disclosed where he kept the keys.

With great effort, Fran lifted the hammer and brought it down on the lock. It bounced and groaned but didn't move. Fran grunted and lifted it again. This time she dented the door. Lewis appeared behind Aaron and frowned. Fran lifted it one more time and screamed with the effort of crashing it on top of the lock. This time it gave way, tumbled to the floor and the door swung open with the force. She let the sledgehammer drop and switched on the basement light, then squinted into the dim room.

"What's she doing?" Lewis asked. "Don said we weren't …"

"No idea," Aaron replied. "But I think she's lost the plot - for good this time." Aaron made to follow her, but Lewis stopped him.

"No, give her a moment. She's … unstable. Give her space."

Fran coughed and waved the dust away from her face as she picked up the rifle and descended the wooden steps into the freezing basement. Lewis and Aaron peered at her from the door.

In the large, dimly lit room, every inch of storage space was used. There were shelves and cupboards neatly arranged. On one side, Don had salted venison covered in muslin cloth. There were jars of pickled and preserved fruits and veg, bottles of disinfectant, bleach, alcohols, fuels. He had a large stash of cement bags, lime and bricks. He had spare rifles, ammunition, old animal traps and tools. Three chest freezers sat in a row and as Fran opened each one, she saw they were stuffed with game and more vegetables. But none of this interested her. She turned to a workbench along the back wall which was flanked by shelving which looked newer than the others.

Still at the top of the stairs, Lewis recognised the shape of glass bottles like the ones they had at school which contained acids, alkalis and alcohols for chemistry experiments. Don had a large Bunsen set up on the bench with tubes, flasks and beakers. Beside them were safety glasses, gauntlets and a small blow torch, all of which had come from his school. A ledger sat open on the desk, a small pencil in the middle of the pages, all illuminated by a powerful desk lamp. Lewis started down the top two steps to get a closer look.

Fran approached the bench and moved the old stool to one side, carefully placing the rifle on the floor. She peered at the bench and the concoctions he was making up until this morning. She looked at his handwriting, his drawings, notes and sketches. She scanned the ledgers and books, some open, some closed, and flicked through each in turn. Then she plucked a dusty old book from the shelf and opened it. Then another, and another. Increasingly frustrated, Fran turned pages and her eyes widened. She muttered under her breath and swore breathily as she worked. Lewis watched her from afar, just as interested in the treasure trove of chemicals and equipment that lay on each packed shelf. He began to descend the stairs as quietly as he could.

Suddenly, Fran sucked in her breath and behind her, Lewis stopped. She slammed the final book shut in triumph and jammed it into her bag. Then she looked onto the floor beneath the countertop. Under the surface was a large metal footlocker. It was shut but unlocked. Fran dragged it out and opened the lid. Bingo. She *knew* it. She knew it was here. And now *she* was going to benefit from it. They were *all* going to benefit. She could do what Don said and stop everything. Stop the war. Stop the draft. Make it all better for everyone. She would be a hero! Fran thought about this for a while and allowed herself a half smile. Yes! The hero!

Now standing behind her, Lewis spoke.

"Fran?" he said gently and she screamed and turned in shock. She had not heard him descend the steps, she was so focused on her find. She grabbed her rifle and pointed it at him.

"No, no, no ..." he said, throwing his hands into the air. "I just want you to be calm, ok?"

He paused as she continued to point the rifle, and Lewis could see her arms shake with the effort. "Please don't shoot me," he added, as an afterthought although it sounded lame, even to his ears.

"Just let me be and I'll be out of here, Lewis," she growled. "I just need to get some things then I'm gone. Don't try and stop me. I've got very important work to do!" Her hands trembled on the rifle, her breath ragged.

"That's ok, Fran, I'm not here to stop you, just ..." He stopped for a long moment and they looked at one another. "You killed

Don, Fran. You killed him," he sobbed but just about kept his tears in check.

"I *know!*" she cried and thrust the rifle at him. "I killed him! I didn't mean to! I didn't want to! I liked Don! He took me in and saved me when everyone else in Scotland thought I was a traitor and a mass murderer!" she sobbed, the tears now streaming down her face, "And now I am! I *am* a murderer and I killed the one man who helped me!"

"Put the gun down, Fran, and we'll try and work something out, ok?" Lewis spoke more bravely than he felt.

"No!" she wailed. "They would never accept that!" she gesticulated to the stairs, indicating the family above them, "They want to kill me now and I don't blame them!"

"No-one wants to kill you, Fran," he soothed.

"I bloody do," came a voice from the top of the stairs. It was Sophie.

Fran turned abruptly and pointed the muzzle of the rifle at her. Then back at Lewis. Then once again at Sophie. "See!" she cried, "I can't go back! I have to leave! Just let me leave, Lewis,' she wailed.

"No fucking way, you murdering bitch," Sophie roared and flew down the steps, barging Aaron to one side.

Fran's eyes widened as Sophie came nearer, and the rifle finally clattered to the floor. She reached into the box. Sophie made a grab for the older woman but Lewis stopped her, throwing his arms around her waist.

"No! Sophie! Look!" he cried, the effort of holding her back almost too much for his aching body. "Look!" he said again and Sophie stopped.

Lewis didn't know much about it, after all, he was just a guidance teacher and the closest he got to warfare was the Xbox on a weekend but he knew instinctively that now, sitting in Fran's hand was a stick of explosives. Fran held it aloft, her arm shaking.

"Just let me leave!" she said with urgency. "I need to go! Now!"

Sophie relaxed in Lewis' arms and he let her go. They both backed off and Fran leaned down to pick up the rifle. She picked up several sticks from the box and placed them in her bag, as her eyes never left Lewis' face.

"Let's go," Fran said quietly, now focused and efficient, just like she used to be in the office.

They left the basement and Fran hooked the keys to the Land Rover into her bag.

"In the kitchen," she ordered. "All of you."

"Fran, you don't need to …"

"Get in the kitchen!" she shouted and pointed the rifle at Lewis. They backed into the kitchen and she closed the door. She raced up the stairs and entered Aaron's room. In her makeshift bassinet, Amy slept on, her sleep no longer disturbed by the sounds of rifle shot, screams and threats. The room was darkened, warmed by the fire in the grate. Fran tiptoed to the bed, picked the crib up and hoisted it off the bed. She grabbed Amy's bag and noticed a bottle of milk. That'd do until she got to town. She walked more slowly down the stairs and slipped out of the back door and into the yard. The chickens scattered at her footsteps and the milkers kicked out at their pen. It had begun to rain once more. She put her rifle and bag into the passenger seat, put Amy in the back, got in and roared the engine to life. She turned into the lane and drove slowly through the mud. *Benefit of all*, she reminded herself. *Benefit of all.*

CHAPTER 22

March
North Sea, travelling East

Izzy dreamt as she slept. In her mind she was in her comfortable, warm bed, the central heating was on and there was wi-fi. She scrolled on her phone and looked at videos of cats and replied to messages from her mother and best friend. She had a dish of ice cream by her side and a glass of prosecco to round off the evening she had just spent with her girlfriends in Dodgers Bar on the High Street. Her feet were warm and her abdomen was flat and smooth. Izzy was in seventh heaven with all the normal her mind could conjure up. But then her stomach began to hurt. Lying in between her fresh sheets and heavy duvet, she grimaced. Then it stopped. And started again. And stopped. Izzy slowly floated to the surface of her consciousness and became aware of her surroundings. She wasn't in bed at home with the heating on. She was still in an old boat, rumbling along in choppy seas. She groaned and pulled her coat around her a little tighter. Then the pain started again and her eyes flew open. What the hell was this? The gripping, tightening feeling squeezed at her abdomen from chest to pelvis. A thrumming, hard pain focused down onto her lower groin. This was it. Was it? Labour. Was it? Izzy didn't have a clue what it was but presumed the feelings were definitely a sign of something going on down there. Oh no, she thought, not now, please, not now. Not on a smelly old boat surrounded by grubby men and defeated women and foul smelling seat cushions and an unwashed floor. Please, God, not here!

The pain released and Izzy was able to catch her breath.

"Callie!" she whispered. "It's started, I think I'm in labour," she said.

Callie slept beside her, rolling with the pitch of the boat.

"Callie!" she hissed again and shook her shoulder.

"Hmm?" Callie awoke quickly; years of practice on night shift, on call and after three boys of her own. "What's wrong?"

"I think it's started," Izzy said quietly. "My labour."

Callie rubbed her eyes. "How far apart are they?" she asked.

Izzy paused. "I dunno."

"Does it hurt a lot?"

"Not too bad."

"Do you feel shivery, shaky, like you're really cold or nervous?"

"Uh, no, I don't think so."

"Urge to push?"

"No."

Callie yawned and turned over. "Time them. If it's every two minutes and they're really painful, let me know. If you get a push urge, let me know. You're probably ages away yet. First ones are always slow." She settled down to sleep once more.

Izzy raised her hands in a gesture that read *what the fuck?* and watched as Callie fell back to sleep. Did she not care? This was bloody important! She was in labour, for God's sake! There would be a flood of water here any minute now, loads of blood and a baby! And Callie didn't care! She had the contractions, surely that meant that birth was imminent. It wasn't like she was going to make a fuss like all those other mothers you see on the hospital documentaries, who screamed and yelled and complained about the pain. She just needed Callie to catch it in a clean towel and cut the cord and it would all be well. None of the wailing and panting. And Callie couldn't even do that!

Izzy sat there for a while, contemplating birth. What should she call it? She hadn't really thought about a name. For a boy, she thought maybe Jack? After her father. Or Ben? She didn't like Oliver or Daniel. Definitely not Lewis, she pouted. Callum? How about girls? Jess? Rebecca? India? Oh shit, here it comes again. Izzy drew breath and let it out slowly as the muscle bands squeezed around her middle. The pain lasted a few minutes and subsided once more. They were about two minutes apart, she thought. Now what do I do? The boat was in complete darkness. She looked around herself at the faces in the cabin; some sleeping, some awake and blinking. All of them miserable and scared. An older woman in the corner snored gently, sitting upright as her two teenage children lay with their heads in her lap. She looked uncomfortable, like she had frozen in place just so that her children had somewhere comfortable to sleep. Yet she was asleep too, upright, one arm around each, still protecting despite the snores. Was this what it was like to be a mother? From selling off all you own to smuggle them in an old boat into occupied waters to escape civil war and drafts and starvation, all the way down to acting as their pillow. Or both at the same time. Izzy grimaced and blew through another contraction. That one felt a bit stronger. She needed water.

Izzy stood up and braced herself against the roll of the boat. She staggered towards the front where she knew the old captain sat and stepped over the threshold into the tiny bridge. It was even darker in here than in the cabin behind and the glow of glass instruments and dials were set in sharp relief to the black night the other side of the windows. The captain sat on a tall, padded seat with his feet on the panel in front of him, his arm outstretched over the wheel. His eyes were closed. Izzy didn't want to wake him. Or did she? How could he navigate if he were asleep? Izzy added all things to do with boats to her list of things she didn't know.

She looked out of the windows in front of her and could see little but gloom. A few faint lights glowed in the distance. Where were they? She looked around the cockpit and saw his water cooler sitting under the dashboard and reached out to pick up a plastic cup.

"What do you want?" The sound of his voice made her jump.

"I just need some water," she managed, although pulled her hand back.

"There's some here," he said, reached behind his seat and in a single movement pulled out a small bottle which he handed to her. His eyes flickered open. "Only one each, though," he continued, "I'm not a charity."

"No, I know, thank you," she said then sucked in her breath as another contraction buckled her knees.

The captain looked at her in horror, as he realised immediately what he was seeing. "Oh, no, I *said* no pregnant ladies, your friend said you weren't going to have it yet!" he swung his legs down and reached out to catch her.

She blew out the pain and closed her eyes. Now this was most decidedly more painful. The squeezing continued as he lowered her into his seat. "Don't touch anything," he ordered.

Izzy couldn't reply. This contraction had taken her breath away.

She stared at the lights in the far distance and concentrated on breathing until it calmed down. She eventually replied.

"I'm not due to have it yet. I don't want this any more than you do!" she whispered as her breathing slowed. She sipped her water.

He continued to eye her suspiciously, one hand on the wheel.

"Where are we?" she asked, eventually.

"About, um, one hundred nautical miles off Scotland," he replied.

"How long to go?"

"About another hundred. Maybe more. Depends what we need to do to avoid the other boats."

"Are we going to Amsterdam?"

"Not quite."

"Then where?"

"There's an island, Texel, off the coast of Holland. We can land at a small port there."

"Is it safe?"

"It's quiet."

Izzy thought about this for a while. "What will happen to us?"

"It's not my job to worry about that," he replied. "But I haven't had any complaints."

"What about the blockade?"

"Out here, there are Dutch ships, not English."

"Don't they stop you and make you go back?"

He chuckled. "No. We are identified as coming from Eyemouth. Scotland. They let us through. They have to, we're refugees from a civil land war. It's kind of the law. If we came out of England, it would be different. Once you're ashore, you can claim asylum. That's the, you know, legal thing to do."

"Have you helped many across?"

He sighed. "More than I can count."

She smiled ruefully. "So you're a pretty rich man by now?"

He stared out to sea and sighed. "Am I?" he asked.

CHAPTER 23

March

On the floor, they listened to the sound of the receding Land Rover and Fran was long gone when they emerged from the kitchen. Sophie ran out to Maggie's room and threw herself on the bed. She sobbed into the sheets as Maggie held her. Don was the closest thing she had to a grandad or even a father. Aaron joined them and they sat together for a while.

Lewis descended the stairs and wandered around the basement looking at the vast collections of end-of-the-world supplies Don had accumulated. He gaped open mouthed at the shelves full of school supplies, chemicals and rare metals. Don must've been back to raid the science technician's stores a dozen times. He peered into the footlocker but was not brave enough to pull out any explosives. Instead, he grabbed a pick and a shovel, went back upstairs and walked sadly outside. The hardest job was just beginning.

.oOo.

After an uncomfortable journey, Fran realised she had been gripping the wheel and gritting her teeth. She tried to relax but couldn't. The roads were mostly empty as she drove towards the western edge of Edinburgh but she took it cautiously. It was gloomy and dour with the absence of streetlamps and she did not want to hit a surprise pothole and send herself or the still sleeping Amy flying. She rolled up to the bridge which ran over the city bypass and looked at the road ahead. It was almost impassable with mounds of rubble piled haphazardly on the tarmac, to presumably repel any visitors, Fran thought as she peered at the mess. Then she noticed that one of the mounds was made of mud and mulch, and it had slowly melted away in the constant drizzle. The Land Rover made short work of the squelchy impediment as she carried on over the bridge. Halfway across, Fran stopped to look at the main carriageway below.

To the north, vehicles had stopped at the hard shoulder, some abandoned in the middle of the road, some were burnt out. To the south, others crashed or upturned. It was deserted and she could see the shadows of a small herd of deer on the road in the distance.

"Wow," she breathed and shuddered. Is this what war looked like from the inside? Was it war? Or just disorganised chaos, waiting for someone to come clean it up, set the whole thing back on its feet and send it on its merry way. She stared for a moment longer into the unfamiliar blackness. Who was coming to clean up? She thought. Who was left?

She crossed the bypass, stopped at a junction at the very edge of the city and considered her options. She had seen only two other moving vehicles, both at a distance, since she left the farm nearly two hours ago but she was now in familiar home territory in a densely populated city. She drove straight on, through the long wide streets of the outskirts, past parks, and rows of houses. There were no lights, no tell-tale smoke rising from chimney pots.

Further in, she stopped again. She was approaching the leafy suburbs of central Edinburgh. To her right she now saw the first signs of life. On a large park some unlucky, or resourceful, people had set up tents - they seemed to be living in as if it were a campsite in the south of France. There were vehicles and awnings erected on the grass and she could see people moving around in the light from strings of bulbs hung on poles. Steam rose from army green cloth tents and she could see gas fires and Trangia heaters making meals and boiling water. Even refugees in a war-torn city needed their cups of tea, it would seem. There were flags hanging limply from makeshift poles, getting wetter and wetter in the drizzle. No-one seemed to be in charge or official, it clearly wasn't an army camp or makeshift hospital - just ordinary people and she frowned at this. It was an ordered scene, but where was the control or accountability?

For that matter, Fran thought suddenly, where was all the fighting or roadblocks or checkpoints? If she was able to drive with no problem into the city, surely the English would be here too? They'd be at Bute House by now, wouldn't they? Or Holyrood? Did they take over the barracks? This thought unnerved her and she looked around, as if they had heard her thinking loudly and come to arrest her for her intuition. Don's house was safe for being cut off from the outside world but dangerously uninformed for the same reason.

All around her, the towering tenement buildings absorbed all the light in the sky. This time of year, the sun rose about six twenty in the morning and set at around six thirty at night and the moon was often covered with clouds. Even during the day, the sun never penetrated some steep sided valleys or roads for weeks at a time in winter and early spring, and it was like living in permanent, bone chilling shadow.

She looked over at Amy, who was now awake and who gurgled and played with her toes in her crib, occasionally looking up at the dashboard lights. She was getting more and more restless with every minute and Fran leaned over and pulled out the milk from her bag to give to her. Amy was just old enough to hold it herself and she began to guzzle happily.

"That's a good girl," Fran cooed, "You're helping Auntie Fran, aren't you? You're my cute little cover story, aren't you? We're going to see Auntie Andrea, aren't we?" she said, one eye on the road, one on her little charge. "And make her pay for all the lies she's told about poor Auntie Fran, aren't we? Yes we are, and then we're going to go back to my flat and never set foot in a filthy muddy smelly farm ever again, aren't we?" Amy watched her with enormous innocent brown eyes over her bottle.

Fran turned her eyes back to the road as she turned a corner to another main junction. There were no streetlights on here either but the reflective paint in the middle of the road lit up as her headlights caught it. Up until this point, Edinburgh looked dark and mostly deserted, a little rough around the edges but essentially, the city she grew up in. Turning into Lothian Road, all that changed. Fran blinked and rubbed her eyes. Cars parked haphazardly at either side of the road were dirty, damaged and streaked with rain, sitting in crumpled heaps or lying on their sides, their windscreens smashed and mirrors torn off. The road was potholed with huge gaping blast holes, streetlamps bent and broken and huge swathes of glass where gunfire had met buildings in a deafening explosion of sharp, shimmering rain. Whatever had happened along this long, wide carriageway, it had finished and the combatants had moved on elsewhere, but the evidence of gun battles and violence was strewn about for all to see. Fran touched the accelerator and continued forward, looking wide eyed and open mouthed at the twisted metal carnage and piles of stone rubble. Her home! Her beloved city had been ripped apart. The dawn air smelled of smoke and drains, of wet tarmac and burnt rubber.

Suddenly, a fox trotted into the road ahead and stopped, his head swivelled towards her. Fran could see two sharp amber eyes staring at her and she pressed the brake with a gasp. The fox paused for a moment, then ran off with a loping gait into what was once a cinema across the road. Fran followed his path with her eyes, then watched it disappear into the darkness behind the rubble.

She rolled on a little further, over the road and onto a smaller street and swept her gaze along the buildings. On both sides, there was damage to every house and garden and business. Stone walls were peppered with holes; gunshots, she presumed, and occasional blast holes, scorched black. In the road ahead, she saw two or three small figures as they raced over the road from one pile of bricks to another, then darted into a darkened alley. She instinctively stamped the brakes and jumped from her seat.

"Hey! Come back!" she yelled. She clambered carefully over a tumbledown wall and tried to follow. She stopped. More footsteps. Suddenly, she heard gunfire just off to the right. She ducked her head and ran back to the car. Fran closed the door and sat in her seat, panting with shock. She closed her eyes and grimaced as the memory of the shot which killed Don flashed before her eyes. Her hand began to throb.

Just then, another two figures lumbered along, chasing the first and Fran could see their breath blowing into the cold air as they heaved along under body armour and excessive weight. A Sec Unit. So they were all still around. Typical that the filthy rats of the Sec Guards would survive. The front one stopped and fired again in the direction of the children, the second one puffing to a stop behind him, hands on his knees. They seemed to give up the chase there, conversed for a moment and began to walk back the way they'd come. Whatever the smaller figures had done to warrant being shot at, they had gotten away with it. Fran held her breath as she watched, the engine idling, the lights dimmed. Suddenly she felt very exposed. She had come to the city seeking revenge and a full apology but had found a war zone. How did she ever think it would be easy?

Staring at the two uniformed thugs with guns in front of her, she desperately wished she were still at home with Don. Pain ripped through her head. Her panic rose. What should she do? If she moved, they would see her. If she sat here, eventually they would hear her.

Too late. They both turned to look at her.

Fran gripped the wheel with one hand, threw the Land Rover into reverse with the other and stomped on the accelerator. They immediately jumped into action and followed, their shouts reaching through the Land Rover's rumble. Instinctively, Fran knew she was in danger and her heart rate jumped. Whatever had happened whilst she was holed up on the farm for months with no news or radio or internet, it had been swift and deadly. She threw the car around to face the way she was going and raced off as fast as the ruined roads would allow. She had to get out of there, find out what had happened, and then return with a handle on how to play it.

She still headed vaguely towards Bute House but for the first time considered that Andrea Taylor would not be there. Was she captured? Was the whole cabinet under arrest? Was someone new in her place? Looking at the mess that had been made out here, Fran wasn't sure she wanted to find out.

CHAPTER 24

Lewis held his lower back as he straightened up. It had taken hours but he and Aaron had finally managed to dig a hole deep enough for Don. The rain did not help and his blistered and freezing hands stiffened and complained. His old injury cursed him as he worked and his limp was more than pronounced when he had finished. Aaron helped him out of the hole and they retreated indoors to warm up.

Sophie, through endless tears, had wrapped Don's bloody and broken body in a sheet and sewn it shut. They moved the now unconscious Pauly into Maggie's room so that they had room to manoeuvre Don out of the area and Sophie shut Maggie's door. As much as she did not want to do this, who else would?

Aaron came into the living room and blew on his hands.

"Is he ready?" he asked sadly.

"If you could call it that," Sophie replied, sniffing.

"I'll get Mr Sinclair, and we'll get it done."

"Ok."

The two men hauled Don out of the back door and placed him as gently as they could in the hole they had just finished.

"Careful with him!" Sophie cried, "You'll … hurt him," she finished with a sob.

Lewis straightened up with a grimace. "Do you think we should try to get Maggie out here?"

Sophie snorted and wiped her nose on her sleeve. "I'm not sure she can get out. She doesn't balance well," she replied.

"We should at least tell her?" Aaron ventured. "We can't keep her door shut for ever, it's not fair. She needs to be allowed to see what we're doing."

"No," Sophie said quickly. "I mean, she's had a shock. Can she handle the sight of Don in a dirty hole? She's really not well. It might, you know, kill her," Sophie struggled to keep her feelings under control.

"She still needs to know what's going on," Aaron protested.

Lewis sighed deeply, "Ok," he said, although he knew it would considerably slow up this excruciating task. He just wanted it to be over.

Inside, in the living room, the fire was almost dead. The air had cooled and the smell of blood and gunfire abated. The three of them looked at Maggie's door. They could hear the sound of Maggie humming softly.

"Aren't you going to open it?" Sophie looked at Lewis.

He ran his fingers through his sweaty hair, "No, aren't you?"

"Bloody hell, Lewis, open the fucking door! You need to speak to her, tell her! Be a man for once!" Sophie hissed at him.

Lewis jiggled from foot to foot; he fought the urge to say 'Sophie! Language!' as he had done so many times in class because she was right. If ever there was a time to man up, it was right now. He took a deep breath and opened the door and Sophie and Aaron followed.

"Oh, Lewis, darling, where have you been?" Maggie held out her hands to him and he took them both as he sat on the bed.

"Maggie, we're so sorry, Don was an amazing bloke and we all loved him," Lewis began. "I can't begin to understand how you must be feeling right now."

Maggie patted his hands, "Are you all alright?" She looked at Sophie, "Eva, are you ok?"

Aaron and Sophie nodded.

Lewis took a deep breath. "Maggie, do you know what happened earlier?"

"What do you mean, dear?" Maggie asked.

"Maggie, Fran shot Don. I'm afraid he's dead. Do you understand?"

161

Maggie moaned and covered her mouth. "That woman shot my Don," she said in a whisper. "I never trusted her!" She shook with emotion.

"Yes, Maggie, I'm so sorry," Lewis replied.

Maggie stared at him and he couldn't look away. She blinked and he thought he could see her thinking hard as he watched her face turned to fury. He had not expected such a response.

"Where is that woman?" Maggie asked suddenly.

"Gone. In the Land Rover. We don't know where," Lewis said. "But we will find her. She will pay for this." His lip began to tremble.

"And my little Amy?" she asked.

"She's ..." Lewis stopped and looked at Aaron, "... upstairs. I presume. She's been really quiet ..."

Aaron looked back at him, his mouth open to reply but he couldn't remember the last time he had seen his little sister. He was so busy with the grave and so shocked at the swift, horrific turn of events, that he had forgotten that there was no-one to see to her. For a split second, no-one moved.

Then, as if they both realised the same thing at the same time, Aaron and Lewis jumped up and raced from the room. Aaron went up the stairs two at a time and threw open his bedroom door. He gasped in horror, as he realised that Amy and her crib were gone.

"Amy!" he cried, expectant of a reply, "Amy!" he bellowed running from room to room - just in case someone else had moved her, but she was gone. Lewis followed him, scanning each room with fresh eyes.

"Amy!" Aaron wailed once more and dissolved into tears. Lewis caught his falling body as he crumpled into a heap on the bed in Fran's room. "She's taken, her. That bitch has taken my baby sister!" Aaron sobbed. "How could I not *know*! How come I didn't check?"

"It's not your fault. we all thought she was just sleeping! We'll get her back!" Lewis took the boy by the hands, "We'll go and get her, Fran can't do this!"

"How? We don't know where she's gone!" Aaron wiped his eyes with the heels of his hands.

Lewis looked around the room from his seat on the bed. He had one arm around the boy, who sniffed and hitched. The room was neat and tidy, the bed made and the writing desk orderly and uncluttered. There were books, papers and a large, leatherbound notebook in the middle, a fountain pen by one side. He craned his neck to see it. This was the book she always wrote in. He reached out and pulled it open on his knees, flipping page after page. Aaron sniffed and looked up. He peered over Lewis' shoulder at the reams of information written there. After a moment, he spoke. "That's some other level revenge shit, right there," he said and pointed to the book. "She was crazy pissed off."

Lewis frowned. "What was she planning?"

Aaron pointed to the book. "Is that why she went and got the explosives?"

Lewis and Aaron looked at one another, realisation dawning.

"She's going to blow them up - all the government people, the First Minister, Andrea Taylor," Aaron said.

Lewis nodded. "I think that's exactly what she's doing. And I think she's taken Amy as insurance so they don't try and stop her."

"What about the English? And the Sec Units? She won't get through," Aaron frowned.

"Probably not, but she is mad enough to try!"

"Well she's not taking my little sister! I have to go get Amy."

"Now, just a minute," Lewis held up his hand, "we have to think before we go after her."

Aaron shook his head, his mind was made up. "Nah, I'm going, this is my sister and no crazy woman is using her as a human shield, for fuck's sake. We'll take a quad. Better still, we'll take the school van. You can drive. Don and I fixed it." He was suddenly struck by the pain of the loss of Don once more but took a deep breath and left the room.

Sitting on the bed, Lewis read on. Fran was one unhinged, unhappy woman. She claimed she was set up. She was the scapegoat. The accusations levelled at Andrea Taylor alone went on and on. Lewis shook his head. It was all madness. How had it come to this? Was it true? Lewis chewed his lip. Who the hell was he supposed to trust?

Lewis allowed his mind to wander at the thought. When he was a boy, before the crash, and austerity, and 9/11, and Covid, and Brexit, he remembered nothing but peace and fun and people being normal and happy. His parents had normal jobs, normal houses and normal pastimes and he and his friends all wanted to have normal toys and grow up to have normal jobs, and houses of their own.

But by the time he was 25 years old, so much future had been taken from him, it was a case of 'making it up as you go along'. He was told to be entrepreneurial and innovative; to make his own luck and own job, to work the grey and black markets to make them work for him. To 'think outside the box' and take voluntary and unpaid work to create a 'better world'. It was all bullshit. Lewis couldn't have innovated his way out of an open door. He hadn't banked on needing multiple skills just to *begin* in life. His parents had set him up for a life behind a desk, mortgage at 27, kids by 30, retire at 65. Now none of that was assured, or even possible. Even the idea of going on holiday, something he really enjoyed as a boy, was lost to his entire generation as Brexit hit, Covid squeezed and the European Union and United Nation sanctions had put a bullet in its head.

Now there was war. He had no idea what on earth he was supposed to do. He had no purpose, not even as a teacher. What on earth could he teach these kids? They were far and away more resourceful and braver than he ever was. They took chances and improvised and stood up for whatever they believed in. And they did it all with so little; no jobs, limited food, no prospects, no information at their fingertips, not even Netflix to entertain them. The UK had become so broken, so quickly, that his generation and theirs had practically nothing in common.

And now. He closed the book. Putting aside everything else, Lewis knew one thing. They had to go and find Amy. She wasn't his kid and Aaron wasn't his responsibility but this small group of people had spent the last few weeks keeping one another alive and sane in an insane world. He owed them his loyalty, if nothing else.

Lewis put his head in his hands and tried to summon his courage to stand. Aaron had fought so hard to keep Amy close; so much so that he had risked his life and freedom to look after her. Lewis was not comfortable with that kind of pressure. "All you need to do is drive that crappy van to Edinburgh, man, come on," he berated himself. "What do you have to lose?" He closed his eyes. "Life, freedom, everything, that's what."

He thought about Izzy and realised he didn't even know where she was, then wondered quite how much more he could let her down. He slowly wiped his face with his roughened hands and emerged looking spent. Nothing went his way. He had avoided the draft so far, avoided becoming a father and yet here he was, *still* trapped by circumstances that swept him along without a life jacket. He sighed and stood up.

Lewis took the book and walked downstairs to Maggie. She was sitting up next to Pauly's makeshift bed on the floor, talking softly to him. He stared back at her; his grateful eyes glassy and cool.

"Fran took Amy. But we're going to get her back, Maggie, I promise."

"Good boy," she said, red eyed, "Go and get our little girl. I will be ok," she gesticulated to Pauly who was stirring to sit up. "And I'll take care of him," her voice wavered with emotion.

Lewis opened his mouth to say something else but closed it again. Right now, what was there to say?

"I'll leave Sophie …" he said, but she interrupted.

"No, you need Eva too," Maggie shook her head, "I have ways of keeping body and soul together, don't you mind."

"Ok," he said, but knew there was no way he could leave her alone with an injured man.

He found Aaron as he finished filling two bottles with fresh milk and threw nappies and a change of clothing into Amy's bag.

"Ready?"

"Let's go, sir,"

Suddenly the lights went out, and from around the corner Sophie raced into the kitchen and skidded to a kneeling halt by the sink.

"Soph, what the …"

"Get down!" she hissed, "They're here! They found us!"

They listened to the night sounds outside the window until the low rumble of revving 4-wheel drive vehicles emerged from the rustle of leaves and the gusting wind.

Aaron peered out of the kitchen window to the yard beyond. The chickens were still outside and they scattered around squawking and flapping as the trucks parked in the yard. Men in black uniforms with handguns and torches jumped from their vehicles and began to search around the pens and barns. Aaron could see their cigarettes glowing and hear the guffaws and murmurs of self-congratulation. Whatever they were looking for, they thought they had found it. He dipped down and joined Sophie and Lewis on the floor.

"Now what do we do?" he asked.

"Fuck knows," she replied and closed her eyes.

CHAPTER 25

Before she could consider what to do next, Fran saw car lights flash in the road ahead. A man in black with a helmet and goggles brandished an assault rifle as he walked into the middle of the road and a flashing yellow beacon on top of a Sec Unit van illuminated his hand as he held it up, indicating to her to stop.

She gripped the wheel. "Oh, no, no, no … please god, no, anyone but them," she murmured to herself then stopped, took a deep breath and glanced at Amy who now chewed at her fists. Ok, show time. She could do this. Politician's face, spin-speech and a look that says, 'I care'.

She rolled to a stop at the roadblock and wound down the window.

"Can I help you?" she asked, sweetly.

The helmeted man thrust out his hand for her identification card but she didn't want to make it too easy for them.

"What?" she said, feigning confusion, "You want money? What?"

He clicked his fat fingers and placed the other hand on his side arm.

"ID!" he said with irritation. "But you can hand over money too if you'd like," he finished with a chuckle, just loud enough for his colleagues to hear. Fran heard titters and rolled her eyes.

She pulled out her driver's licence and handed it to him. He shone his torch in her face and then at the licence. Then he grunted and shone the torch at Amy who screwed up her face. She immediately began to fuss and hitch. Fran let her continue.

"This your baby?" he asked her.

"Yes," she replied more loudly, Amy's cries now rising in the background.

167

"Where are you going?" he asked, "It's after curfew."

"Sorry, what?" Fran cupped her ear and pretended she couldn't hear above the noise.

"I said, it's after curfew, you shouldn't be out. No-one allowed out after dark until 10 am!"

"Oh, I know there's a curfew, thank you." She nodded, feigning ignorance of his larger point.

Amy was now yelling throatily. She was tired and wet.

"No, I want to know where you're going ..." he shouted.

"Fucking Hell, Tommy, let the bitch go, fuck's sake, it's giving me a headache," his colleague interjected. "She's clearly too old for the draft, let her go."

The two men stepped back and waved her through and Fran wound up the window with just a little disgruntled harrumph. Too old, my arse, she thought, I'll be running this country soon, you little ned. Fran bristled as she drove. She did not want to explain herself to some low-ranking grunt while he pointed his over-important gun at her. If she *had* to give herself up to the authorities to get back into Bute House, then it was going to be to an officer of some importance, not some undereducated pre-pubescent squaddie or a trained Sec Unit gorilla. She was now metres from Bute House and moments from taking the bitch down. No-one was going to get in her way.

Fran drove a little further towards Charlotte Square, where she saw the inner blockade for the first time. She stopped and sat for a while in the Land Rover with Amy's screams ringing all around her as she peered at the barbed wire and searchlights. On the other side of the fence, the tall windows of Bute House shone through the darkness.

Now this was new, she thought, as a green clad Scottish squaddie approached her.

"Help you?" he asked.

Fran cleared her throat. "I am Francis MacDonald MSP. Minister for Europe. I would like to see Andrea Taylor." She held up her official parliamentary pass so that he could read it and he nodded. He stepped back and spoke into a walkie talkie clipped to his shoulder. As he did so, others swept the underside of the vehicle with mirrors. One opened the back doors and looked in, another popped the bonnet.

Fran turned to comfort Amy. Poor kid needed a change. Fran dug into the side of her crib to draw out a fresh nappy and her hand closed around something, Don's gift to the war effort. She pushed it down deeper, there would be a time for that particular threat, and pulled out a cloth nappy. As she changed Amy, she watched as the squaddies finished their security sweep and then stepped out of the way to let her through.

"Up there," he pointed, "There's not much traffic but please adhere to the rules of the road and all the one-way systems."

"Thank you Private MacAdam," she said in her best ministerial voice, after glancing at his embroidered nametape, as if she were bestowing him a favour by knowing his name. "Good job."

She rolled on through the fencing and they closed it behind her.

Fran instantly felt calmer. Inside the inner blockade it was as if nothing had happened. There were no shell holes or bullet holes in windows and walls, no overturned cars or random rubble fires. Whatever happened in greater Edinburgh, it most definitely did not happen here. She drove straight to the door of Bute House, stopped and pulled on the handbrake. I'd usually turn up in a black Mercedes, she thought, then it would drive away - but not tonight. She was just going to leave the Land Rover outside the front steps right on top of the double yellow lines and march straight into her office and demand an explanation. If it proved not to be forthcoming, she would bloody well shoot it out of her. Fran pulled Amy's basket from the front seat and started up the steps, a determined frown on her face but just before the top, she stopped as half a dozen uniformed soldiers stepped out of the building and pointed their weapons at her.

For a moment, no-one moved.

"How dare you!" she finally exploded, standing as tall as she could, "I am an elected official and you will let me pass!"

"State your business," came a deep voice.

"Fran MacDonald, MSP. I am here to see Andrea Taylor. Put your guns down and let me in."

"Turn around. We will escort you from the area. Your access is not authorised," a gruff, military voice stated.

"Oh, it is now," came a different voice from inside the hallway. "Sergeant, let Ms MacDonald in, please."

They lowered their guns and stood back. Andrea Taylor emerged from the shadows and smiled at Fran; her hand outstretched in a greeting which indicated she wanted to shake her hand. She looked pristine, in a red trouser suit with patent heels and a silk scarf at her neck. Her hair looked like it had been recently cut and styled and Fran touched her long, unkempt bob, now secured in a ratty ponytail.

She stared, unsure what to do next and when she thrust out her hand and consented to a handshake, Fran knew her grip was weak and clammy, her fingernails cracked and dirty after months of little soap and no expensive hand creams.. She opened her mouth to speak but couldn't. Why was Andrea Taylor waiting at the front door? How did she look so unaffected by all the carnage around her? Like so many before her, Fran felt instantly intimidated by Taylor's unflinching demeanour and surety.

"And who is this little darling?" Taylor went on, peering into Amy's basket. "Oh, Fran, you weren't ... were you? Is she yours?" Her confusion, Fran saw, was evidently underpinned by amusement. Obviously, the very idea of Fran being pregnant was, to Andrea Taylor, a ridiculous notion and Fran suddenly remembered why she was here. She pulled the basket away and held it behind her legs.

"She is my ward. Her name is Amy."

Taylor smirked, "Sergeant, take the child and make sure it is fed."

"No!" Fran yelled. "Amy stays with me! She's my responsibility!"

Taylor stopped him with a raised hand. The smile had gone.

"Ms MacDonald," she began through gritted teeth. "If you want to talk around the table with the big boys and girls, then I suggest you get rid of all distractions." She moved closer to Fran who instinctively turned away to protect Amy, "... because you're going to need every single wit you have left to keep yourself out of jail, Fran."

Fran regarded her with cold, black rimmed eyes.

"I'd rather take my chances with the child than without," she growled.

Taylor said nothing for a beat, then clapped her hands together in supposed delight.

"Then I guess we will have a cute little visitor to our Cobra Meeting tomorrow!" she exclaimed, like it was the most natural thing in the world and Fran's visit a social and welcome one. "Come, Fran, let's get you something to eat. There's lots of people here who are eager to see you again." She held out an arm to guide her inside and with a beam, welcomed Fran MacDonald back to Bute House.

CHAPTER 26

Aaron and Sophie both sat on the kitchen floor as Lewis lay in the hallway.

The door handle rattled. A knock, swift and hard. Everyone inside held their breath.

Shuffles and grumblings. Another try at the door handle. Thank God Don trained them to always lock the doors, Lewis thought as he squeezed his eyes shut.

"Holy shit! Look at this!" a voice came across from the barn.

Boots trudging away from the house. Whoops of joy, a tumble of chatter, exclamations of pleasure.

The Sec Unit had found the shelves in the barn where Don brewed and lay down his own beer, another side hobby for the chemist of Wolf Craigs. From the kitchen, they could hear the pop and fizz of bottles opening and the delighted lip smacking and sighs of happiness when they realised it was not-half-bad. Beer was incredibly hard to come by, even on the black market. They began to drink and, from the sounds that permeated the darkened kitchen, they showed no signs of stopping. Sophie, Aaron and Lewis lay there and waited, listening to shouts and cat calls and what sounded ultimately like a mini fracas. They seemed to be fighting amongst themselves. One van left and the barn returned to quiet for the night.

After an hour had passed, Sophie peered over the kitchen sink and through the window at the darkness. There was now no movement outside although a van still remained.

"Should we wait til they've gone?" Aaron asked.

"We can't really do anything until they have," Lewis replied with a croak.

"They'll know *someone* is in, surely." Sophie hissed. "There's obviously someone living here. What are we going to do? We can't just sit here! They'll try to get in again."

"I don't know," Lewis whispered. "Some of them left. Maybe the rest will, too. I've no idea."

"Well *think*!" she hissed again. "We'll all be drafted! Or shot! There's no baby so Aaron's screwed and it doesn't take three people to look after Maggie so at least two of us are heading off to the barracks tomorrow! Or jail! So who is it to be?"

"We're a farm," Lewis replied. "Surely we can all stay here?"

"For God's sake!" she cried, "We have a basement full of dynamite! We are *all* armed! There is a rug in the living room covered in blood and there is an English squaddie in Maggie's room! Even the Sec Units can make something out of all that! All they'll see is people to arrest and shoot! Think of something!"

As she spoke, Aaron got up from his crouch and took a deep breath.

"Aaron, what are you doing?" Sophie pulled at his trouser leg.

"Someone needs to go get my sister. And we need to get rid of the Sec Unit before we can go do that. Someone needs to look after Maggie and Pauly. I see three people and three jobs. I'm going to get Don's gun and take Pip into the hills. We'll fire off a couple and make a run for it. I'll head for the pens up the hill. These fat bastards will all run out of breath before they get halfway up. But it'll be enough of a distraction for you to go get Amy, Mr Sinclair."

"What? Me? But I can't ..." Lewis began.

"You're the only licensed driver. You can take the van. When you start it up they will probably hear you and come running but I've got an idea for that. Go get her and take her somewhere safe and take care of her for as long as necessary." He swallowed. "Sophie," he turned to her, "You can go too, so you can get back to your mum,"

Sophie looked at him. He was willing to sacrifice himself so that everyone else had a shot at freedom and happiness. And he was such an idiot at school, she remembered and smiled ruefully.

"No," she said, shaking her head, "I need to save this family first, then I can think about mum."

"You sure?" he asked.

She nodded, "Sure," she said.

"Ok, then you need to secure the house so they can't get in. We don't know what they'd do to Pauly if they captured him. Keep Mol, she's a good guard dog."

"I know what I'm going to do," Sophie nodded her head at Aaron. "Don't worry, I'll sort it out," she said and began to crawl out of the kitchen.

"What if they catch you?" Lewis asked Aaron as he filled the rifle with shells. "You'll go to jail or be drafted. You'll lose Amy."

"It kind of looks like I've lost her anyway, doesn't it," he replied, his chin wobbling only slightly. "Now there's other reasons to fight; to get you out and save Amy, to save Pauly, to protect Maggie and Don's farm. To give Maggie something to live for."

Lewis closed his eyes and leaned his head beside the doorjamb. Where the hell did these kids get their resilience from? It was dark outside, they were surrounded by armed Security Units and who knows, possibly the English too. Don was dead and Amy missing yet they still came up with a clear plan to save the day. Lewis couldn't believe it; he was petrified into inaction just by the presence of other people at their little haven. He didn't want to go get Amy, he never wanted to set foot outside this valley ever again! Yet here was Aaron, about to throw himself into the darkness and the rain and start firing! And Sophie, with her self-assured nods and declaration to save her new family *first!* As if she were then going to race off to town and save everyone else!

Lewis took in a ragged, shaky breath. A few months ago, he would have happily taken credit for the way the kids in his school had turned out but he knew now that he had only played a small role in their lives, and the same even in his own. However, if he didn't play his part this time, the whole thing would fall apart. If he didn't go get Amy, who would? He thought that Fran *probably* wouldn't blow herself and Amy up in the Land Rover but nothing was for sure. Aaron was saving *his* arse from the draft. He owed him. He owed Don. Let's face it, Lewis, old buddy, he told himself, round here, you owe *everyone*.

CHAPTER 27

Izzy picked her way carefully around the legs and feet strewn around the floor in the cabin. She was between contractions and the captain had suggested she took his berth at the back. He held one arm as he walked alongside her and opened the thin door to the small room so that she could sit on the bed. The whole bedroom was just one bed, a closet, a table and a port hole. There was a pull switch light over the small pillows and a bottle of water on the side, secured by an elastic cord.

Izzy flopped on the bed just before the wave of pain began again.

"Go get Callie, please," she managed through each shallow breath and the captain stumbled off to find her.

A few moments later, Callie entered the room, yawning. The contraction was over and Izzy lay weeping on her back.

"How are you so calm?" Izzy blubbered, "This is the scariest thing that's ever happened to me, and I've been shot at by the English!" She sniffed lavishly and wiped her nose with her sleeve.

"I'm a nurse," Callie sat beside her. "I've seen it all before," she smiled and patted her hand. "People had babies in all kinds of places for millennia and then just went back to their business. You're not the first and you won't be the last."

"Don't we need towels and hot water and stuff?" Izzy asked, vaguely irritated that Callie wasn't indulging her misery.

"We could use some clean towels and some water, yes, but possibly not yet." Callie yawned again.

"Are you sure?" Izzy replied in a strangled voice as the pains started again.

"Now," Callie began in a soothing voice, "Breathe deeply and calmly, do not try to tense up against the pains and don't try to push or stop them, they'll come anyway. Deep breaths will help to control the pain. In … and out … and in … and out …"

Izzy tried to follow suit but the tightening across her belly was becoming excruciating.

"I have to get up," she declared and hoisted herself off the bed.

"Easy now," Callie soothed and moved out of her way. Izzy paced restlessly as best she could in the tiny space and leaned onto her hands on the bed when the contractions came and went.

"I can't sit down, I'm too …" Izzy moaned.

"Restless?" Callie asked,

"Yeah, I feel shaky, a bit sick, a bit nauseous."

"Ok, missus, back on the bed, it's not long now," Callie ordered just as a gush of water burst down Izzy's leg and onto her boot.

"Oh, no! I couldn't stop it," Izzy cried.

"It's normal, don't worry, up you go. Now's the time for water and towels and other stuff. I'll be back in a mo."

"No! Callie don't leave me!"

Callie had gone.

Izzy lay back on the pillows and moaned. This was just the worst day of her life bar none and she was going to kill that bastard Lewis Sinclair the moment she set eyes on him again. Which was probably never, she thought and burst into tears. Why was having a baby so messy and dirty and wet and painful and so … so organic? And bloody inconvenient. The pain began again.

She tried to call for Callie but it came out as a strangled gurgle. She gripped the bedclothes beneath her in an effort to counter the pain as her body suddenly took it upon itself to push downwards into her pelvis. Izzy grunted with effort and grimaced at the pain. She looked down at her belly; it looked different, like it had shifted and changed shape.

"Callie, for God's sake!" she managed to mutter as the pain withdrew momentarily, "Help me!"

Callie returned just then with towels and tissues and her bag.

"Don't leave me again!" Izzy said and tugged at her sleeve.

"Sorry, doll, I had to get some things, and I'm going to need that arm," she said, brusquely, in what Izzy recognised as her charge nurse voice. Izzy let go.

"Right, ok," Callie mused, "I can see baby has shifted, have you pushed?"

"A bit."

"Yup, baby has moved right into position, so it's all good, but I need to examine you, ok?"

"Why?"

"See how far dilated you are."

"How?"

Callie indicated by holding up three fingers.

"Eww, for the love of …" Izzy began but the contraction began again.

.oOo.

In the cabin beyond, no-one slept on. Every person sat or lay wide eyed staring at the closed door or at one another. Every time Izzy grunted or moaned, the women winced and the men buried their faces. The captain sat in his chair once more grimly trying to ignore the noises behind him. Just a few more hours would see them onto the quiet beaches of Texel Island and he could make this his last run ever. Running refugees into Europe was easy, listening to a woman give birth was quite another matter. He steadied the boat with one hand on the wheel and with the other placed binoculars over his eyes and peered into the complete blackness of the North Sea. It had been a calm enough crossing for once and he had encountered no other vessels within miles. Everything would be perfect if it weren't for that … he grimaced as her heard Izzy cry out in a throaty, primordial roar. He swallowed hard.

.oOo.

"A bit further, Iz, just a bit further!" Callie cried, "It's coming! Don't stop!"

Izzy squeezed her eyes shut with the effort of the final pushes.

"I can't do it, no more, please!" she cried out, panting.

"You're so close, come on, one or two more contractions and we're there," Callie promised.

Almost immediately, Izzy felt the familiar tug again and she gritted her teeth with the effort of pushing.

"Crowning! I see the head!" Callie said, "Slowly now, pant, pant, don't push ..."

Izzy panted as best she could with the rising new pain that felt like a hundred paper cuts where the baby emerged and she tried to pause but the baby would not be put off. Izzy felt the head pop out and Callie lifted the shoulders as it twisted and wriggled free. Izzy let out a huge, ragged breath as the weight and the pain of the last few hours fell away. She was covered in blood and everything was wet but it was over.

"Here's your baby. It's a girl!" Callie lifted it onto Izzy's chest and Izzy clutched at the child. It was slippery and filthy and it was getting her shirt all gross and dirty. She had to hold it in place because if she didn't, it would have rolled off with the pitch of the boat. Izzy began to cry. Her arms ached with all the effort and the last thing she wanted was a screeching baby. She just wanted to sleep.

.oOo.

Outside in the dim cabin, a smattering of applause and murmurs of relief filled the once silent air. There were smiles and back pats. They listened to the sound of Izzy's baby crying and the boat engine thrumming and, for a moment at least, they weren't on a small boat escaping a civil war and austerity and sanctions and government disagreements. There was a hopeful new soul aboard, the mother was safe and just for a while, some of them felt akin to normal.

CHAPTER 28

"Now, you light them, then throw them, ok? Don't hold onto them. Understand?" Aaron instructed Sophie. She shone her torchlight at his face and it illuminated the entire basement.

"How do you even know all this?" she whispered.

"Don told me," he replied and handed her a cloth bag filled with explosives.

"I thought we weren't allowed down here?"

"Don said someone should know. He said it was safer if ... someone knew ... not everyone."

Sophie took it carefully. Never in all her life did she think she would see actual dynamite thingies. This is awesome and scary at the same time, she thought.

"Come on," he said and they headed back upstairs.

They returned to the kitchen where Lewis kept watch.

"They haven't moved from the barn yet," he reported. "I think they've drunk most of the beer so they'll be hungover at least."

"Right," Sophie began. "Aaron, good luck. Hopefully see you when you get back." She embraced him with one arm.

"What's the plan?" Lewis asked, his eyes now fearful. This was it. The moment of truth. Hero time. Lewis felt sick.

"Sophie's staying here to take care of Maggie and Pauly, but he needs to be out of sight." Aaron explained as he filled his pocket with dog biscuits. "She's going to protect the house with this," he pointed to the explosives as Sophie held one up. "Until I can get back. Then we'll work it out from there."

Lewis pulled a face.

"I'm off into the hills." Aaron continued, "Once I'm gone a while, I'll start to pull off a few shots. That should bring 'em running. Or send them away. Either way, that's your cue to take the van. Only problem is, it's parked just behind their van. You'll have to gun it."

"But where am I going?"

"Fuck's sake, man," Sophie hissed, "To get Amy!"

"I know that," he replied, "But where?"

"I don't fucking know!" she replied in a teeth gritted whisper, "Fran's a mental case politician who wants revenge! You read her diary! Where would you go?"

Lewis stared at her and opened his mouth to reply when there came the first knock at the door.

They all froze.

"We're too late!" Lewis mouthed in a near silent cry, "It's too late!"

Sophie and Aaron looked at each other. "Back doors," they said in unison and both sprinted off into the house. Lewis heard Aaron call to Pip, heard the back door open and close softly and heard Sophie enter Maggie's room and speak to her with urgency.

Lewis was left alone in the kitchen, lights off, with the Sec Units just the other side of the door. They knocked again, louder this time. What should he do? Let them in? *No, bloody hell, Lewis, pull yourself together,* he thought. *You've got to get out of there. Keys, blue book belonging to Fran and go. Just go.*

I'm scared.

You're always scared. Just go.

Another knock. Voices. The shuffling of feet.

Someone tried the door handle.

What are you waiting for? For God's sake, go!

Just then, the sound of a gunshot filled the air to the east. Aaron must've sprinted up the hill towards the upper paddock in record time, Lewis thought. The men outside swore and made surprised noises then moved off in the direction of the noise. Lewis watched as their torch lights swung through the air towards the hillside, but he knew they wouldn't find Aaron in a hurry. The boy had spent a long time in hidey holes in the brush.

Pip barked. Lewis swallowed. Another gunshot.

The men moved further away, jogging now through the back gates into the hills beyond.

Lewis grasped the door handle. He bent down and looked through the old keyhole and saw nothing but darkness. He stood up straight again and took a deep breath. The van was in the yard outside. It was practically parked next to the Sec Unit van. He had no choice but to just leave the safety of the house, walk across the yard, get in and start her up.

Gunfire. Returned shots. More barks. Lewis squeezed his eyes shut.

Lewis turned the handle and opened the door a sliver. The cold air pushed the door a little more and he stopped. If anyone was out there, they would see him now. He took a deep breath and opened it wider, just far enough to slip out. He shut it behind him as quietly as he could. The yard seemed deserted, and he could hear yells and shouts and gunshots from the hillside beyond. Lewis raced on tiptoe to the van, keys clutched in one hand, Fran's book in the other. He screwed up his eyes with fear. He snatched open the door and threw himself into the driver's seat. If anyone were still around, he didn't see them, concentrating only on jabbing the keys into the ignition and racing away.

Another gunshot boom ricocheted through the valley air and Lewis used the noise to rev the van and turn it around. Screams permeated the air and Lewis was sure Aaron had hit one of them. He headed out of the yard and drove as fast as he could down the dirt track. It was still sticky and rutted with mud but passable and much easier than coming up, as he had months before. Lewis drove as hard as he could, the lights off and with hands gripped on the wheel.

"Please, please, please," he begged, manoeuvring the van over cattle grids and through potholes. "Please don't see me! Please see them not me! Please don't follow me ..." but then checked himself.

"Jesus Christ, man, what are you doing, what are you saying?" he asked out loud. Then he slammed on the brakes and came to a slithering halt.

It was suddenly clear to him that they were doing this all wrong.

Once he left, Sophie and Aaron, and possibly Pauly were all going to die. They would not stop at chasing Aaron and they would force their way into the house. Once there, the chances of them showing any mercy would be slim. After all, they'd been shot at, and Aaron was a handy shot.

Once he left, Lewis thought, their last line of defence had gone.

He took a deep breath. Amy was safe, sort of. Fran would not let harm come to her, if for no other reason than she was a good human shield. Getting her was not a priority, despite what Aaron said. Saving the people in the farmhouse was the priority, Lewis knew that now.

If the Sec Unit *didn't* follow him, then Aaron and Sophie were surely next in the firing line.

He stopped. Their plan was backwards. He *had* to get the Sec Unit to follow *him*, not Aaron. Sophie and Aaron wouldn't be captured, then they'd be shot. Shot dead. Pauly would be next. Maggie would be alone and vulnerable. He would give her three days before she was dead too. And the dogs. Lewis's eyes prickled with anger and fear. *Bastards!*

The English weren't his enemy, neither were Europe, or New Britain. It was every small minded, bigoted little mini-Hitler who roamed the streets with guns wielding them like nuclear weapons. It was hatred and division and greed and money and the need to identify and close off into little boxes and throw bombs from behind the supposed good and righteous walls of the elected few. It was every vote and every move towards a divided, angry blaming state that handed the reigns and unlimited power to the corrupt and remorseless. He hated himself for not doing anything at all to stop it.

When the NHS collapsed, and as people died untreated in their homes, he needed to access surgery for his leg so used up Izzy's health credits, earned through turning up for work even though her wages were cut. Because of his selfishness, she had no credits left when she really needed them. When all the foreign-born students at school left, he shrugged; fewer essays to mark. When the schools reduced the timetable, he rejoiced at having less work to do. When the internet thinned out so much it was almost unusable, he piggy backed off the fire station up the street. When they closed, he only complained that he could no longer play *Apocalypse Storm: Inbound.*

At no point in the last ten years did he question anything he saw around him. The State didn't take away Izzy, he pushed her away with her inconvenient pregnancy. He didn't lose his job or purpose, he ran away from it. He let it all happen just so that he could get a takeaway on a Friday night and longer pub opening hours.

"Fat and drunk, that's all I became. That's all I stood for. Me, my friends, my entire network. We did nothing. We were our own worst enemy."

He stopped. "Fuck it."

Lewis looked in the rear-view mirror. This was risky, but not a total loss. He slammed the van into reverse and began to slide back up the slope towards the yard. All the way, he kept his hand on the horn, the beeping loud, screeching inside his head. The engine squealed in protest; it hadn't been used this hard for a while.

.oOo.

Aaron hid in the gorse with Pip and watched the Sec Units puff and pant up the hill. They had all slowed to a staggering crawl, except that one - he looked through his sights – a small, runty man with a bald head rolled around clutching his shin like a theatrical footballer looking for a penalty. Get up, ya rally, he thought, it's just a flesh wound.

He chuckled to himself at their feeble efforts to alternately hide then race up a bit further. He could smell the stink of alcohol from where he was, and each man looked like he'd had a skinful. Aaron looked through the sights at a fat, middle aged man in black who held onto the fence as he forced one foot in front of the other. He collapsed against a large boulder and breathed heavily, his shaking hands fiddling with his side arm. He could barely get it out of his holster. Aaron trained the sights on him and whispered, "Boom," as he pretended to pull the trigger. Pip crawled under his arm and he felt her warm fur and cold nose on his palm. He put the gun down and patted her. Pip panted, her tongue hanging out of the side of her mouth for a moment until abruptly, she stopped, raised her ears and cocked her head on one side. Aaron read her signal and pricked up his own ears. It was then he heard the school van horn, the engine revving high. What the hell was Lewis doing? Aaron squeezed off another shot to distract his pursuers, mindful not to hurt anyone this time. The shot disappeared into the misty gloom and the Sec Unit took cover once more, grateful for the rest.

Aaron could still hear the van. That bloody idiot would have them all running if he didn't shut up! He was *supposed* to be going to get Amy whilst Aaron distracted them! Sophie was right, she always said Mr Sinclair was a loser, he couldn't get anything right. He watched the men from his perch on the hill, they were just visible with the lights from the barn in the yard and the weak light in the sky as they turned towards the noise Lewis made. They shouted in confusion, waved their arms about, spoke on radios and eventually all darted down the hillside as fast as their old, flabby legs would go.

His plan to get them to follow him to allow Lewis to drive away had been sabotaged by the idiot himself. He looked through the sights again and was incredulous to see Lewis get out of the van and run back into the house. *Was he mad?*

"What the...?" he exclaimed and watched the door to the house. The dark figures were only jogging halfway down the hill, he could see that, but they would be back in the yard in no time. Did he chicken out? Did he give up? Is he that much of a coward?

"Bastard," Aaron said simply. He put the rifle down and put his arm around the dog. He had to get back to the house, it would soon be swarming. They would capture Sophie and Pauly and …

Just then, the door opened once more and Aaron watched as Lewis bolted out of the house and ran back to the van. A shout went up from one of the Sec Guards: he'd been spotted!

"Oh, shit," Aaron murmured as he watched the Sec Guards move a bit quicker, he frowned even deeper as Lewis roared the van back into life. This was hardly the quiet getaway they had agreed on. What on earth was he doing?

Just outside the yard, Lewis watched them pursue him. He almost felt like taunting them, just like they taunted people on the streets with their guns and seemingly unlimited power to harass and detain.

"Come on, you bastards!" Lewis said through gritted teeth. "Come and fucking get me!" He whooped with manic joy and began to laugh.

Lewis watched as men in black ran towards him through the mud and effluent from the cow shed and threw themselves into their black van. They were following him. Good. He slammed the van into first gear and roared off down the hill once more, used to the unique patterns of ruts and holes in the track. The Sec Unit van started up and the lights illuminated the yard and farmhouse, sweeping onto the track with a jolting, uneven gait.

Lewis moved to second gear, then third and roared over the cattle grid onto the tarmac. He checked the mirror. They were a little way behind him but still coming, further and further from the kids. He hoped that Aaron would forgive him; he was sure Sophie would roll her eyes and call him a loser and Maggie would … Maggie would beam at him and delight in his limited company despite his shortcomings. He felt a stab of shame and hurt. How much more could he have done to prevent Don's death? Using himself as bait in this cat and mouse game was the least he could do to save them. He shook his head. What an idiot! I'm such a selfish, stupid moron! Why did I always leave the thinking to Don? To everyone else? No wonder Izzy buggered off. She knew what a terrible father I would have been.

Lewis raced through the hills onto larger and wider tracks, following the route that Fran had taken earlier. The Sec Unit followed at a considerable distance now and with each bend in the road, he could comfortably lose them. He knew this area well and darted through the rubbly trails with ease.

.oOo.

Aaron slipped in through the back door and closed it quietly. "Sophie!" Aaron called, "It's me! Are you there?"

He listened but heard nothing except Pip drinking from her bowl. Mol trotted out to greet them and both dogs wagged. Aaron moved through the house to Maggie's room and opened the door. It was dimly lit inside but he could make out Maggie in bed.

"Maggie?" he said softly.

The overhead light went on and Sophie emerged from behind the door. She put her rifle down and let out a deep breath.

"What happened?" Aaron asked, looking at each of them in turn. Maggie's eyes twinkled and she held out a hand to him. Sophie looked worn out but determined, her eyes dark and hollow. Pauly was awake, sitting up and half naked. His eyes were glazed and skin pale, his breathing fast and shallow.

"Lewis came back," Sophie said. "A crazy Lewis, all shouting and wild eyes!"

"What did he do? Did he go get Amy?"

"Yes. He said he was going to Edinburgh get Amy. And in order to get even closer, he took Pauly's uniform."

CHAPTER 29

March 2025

After a solitary meal in the Bute House kitchen, Fran went to find somewhere for them to sleep. She did not want to sleep upstairs in the guest bedrooms, she felt too exposed, so Fran returned to the wing of offices, now deserted for the day, pushed open the door to her old office and peered into the darkness. She had slept here a few times in periods of great pressure and overwhelming workloads and knew it was comfortable. She and Amy would be safe here.

As she opened the door wider, the room looked like it had not been used since she left over four months ago and it smelled musty and damp. She switched on the light and placed Amy's bassinet on her desk then lifted the baby from it onto a rug by the fireplace. The grate was swept and still, no logs or kindling had been arranged there as it once had and there was a small breeze of cold air from the flue.

Fran turned back to the bassinet to extract her prize. Then she paused, turned back to Amy. Was she cold, lying there in the draught?

She turned back to her task but her mind couldn't focus. She shook her head and tutted, then strode back to the fireplace to close the flue and place the ornate fire screen in front of it. Then she knelt down to check Amy's fingers for warmth. She was ok but Fran decided it was better to keep her jumper on. Amy gurgled and grabbed her feet, dribbling from her gummy mouth. Must be teething, Fran thought, I should get you a teething ring or toy to chew on. She stood up to search the room for something suitable and began to rummage in a drawer by her desk. She found an old, twisted leather bookmark and gave it to Amy who immediately began to chew and gnaw at it. Fran sat there for a while and smiled indulgently at her.

"It's time you were asleep," she said and Amy blinked at her, then rolled over onto her stomach to grab at the deep pile of the rug.

"Precious," Fran muttered, then stopped. She peered at the fire screen and then at her desk. The old, Georgian building was peppered with fireplaces, the only source of heating in the large house. That was it. That was the plan. The fireplace. The huge, six foot tall, wide open fireplace in the meeting room suite, the ornate sandstone grate flanked with two stone dogs and intricate wrought iron patterns. The one that could hide a man, no, several men, if it came to it, in times of war. One that was lit whenever there was a meeting scheduled, a ritual which had arisen when the gas pipelines were stopped when no-one was allowed out to the rigs to work and the refineries were attacked. The one Fran knew that Andrea liked to have roaring on behind her as she sat down with a flourish at the head of the large meeting room table. She probably thought it was part of her mystique, Fran scoffed, the Thane of her own personal Highland castle. Then she squirmed as she remembered how much of that pomp and ceremony she had embedded in her own life before the ultimate betrayal.

She had to do it at just the right time, when Taylor sat herself in the big chair and declared herself the victor, despite whatever evidence there was to the contrary. Andrea Taylor would stop at nothing to nail Fran to the wall for the downing of the flight from London. She had to get rid of Taylor to give herself a fighting chance in the international courts if it came to it.

"Auntie Fran is a genius!" she said to Amy in a sing-song voice and went to begin the job of remaking Amy's bassinet, before waiting for the work to stop, the Ministers to go back to their rooms and the corridors of power to fall silent before she began her dirty task.

CHAPTER 30

Callie held the baby whilst Izzy calmed herself down. She had been sobbing for almost an hour now and Callie was almost at the end of her patience.

"I can't do it, Callie," she sniffed.

"Yes, you can."

"I don't want to do it, then, is that better?"

"Not at all. Look. I know you are exhausted and hormones are running like crazy around your body but you have to step up!"

"I didn't want this baby, though!"

"But you have it now," Callie growled through gritted teeth. "It is no-one else's responsibility. You've had more than enough time to come to terms with it."

"It's six weeks early!" Izzy cried and fell onto the bed into a heap of more tears.

Callie rolled her eyes. Lewis and Izzy were made for each other, couple of big babies wanting someone else to take control.

"Remember how you got to the refugee centre? How did you manage that?"

"With a car. And no baby." She pouted.

"Oh, for Pete's sake." Callie had had enough. "Fine, we'll get rid of the problem then." She stood up, hoisted the baby onto her shoulder so that she could open the door and left the room. A moment later, she returned, her arms empty.

"Where is she?" Izzy asked.

"I took care of one of the problems. The baby. Not your problem anymore."

"What did you do?" Izzy wailed and made for the door.

Callie caught her and set her back on her feet. "I just made your life much easier. Now clean up and get dressed. Do you have any sanitary towels in your bag? If not, try mine." She pushed Izzy back onto the bed, turned and opened the door.

"What did you do?" Izzy repeated and began to scream. "My baby! What did you do to my baby?!"

"Get. Dressed." Callie said through gritted teeth and closed the door behind her as she left. She could hear Izzy wailing but walked away calmly.

Out of the small, dirt streaked window, Callie could now see land. Finally. She peered at the sliver of darkness between the brown sea and the weak grey light of an early spring dawn. Here was safety and hopefully, although she had pushed all thoughts of them out of her mind lately, her husband and youngest son. She knew there was no guarantee she would find them soon, possibly ever but she had to try. Then turn her focus back to Scotland to try to find her older boys. What a mess. Izzy just did not understand the pull your children had on you. How you would do anything and go anywhere if they were in trouble. No amount of obstacles would deter a parent, whether the children were large and bearded like Matthew and Elliot or small and vulnerable like her little diabetic Josh.

She gathered the baby and the blanket from the passenger who now held her – she had been passed around in a celebratory manner by most of the women and some of the men – and sat down. The child made small noises and crumpled her bruised and reddened face. She had just been through the trauma of birth and would soon be faced with the trauma of being abandoned on a beach on a small island off the coast of Holland. Callie smiled at her. "Things can only get better from there, kid," she said then looked up.

Izzy stood over her, her face puffy and streaked with tears after hours of effort and strain, first from the birth, then from the effort of such acute misery and shock. She held out her hands for her child. Callie smiled at her and handed over the baby, then stood up so that Izzy could take her seat.

Izzy cradled the baby. She was redressed in trousers and a sweater, boots on her feet and the large greatcoat draped over her shoulders, she could have been any mother in any maternity unit in the world, sitting up in bed, exhausted yet proud, staring into the face of her newborn.

"I thought you had … you know," Izzy said.

"Do you really think I would?"

"No, but," she sniffed. "People do strange things these days."

Callie and Izzy looked at the baby for a while.

"Now do you understand why I do the things I do?" Callie asked. Izzy nodded.

"She's called Caroline," Izzy said. "After you."

CHAPTER 31

Andrea Taylor lunched on Scottish Salmon and new potatoes farmed in the Kingdom of Fife. She wiped her mouth on the finest linen napkin and smoothed down her tweed skirt with finely manicured hands before rising to pour more wine. She crossed the dark, underlit room and mused that the ambience could be improved by a window or two onto a glorious tree lined capital street but settled for a large glug of claret and a seat by the roaring fire.

Even a Sunday spelled work for a leader at war, and she picked up a sheaf of papers and began to read where she had left off before she ate. She placed her glasses on her nose and started, *From the Desk of the Right Honourable* ... then put them down again with a sigh.

"Damian!" she called into the darkness of the adjoining room, "I need you."

Her secretary came through almost immediately, yawning, wearing jogging bottoms and a hoodie. He held his large diary in one arm and a coffee in the other.

"Off duty?" she enquired in a sarcastic tone.

"Yes," he replied simply but sat down and opened his note pad. "What do you need?"

"How is the central perimeter holding up?" she asked, peering at the ruby wine in the glass which sparkled in the firelight.

Damian sighed. She asked this question almost every hour. "It's fine. The last engagement was," he looked at his watch, "... six hours ago on the blockade along the High Street, not far from the castle. Captain McGurk who's been in charge up there for the last three days says he thinks New Britain troops are testing out the strongest point before they push through," he swallowed, "Which he says they will, with not much trouble. He thinks …"

She turned to stare at him and he stopped. Andrea Taylor was not in the slightest bit interested in what other people 'thought'.

"And the rest of the outer city?"

He rubbed his weary eyes before he looked at her. "Carnage," he said. "There are engagements between the Sec Units and New Britain troops all over the place. New Britain are camped in the hills around the city, and Sec Units are preventing people getting to refugee centres in the south and the east so they can arrest them and take some of them to be drafted. In between there and here, it's everyone for themselves. There's looting and mob rule. Loads of people have tried to get through the blockade into the central area. They can see it's much safer in here than it is out there. So they can't get out of the city and they can't get to safety. They're trapped between Scottish troops with the barbed wire keeping them away from the politicians and the New Britain troops preventing them from leaving the city. All the time, the Sec Units are raiding homes, dragging people to the barracks to do their draft duty and shooting looters."

"And outside of Edinburgh?" Her face was impassive, she stared into the distance.

"Same story. At least, the same story from the people we can reach. People being drafted, but … um … we are running out of uniforms and guns, there's no-one to properly train them. So the new Scottish troops look … well," he sucked on his teeth. "They look like guerrilla fighters with guns. They're not uniformed, they're not equipped. They are just armed, the Sec Units we spoke to made sure of that."

Andrea Taylor nodded, steepling her fingers. Some good news, then.

"Communication is going down all over the country," he continued, looking distractedly at his notes, "It was patchy before but now we haven't heard from the Borders or Dumfries or

Jedburgh or Lockerbie in hours now. We can only guess at the numbers lost outside the city." He finished quietly, the momentous horror of what he had to tell her draining him of strength. He took a deep breath and blew out slowly, in an effort to compose himself.

Collateral damage is what she thought. "Thank you, Damian, that is all," is what she said.

.oOo.

Sophie stirred the soup whilst Aaron cut the bread. Despite some sleep since the Sec Units left, chasing after Lewis, they were both exhausted and ravenous after hours of hard work and the unhappy task of saying goodbye to Don. The radio on the windowsill played crackly music interspersed with news updates and broadcasts from Westminster. Occasionally it went silent.

Sophie sniffed and wiped her nose with a sleeve. "Do you think he found Fran yet?"

Aaron continued to cut and butter the bread.

Sophie continued, "Because I will kill her when I find her. Mr Jack was a lovely ..." She couldn't finish as the words caught in her throat. She sobbed for a few moments, then hitched and finally sniffed again. She pulled out her cloth handkerchief and wiped her nose. "Aren't you desperate to know where Amy is? I know I am." she continued. "I'm sure Fran wouldn't hurt her because she was always rocking her and cooing at her. Just, after what happened ... I think we should go and try and find her as well. Lewis is probably crying in a layby somewhere," she grumbled, rolling all the possible options they had left over in her head.

Aaron didn't reply but placed the bread on a tray and arranged four bowls for soup. He picked up the dog's bowls and threw in the scraps along with the bones and skin from yesterday's dinner. Pip and Mol both charged through at the sound of their bowls being placed on the floor and they ate fast.

Sophie ladled the soup into the bowls and grabbed a fist full of spoons.

Aaron finally spoke.

"Do you remember when Mr Jack went part time after Maggie got sick? I think we were about S3, about 13 or 14? He went away for a while, then came back again?"

Sophie nodded.

"He was the best teacher I'd ever had. I was always in the dumb groups with all the ned kids who didn't care and didn't want to learn anything and I just sort of," he shrugged, "… got caught up with that and decided it was easier to muck around than work. Mr Jack, he changed that. I never mucked about in his lessons, I really wanted to please him, wanted him to be proud of me."

He sat and both dogs pressed their heads into his legs, looking for a head scratch, which he obligingly gave.

"And then I wanted him to be proud of me in other things and other subjects so I started to do more work for other teachers. It sort of was like a snowball effect. More and more people said how good I was being and they were all proud of me. Then Amy was born and mum had such a bad time, with the food shortages and that post-natal thing women sometimes get and our dad going to Jamaica and not being able to get back. I felt I needed to be a, like, a bigger man."

"I remember," Sophie sat with him, the steaming soup bowls between them, the smell permeating the kitchen.

"So I did. And I thought I was doing a good job, looking after mum and doing well in school and taking care of Amy."

"You *did* do a good job, Aaron, everyone could see that," Sophie soothed. This was the first time he had spoken about his mum since she'd known him.

Aaron took a deep breath. "She still left. She asked me to look after Amy and walked out of the door. She left us and I have no idea where she went or if we will ever see her again. We were alone for days and I had to grow up more than I ever thought I could. It was hard you know," he looked at her, and she nodded. "It was hard doing the basics, and I had to bring her in to school because it was warmer and there were lots of people who wanted to help me and could look after her so I could study. The kitchen ladies always gave her milk and stuff. When I was arrested that one time, Mrs MacHale took her in right there and then."

"I remember her in English, sleeping in her buggy," Sophie smiled.

"That's when I started seeing Lewis, Mr Sinclair, a bit more because he was guidance and gave me vouchers and numbers to call and helped out with doctor appointments with her, and that." he fiddled with the bread and broke of little pieces which he dropped onto the table.

"And I went to live at the school after it closed because it felt, just, safer. When Mr Sinclair came and we all had to leave, I was willing to go with him because, well, I thought he had a plan, or could look after us or knew what he was doing, even though he didn't really."

Sophie rolled her eyes but said nothing.

"To be honest, I just didn't want to be alone anymore. And when we came here I was extra relieved because I knew Mr Jack could help and would know exactly what to do. That's also when I realised that Mr Sinclair might be a teacher but he wanted Mr Jack's approval just as much as I did. Mr Sinclair didn't really know how to do anything, he always asked Mr Jack. He was always happy when Mr Jack said something nice to him. He was just like me, except for one thing."

"What?" Sophie asked.

Aaron frowned, struggling for clarity. He knew what he wanted to say, but wasn't sure he could make himself understood. "Amy. He didn't have an Amy. He spent his whole life with no-one to take care of except himself. Not like you and me and Mr Jack. He never struggled for anything, until everything went to crap with the sanctions and all that stuff and *everyone* began to struggle. He doesn't know what it's like to really be responsible or in charge or just have to keep going because there's literally no-one else to do it except you."

"What are you getting at?"

"Well, I think that he came back to get the Sec Guards to follow because now there's no Mr Jack, he finally felt responsible for something and there was literally no-one else to sort it out. I think he worked out that they would've killed us if he'd left. I only worked that out afterwards. So he became Mr Jack."

"He wishes," Sophie said automatically, then checked herself. "Do you trust he'll get her back?"

"I think I do. He took Pauly's uniform. He must have a plan."

They sat there for a moment, old music tinkling from the radio, lost in thought.

"Should we go and help him?" Aaron asked, finally.

Sophie considered for a moment, as she bit a fingernail. "I don't think we can. Not both of us. Pauly does not look well, we have to think about that. And Maggie. I guess we are in charge here now."

"I suppose you're right," he sighed. "Food first, then we'll think," he said and they both took the cue to scoop up bowls and trays and took them through to the bedroom.

Aaron pushed open the door with his elbow and Sophie went through first with a tray. Maggie was not in bed. Sophie stopped at the door and stood for a second, nonplussed. Where would Maggie go? Where *could* Maggie go?

Right then, Aaron sucked in his breath and stared at Pauly.

From his makeshift cot in the corner of the room, slung low to the ground and rumpled from all the effort of removing his jacket and shirt, Pauly lay back on his pillows with his rifle cocked and aimed right at them both.

Aaron stood still. Pauly looked terrible, much worse than last night, with blotchy skin and sweat dripping from his chin onto the covers. His hands, and the rifle, shook with the effort. Next to him, Sophie stood stock still, shocked at the sight of him, her hands gripped around the tray.

"Pauly," Aaron began softly, as he took a step into the room, "We want to help you dude," but Pauly shook his head. He cocked his head towards the open door behind them.

They didn't move any further. Pauly continued to hold the rifle up, eye to the sights.

Just then, out of the corner of his eye, Aaron saw a small movement behind the opened door. Instinctively, he knew it wasn't Maggie. He stepped out of the line of fire, shoving Sophie along with him. She didn't protest but the soup spilled onto the tray and her hands and she grimaced at the scald. Behind the door, a Security Guard emerged slowly, his own gun pointed back at Pauly. He was stocky and short, his black uniform straining at the gut. His filthy boots indicated that he was one of the men who had chased Aaron up the hill into the crags but was clearly left behind when the vans all left. Finally, he must've sneaked in.

"Put the gun down, English scum," the Sec Guard growled. His handgun also shook under an ever-tightening grip.

"I'm warning you, sir," Pauly returned in a weak, raspy voice. His throat sounded dry and hoarse. "Please lower your weapon. There are civilians in the room. Please allow them to leave."

Sophie started to back out of the room but the guard yelled at her to stop.

"Don't move, bitch," he shouted and Pauly hitched his rifle up higher on his shoulder. "I'm a civilian too, bastard. You can't shoot me."

"Let them leave." Pauly repeated. "The moment you take your gun from me and point it at them, I shall be at liberty to shoot. You are not an enemy combatant but your engagement with me indicates that you are fair game."

The Sec Guard advanced slowly.

From his position between them, Aaron could now see how much of a mess Pauly's leg was. The break was straight but the

200

whole lower limb was swollen and stretched, fiery red and angry. He wasn't going to walk on that for a long time. He returned to stare at the guard.

"Pauly, what do we do?" Aaron asked.

"Keep back, Aaron." He spoke to the Guard again. "Sir, you are in a civilian household. Please put your weapon down. You are engaging the enemy, but please allow the children to leave." Pauly drew in breath. Speaking obviously caused him pain and Aaron wondered how much longer he could hold up the heavy rifle.

"No!" the Guard cried. "That one's dangerous," he indicated Aaron. So, he had been up the hill, thought Aaron. Must've caught a shot, or a fright.

Just then, a high sing-song sound emanated from the living room beyond.

"Oh, yes, my darling," Maggie was saying, "I've lived here for many years now, since we got married back in 1989, and both boys grew up here."

Sophie thought Maggie must be talking to herself until a deeper, gruffer voice replied. Sophie sucked in her breath. *Who the hell was that?*

"Well, aren't you a bonny lad!" Maggie said now. "I know a young girl who would love to meet you!"

Maggie entered the room on the supporting arm of a young Sec Guard. She was wearing Don's old housecoat and slippers and an old scarf around her neck. She glanced at Pauly and then at the other Guard behind the door then began to laugh.

"Oh, boys!" she cried, "No time for fun and games. We have guests!" She patted the Guard's gun with a skinny hand, and he lowered his arms as she passed on her way to the bed, although he didn't take his eyes off Pauly. She grasped at him and, now, between two guards, she allowed them both to help her onto the bed and under the covers.

"Did either of you boys go to school round here?" Maggie asked, conversationally. "If you did, you'll know my Don. He's a wonderful teacher and did a great job on all the naughty boys." She smiled indulgently at them. "Although, I'll bet you were both as good as gold, weren't you, son?" she gripped their hands tightly as the younger one replied in deferent tones. The older Guard who had pointed his gun at Pauly now eyed Maggie. He tried to pull away from her but she held on with her bony fingers. She continued to gibber nonsensically, her questions darting from one to the other.

Pauly lowered his rifle in relief and sat back in his bed.

Aaron looked at him. He looked terribly pale and sweaty, his undershirt soaking wet and stained with vomit. His breathing was fast, his skin blotchy.

"Oh, Jesus," Sophie breathed, as she knelt beside them, "How long has he been like this? What the hell happened?"

Aaron pulled back the covers to show Pauly's broken ankle, swollen and red. The skin looked angry, mottled and dark.

"Shit, he's got an infection," she whispered. "He needs antibiotics," Sophie said, decisively.

"We don't have any!" Aaron shook his head.

"So we need to go and get some!" she hissed. "This is why we need to go into town, not just to find Amy!"

"We can't both go into town, we have slightly more pressing matters! Maybe the guards can take him, get him help?"

"... and this is my granddaughter, Eva and my grandsons, Aaron and William ..." Maggie was saying, still holding tightly to the two Guards. "They run the farm and look after me so well," she smiled at them all as everyone in the room regarded each other with suspicion and distain.

"Ma'am, they all should have gone to join the army. You know, the draft. We need to take them away with us," the younger Guard said.

"Dodging the draft carries a shoot-on-sight policy, ma'am. We have to take them in," the older one insisted as he tried to extricate his hand from hers.

"Shoot my babies? I don't think so!" Maggie's face widened in shock. "Why, what are they going to do in this new army? All the other men did was pretend to throw bombs and shoot up in the Pentlands, right over there it was. War Games, they called it and great fun it looked too." She smiled again, "Unless you were a sheep, then it was very scary and it took us ages to get some of them back after big explosions." Maggie laughed. "My Don, he used to take old Mol for miles into the hills to find lost sheep. They came back so filthy! Just for a sheep, mind! Luckiest, most spoilt sheep in Scotland!" she inclined closer to the younger man, "And most spoilt dogs, too!"

"Ma'am," the older Guard tried to return the conversation to the draft, "We have to take your grandchildren. If they resist like this one did," he indicated Pauly, now flat on his back with his eyes closed, "We have no choice but to shoot them as deserters, just like in the war. We haven't got time to waste. We need every person we can get"

"We aren't in a war, young man!" Maggie exclaimed.

"We are, though," he returned, "Against the English." He turned to Aaron and Sophie, "Please make her understand."

Sophie shifted her weight onto one leg and folded her arms, returning his stare.

"Oh, nonsense, who will take care of me if they go? And the farm? Tell you what, I could really use a cup of tea. How about it, boys? Tea? Homemade bread and apricot jam? Sound good? Eva's a good cook. You must've been working hard, you were all making such a big racket out there last night!"

The older Guard widened his eyes. He considered her offer for a split second before his stomach got the better of him.

"Sounds good, Maggie," he relented, "We'll have tea before we head off - but I insist we all go."

"Aaron, Eva, hen, go make our guests some tea and slice some bread. Can't have you all going off to fight on an empty stomach."

Sophie and Aaron stopped for a second, eyeing the two Guards. Maggie had one on either side of her, holding hands, looking up at them both like a proud, indulgent grandmother looks at her graduating grandchildren. They hesitated.

"Go on, now." she said and nodded imperceptibly. "And take the dogs too, they need fed."

"But I just ..."

"Off you go, now." Maggie interrupted him. She looked at them significantly.

"Off you go, Sophie," she said, firmly.

They hesitated a moment longer.

"Pip, Mol," called Aaron.

They hurried out of the door into the kitchen.

"What the fuck?" Sophie said as she picked up the knife to saw at a new loaf of bread. "Is she ok?"

Aaron placed the kettle on to the stove then held onto the cupboard door where they kept the tea bags. "I ... I don't know," he had to confess. Neither of them had heard Maggie talk at such length before. What has she done?

"Let's just make tea and see if we can't talk them round. Persuade them to let us stay. Maybe even get us some antibiotics for Pauly." he shrugged but still didn't open the cupboard.

"Yeah, right," she replied. "Get a grip, Aaron, they have orders to shoot us! I'm pretty sure they haven't just received new orders to be sweet and reasonable to everyone. Tea and jam pieces won't change their minds." She looked at the knife in her hand and the realisation dawned.

"Maggie practically kicked us out of the room," she said.

Aaron turned to her. "She was pretty adamant that we left. And took the dogs."

"Are we supposed to escape?" Sophie stared at him.

"Do you think she understands what's going on?"

"Maybe. It's just, the last thing she said," Sophie said, flatly. "For the first time ever, she didn't call me 'Eva'. She called me 'Sophie'."

She put down the knife. "I think she knows exactly what she's doing."

They looked at each other for a moment longer then bolted for the door, followed by Pip and Mol. They went as fast as they were able, making as little noise as they could. Aaron picked up his rifle by the door and Sophie dragged her large Greatcoat over her shoulders and grabbed the quad keys, mindful to grasp them in a way that didn't make them jingle. As she did so, she noticed Fran's car keys were gone.

They opened the door and tiptoed out.

CHAPTER 32

Lewis shrugged his arms into the jacket and did up the buttons with one hand as he drove. It was a bit tight but it fit convincingly enough. He turned a corner into a familiar old disused farm track and drove as far up as he could before he jerked on the handbrake. They wouldn't see him from the road, he knew that, and besides, he was convinced he had lost them a few miles back before doubling back. The Sec Units, with their blaring sirens and bright lights had, he knew, turned off right some time ago, presumably following some other poor unassuming soul. He sat for a while, just to make sure he was completely alone.

After a while, with the morning gloom subsiding, Lewis took a deep breath and sat up. This must be right, he thought, as he jumped from the drivers' seat and looked around himself at the old bent trees and abandoned industrial farm units, it fit her description perfectly. He pulled his backpack onto his back and rummaged in his pocket for the keys, then began to walk further up the rocky road. Despite her not knowing the name of the road or the farm or the track, he found Fran's abandoned car quickly. He pressed the lock button on the key and it immediately whooped and flashed its lights.

"Bingo," he muttered. A fast car with lots of petrol and a number plate that opened doors, or gates, or blockades, whatever, he thought. He jumped in and turned over the engine. It shuddered for a few seconds but then burst into life, thrumming dutifully at his request. He adjusted the seat and mirror and threw it into reverse. He rolled slowly towards the tarmac road and peered out both ways. It was clear and he roared off towards the city.

Half an hour later, just before he reached the outer suburbs, Lewis abruptly turned a corner and the car began to climb up the hill just south of the city. When he could go no further, he rolled to a stop, got out and he stared out at the devastated city in front of him. From where he stood, he could see most of Edinburgh, from the bypass in the south to the Leith Docks on the Forth. Nothing had escaped damage. Puffs and columns of smoke drifted upwards from every quarter, spires had toppled and even the Castle looked different with walls missing and buildings damaged. The once green parks looked barren and empty, with all the trees cut down for fuel and whole swathes of the city were now blackened blank spaces. Lewis sucked in his breath, horrified at the desolate and ruined city. How on earth was he supposed to find *anyone* in that ransacked place? Did Bute House even still exist? Were Fran and Amy even still alive?

He took a deep breath and walked back to the car. He had made a promise to Aaron to find Amy. He had Fran's blue book and could use it as a bargaining tool. He had Pauly's uniform to open the enemy lines and a Scottish accent to open the defensive ones. If all else fails, he thought, I have Don's dynamite although he dismissed the idea of using it as quickly as it entered his head. He might be about to do something spectacularly dangerous and stupid, but he didn't have a death wish.

He turned back down the hill to face the outer blockade, the English, a possible shooting, imprisonment or death. He chuckled ruefully and thought, for perhaps the first time, that signing up all those months ago might have been the more sensible option.

.oOo.

Sophie and Aaron scurried fast but quietly through the yard, followed faithfully by Pip. They tiptoed around puddles and jumped the larger holes. Aaron reached the quad first and grabbed the handlebars. He leaned over it and pushed, the wheels began to turn and the quad rolled out of the yard onto the dirt track. Pip automatically jumped onto the back and lay down, still alert to the bumps and dips of the road. Sophie ran behind, clutching the rifle.

"Mol! Where's Mol?" Aaron cried in a harsh whisper, still pushing hard.

"She was here a minute ago," Sophie replied, slightly out of breath. "But we have to go on! She'll follow if she wants to."

They lumbered towards the open gateway and the cattle grid, the quad bouncing on the uneven road then bumped across it as fast as they were able.

"We'll take the western track!" she called into his ear, "I think I know where Lewis might be!"

Aaron grunted, started the engine and roared away as fast as the quad would manage.

Inside the house, Maggie continued to chatter.

"Did you know that phrase, 'an army marches on its stomach', boys? Well, it is certainly true when you're running a farm, like here." Maggie held tight to the two Sec Guards. They looked at one another, slightly helplessly, neither of them wanted to pull away and upset the old lady in front of them, as inconvenient as it may have been to stand there in her iron grip. The older one eyed Pauly, but he had laid back down on his cot, sweating and pale. If he was a threat before, the Sec Guard didn't think he would be bothering them again. Beyond the door, a high pitched whistle slowly gained volume.

"I don't think he's very well," the younger one said, and turned to Pauly's cot.

"My poor William, he's so tired with all the fighting. But we'll fix him up, won't we, boys. He'll be as right as rain with some tea."

The whistle continued, louder now.

Maggie spoke again, "Of course, my Don will be back soon to take care of everything," she said, and the two men looked at one another. They knew Don was not coming back, they'd seen the grave. "You'll see, he'll straighten everything out."

The whistle became urgent.

The older Sec Guard opened his mouth to reply but suddenly clamped it shut and frowned.

He fumbled with his gun, pulled his hand away from Maggie's and stammered, "Kettle!" The gun became tangled in his webbing vest and toggled sleeves and he grunted as he continued to pull it.

The younger Guard reacted to his panic, despite not quite understanding what his problem was. "What's wrong?" he asked, wide eyed.

"Kettle! It's still on! They've gone! They must've gone!" He dragged his gun free of his vest and held it aloft. Then both men made for the door.

"I don't think so," came a voice from the bed.

The Sec Guards turned and once more faced Maggie; hands clasped in her lap around an old-fashioned handgun.

.oOo.

Lewis approached the city from the south, with little in the way of obstruction. He drove towards the outer blockade, just outside the bypass, rolled to a stop and got out. There was one New Britain soldier who manned the road with another who sat in an armoured vehicle to the side. He looked to Lewis like he was taking a coffee break and Lewis' mouth began to water. It had been months since he'd had coffee, Don only had tea left now.

"Alright?" the squaddie called and sauntered over.

Lewis could've punched the air. Scottish! The man was Scottish!

"Alright, mate," Lewis returned not disguising his accent.

The squaddie hesitated slightly at the sound of his voice then looked more closely at the uniform and decided it was safe. Lewis tried not to let his relief show.

"Do you want in?" the man nodded towards the city.

"No' really!" Lewis laughed and leaned on the car bonnet, ankles crossed in a relaxed manner. He took out some rolling tobacco and papers, "Smoke?" he said.

"Oh, yeah!" the squaddie replied and Lewis handed over the finished cigarette before rolling one for himself. They both lit up and inhaled, then let out streams of sweet smoke.

"That hits the spot, don't it?" Lewis said, eyeing the squaddie. He can't have been much older than Aaron and Lewis had no problem regarding him as one of his old students. He might not know much but Lewis knew how to speak to teenage boys.

"You frae Edinburgh?" Lewis asked.

"Aye," the squaddie replied.

"Where d'ye stay?" Lewis asked, after a moment.

"Niddrie."

"So this smart part of toon will no be familiar to ye?" Lewis said, and dug the squaddie in the ribs with a grin.

"Cheeky cunt," the squaddie muttered but smiled back. They continued to smoke.

"Nothing smart left in Edinburgh," the squaddie said, after a while. "If you've no been, like?"

"Ah've been in the hills. My Sergeant had orders frae the top tae send me doon tae bring this car," Lewis lied smoothly. "It's supposed to belong tae a cabinet minister, ken, the one who's wanted?"

"Oh, aye?" The squaddie turned and looked at the Mercedes he leaned on.

"Ah'm supposed tae give it tae a Captain ... um ..." he pretended to search for the name, despite knowing it full well. Pauly had told him the name of his Captain and Lewis lied fluidly. If there were any questions asked, he had answers at the ready. "Captain Johnston. I'll be looking fae a lift hame, mind!" He laughed and the squaddie joined him.

Lewis ground his cigarette underfoot and wiped his hands.

"Right, so ah will be back through this way later," he paused. "Them new Scottish troops been giving you hassle?" he asked.

"Nah," the squaddie replied, walking towards the gate to open it, "They're all in the inner blockade, or down at the border on the roads. We don't see 'em no more, not since ah've been here. We're just here to check who gets in or oot o'the city. It's those fuckin' Security Units, watch out for them bastards. Cunts one and all, man. They'd shoot you in the back before asking questions. Thanks for the smoke."

Lewis got in the car and drove through the gate with a wave. He watched the soldier close the gate behind him and shook his head. "The enemy of my enemy is my friend," he muttered, then frowned as he tried to think where he had heard that phrase before.

He drove northwards through the disarray that was south Edinburgh. He saw, as Fran did just a short while ago, that the fighting had been intense in pockets, non-existent in others and everywhere was deserted except for wildlife, the occasional scampering looter and displaced refugees, camped in parks, hunched over steaming pots or camp fires. He headed to the centre, shaking with nerves now but confident he was close to his prize.

.oOo.

"Fuck's sake man, you aren't going to shoot anyone!" the older Sec Guard laughed at Maggie.

"Try me," she said in a low voice.

"Ok, I will," the younger one said and raised his gun to shoot.

"Mol, squirrels," called Maggie, quietly. Mol appeared from under the bed, jumped up onto it and stood in front of the Guard. She wagged her tail in warning. Her big brown eyes stared, her haunches poised and covered in black and white hackles. She began to growl.

"Mol and Pip have danger words. If I say 'squirrels', Mol knows I mean business." Maggie stated matter of fact. "My Don made sure of that."

"Your Don is dead!" the older Guard shouted, but he backed away from the dog, "Get that through your thick, demented head!"

"Yes, I know," Maggie said. "But Mol's guardianship is not the only thing he left us."

Maggie sat up straighter in bed and opened Don's old housecoat. From the inside pocket, she drew a plastic box, covered in tape. It could've been an old mobile phone except for the wires and solder adhering to the outside.

Both men gaped. They had never seen anything like it before, except in movies.

"Is that a ... detonator?" one of them stammered.

"Is it real?" the other one asked.

"Is this place wired up?" They both looked around for evidence of explosive, wires, anything to make the threat real.

"She wouldn't dare, she'd die too, and him," he waved towards Pauly, and Mol snapped at his hand.

"You'd kill yourself and the kid and the dog," the older Guard said, scoffing.

"My Don always said we had to make plans. That's why we live here, out of everyone's way. When the world fell apart out there, he told me about the final plan. If we were ever under threat, my Don said, I could use this," she waved the small box.

"Fucking fruitcake," the older one said but began to retreat from the dog and the bed.

"Are you boys going to sit down or make the tea?" Maggie asked. "That's the two options."

"Fuck this," the younger one breathed. Before anyone could react, he squeezed off a shot at Pauly who recoiled as he was hit in the shoulder. He screamed in pain. Blood spread quickly around his pillows, and he balled his fists in agony.

"I'm in fucking charge, and I'm going to shoot me some deserters!" the younger one shouted and turned to leave, the older one in tow, his face lit up with delight at the gunplay.

Maggie looked at Pauly in shock. He nodded.

"Do it, Maggie. Just do it." he stated and fell back, his eyes closed.

Maggie reached into the bedside drawer and placed the detonator onto a larger unit.

"Mol, squirrels," she said again and Mol bolted barking from the room, just as the air drew in, then pulsed behind her.

CHAPTER 33

As he drove, Lewis discarded his uniform. If there were Scottish soldiers about, he did not want to be stopped, and even less so by the Sec Units. The squaddie had mentioned the inner blockade. Lewis wasn't sure what that meant. He turned the wheel left and right to avoid the potholes and blast holes in the roads as he drove towards the West End of town. Water leaked from damaged underground pipes and ran down the roads into blocked drains, then continued until they found holes to convert to oily little ponds. Smashed shards of glass carpeted the pavements and roads with twinkling crumbs and the front of every shop was littered with half looted, half dropped bags and packets of food, spilled drinks and empty cartons. Inside the shops, Lewis could see empty shelves and mangled tills, where looters had struggled to access the cash inside. What good cash would do these days, Lewis muttered to himself.

Closer to the centre, every tenement building looked dark and uninhabited. Lewis could sense that he was being watched, how could he not be? He suddenly became conscious of the expensive car he drove and he tried to speed up, the roads making it impossible to go too fast. He passed small pockets of people, either huddled together around fires or children playing in the rubble piles, dirty and often coat-less.

Lewis drove on and pulled up in a dark side street outside a bunch of shops. He was too tired and hungry to go any further.

He switched off the engine and looked around. The street looked deserted, but he had to be careful. He fumbled in his coat pocket and pulled out a few coins. If anyone asks, he was going to pay, he thought to himself. He was sure that wouldn't happen. Every shop he had passed had been abandoned. He opened the car door and closed it as quietly as possible. Then he locked it, just in case.

Across the road was a pharmacy. He looked at the door and windows - it was locked and the shutters were intact. Next door, a small newsagent store had obviously been turned over more than once. Lewis walked in through the open door and peered into the dark interior. Clearly no-one was home. He scanned the shelves for something convenient to eat but there was very little to choose from. He chose a jar of olives and then reached into a small freezer to pull out a pack of half baked bread rolls. It would have to do.

Back at the car, he slipped down in the seat, covering himself in his coat up to his chest to keep warm. Then he reached over, unzipped the backpack and pulled out a bottle of water to help the food go down. He ate slowly and peered out at the close. Green moss and slime grew up the walls near the broken old downpipes and weeds grew through the cracks in the pavement. He remembered vaguely that he and Izzy went to a club near here before it closed. Rio? Reno? He couldn't quite recall the name. Izzy skimmed through his memory but he pushed her away and reached for his tobacco. The streets were deserted here, the air quiet and still although the tang of woodsmoke from fires permeated the car. He finished his cigarette and gulped a few swallows of water before settling down again, his eyes now tracking a distant plane, far above, its lights blinking in the cloudy blue sky. Then Lewis closed his eyes and slept, truly alone for the first time in his life.

CHAPTER 34

Aaron and Sophie rode towards town along the Pentland paths rather than risk the open road. It was safer that way, they surmised, it was much quicker than driving to the tarmac road and besides, Aaron knew the paths and tracks well after working the sheep with Don. Pip lay crouched on the back, balanced expertly on four solid paws. After a while, they rounded a long, sloping pass past a deserted cattle shed and a copse of low, craggy trees.

The streaming cold air had frozen both their worried faces and Aaron's fingers stiffened around the handlebars. They were closer to the road here and they continued more cautiously for a while until Sophie tapped him on the shoulder and called in his ear.

"There!" she said, pointing towards the shed, "Look at that! It's the bus! I knew it!"

Aaron turned downhill and they stopped by the old school bus, parked deliberately under the trees, away from the track. Sophie jumped off the quad and Pip followed. She tried the door which opened easily. Immediately the familiar smell of the farm, and of Lewis and even the school drew into her nostrils. Aaron joined her as she stepped up into the van and Pip jumped in behind.

"Her keys were gone. Fran's, I mean. I knew he'd taken them. I knew this is what he would do! He's taken her car. Maybe he's not so useless after all," Sophie snorted.

The air felt warm inside, compared to the rushing frigid breeze and Sophie let out her breath. Pip stood up on the seat and shook out her fur. They both looked out of the window and contemplated their next move.

"What do we do now?" Sophie asked. "Where do we go?"

Aaron flexed his frozen fingers and grimaced.

"Where is there?" he asked. "I mean, where else is there but the farm …"

Just then, a deep, rumbling boom flooded the valley before them. In the distance, a flash of light followed by a ball of black smoke rolled into the air. They both watched, open mouthed. Pip pricked her ears and cocked her head to one side.

Sophie sucked in her breath. "Oh, Maggie, no …" she breathed, her hands over her mouth, her eyes wide with shock.

They both knew it was the farm. With the smoke rising and the light now a low, orange glow, Aaron and Sophie knew they had lost the only secure place they had known in years. The smoke continued to rise, black and billowing and Sophie swallowed. Her throat was sore and dry, her head ached. Maggie was her friend, like a grandmother and a mother, even though Sophie looked after her, not the other way round. She might have been a bit muddled and forgetful but she never raised her voice or got upset. Maggie loved everyone. Don took care of everyone. And now they were both gone. Sophie dropped her head into her hands and sobbed.

Aaron hung his head and wiped away the tears from his cheeks with the heels of his hands. He sniffed and hugged Pip, who whined at their distress.

Two days ago they were a family. Dysfunctional, unrelated and stressed, perhaps, but a secure unit from where they could all look out and feel safe. Now they had a van, a dog and each other. Once again, like before, their lives had shrunk. Once again, like before, they knew they had to keep going.

"We'll stay here today," Sophie said, after a while. "Think about it tomorrow."

Aaron nodded his head, drew up his knees and hugged Pip close. Sophie looked at the glow for a little longer then turned away, shivering and nauseous, unable to watch any more.

.oOo.

Lewis awoke in the weak light between the tenements. He had not meant to sleep so long. It was an expensive car and sleeping in the driver's seat was very comfortable. It smelled vaguely sweet, like pine air freshener and the tinted windows kept him away from the immediate eye of looters. The street outside was still quiet but a vague smell of blocked drains gave him the incentive to move. He reached for his water bottle and took a slug, then turned the key, looked in the mirror automatically, even though there was clearly going to be nothing coming, and drove slowly away. No-one was out. Lewis knew the city must be filled with people but they were all very much keeping out of the way.

Eventually, he approached the road leading to Charlotte Square. He could see Bute House from where he sat and he took a deep breath. This was it. The blockade was indeed there as the squaddie had said and he rolled down his window as he came to a stop.

The soldier at the gate trained a rifle on him. "Name?" he said simply.

"Lewis Sinclair," he replied, his hands raised.

"Do you have business here?"

"I have something that belongs to Fran MacDonald MSP. I believe she's inside. She needs what I have here," He stared straight ahead, afraid of what the soldier could do if he didn't like Lewis' face or tone of voice. They probably weren't as bad as the Sec Units but Lewis was disinclined to find out.

"Hold on," the soldier replied in a gruff voice and turned to speak into his radio. The other soldiers checked the underside of the car and shone torches into the back. One asked Lewis to open the boot. He peered in, rummaged around for a moment then closed it with a slam.

A few minutes later, the first soldier returned. "Do you have any ID?" he asked. Lewis pulled out his old driving licence and the private nodded and turned away again.

"Tell her I have her car, too, if that helps," Lewis called and the soldier glanced at it.

After a moment, he returned and motioned to the other soldier to move the barriers. Lewis drove slowly through and up to the door. He got out and was about to climb the steps when the house security flew through the door, handguns pointed at him. The sky was still a gloomy dark grey but he could see at least five people intent on shooting him.

"Whoa!" he cried and stretched his arms upwards as fast as they would go. In one hand he held her blue book, in the other, the car keys.

"It's ok, Sergeant, he's here to return my property. Let him be." Fran emerged from the doorway, Amy perched on her hip.

"Fran," he said, "I'm here to do a deal," he began but she cut him off. She did not want her business discussed in front of the grunts.

"Come in, Lewis," she said quickly, "I'm sure you haven't had breakfast, you must be hungry."

The guards lowered their guns and let him climb the remaining steps. He eyed them as he slipped past into the house, then followed Fran down a series of corridors until they reached the door to her office. They both entered and Fran shut the door behind him.

"Lewis, you've saved my life," she said and made to take the blue leather book.

He held it up out of the way, "Not so fast, Fran, I haven't just come to give you this like you forgot your packed lunch or anything. I want to trade."

"Amy?"

"Of course, Amy." He tutted.

"That's ok, isn't it baby girl," Fran cooed as she bounced Amy on her hip, "You've helped Aunty Fran so much, haven't you? With your smuggling and crying and keeping my goodies safe."

Lewis pulled a face. Fran sounded clearly unhinged. He looked at the book in his hand.

"I read this," he stated simply. "You have some serious revenge issues, Fran."

She put Amy down on the rug by the fireplace and sat next to her.

"Of course I do, Lewis, I always told you, I was framed. This is my proof of innocence. My diary, notes, minutes of meetings, receipts, phone calls. I didn't do it. SHE did. And much more besides. I want a part of the new Independent Scottish Government, Lewis, and no small matter of mass murder is going to stop me. People have been elected into the top spot with worse. And I'm going to stop her doing worse. I'm not the bad guy, here, Lewis, Andrea Taylor is."

"Fran, you killed Don. No amount of spin can change that." Lewis shook his head.

"An accident. I - I didn't mean to, I thought he was going to hurt me. It was self-defence," she grappled with her explanation until it covered all possibilities.

"Don was your friend," Lewis held her gaze.

"Don was no saint, Lewis," Fran turned away and bit a nail.

"He saved you."

"I *know!*" she sniffed. "And maybe that's ... that's why I'm doing this," she started to cry. "He was a good man to me and he died for no reason – he shouldn't have grabbed the gun." Fran straightened up and wiped the tears away. ". I need to stop Andrea Taylor before more good men die. We never needed to go to war. All of this is her fault, don't you see? From the very beginning! She just wanted more power and was willing to do anything, compromise anyone to get it. The Sec Units don't need to be so cruel, but they are because of the precedent. Allow it once and it happens again and again. She's allowing ... no, she's actually *encouraging* all this violence." Fran sat down and wiped her eyes. "I mean, I can understand why she wants out of New Britain, we were being punished for the sins of Westminster - but were they guilty? Do we know who was really to blame here? What was left of Scotland is all gone. There's nothing left and it's all her fault."

"There's plenty left, Fran. There's loads of good people left. Look at Aaron and Sophie, good kids. No-one wants to fight. It'll be over soon, I'm sure." Lewis almost started to feel sorry for her.

"Yes," she sniffed, "Yes, it'll all be over soon." She looked at the baby and saw that she was asleep. She smiled. It was far too early for her to be up yet. She rose and picked Amy up with a practised hand then put her in her bassinet, covered with the blanket. She tucked the leather bookmark and a half drunk bottle of milk beside her and turned to Lewis.

"Do you want breakfast? They've just opened the kitchens," she asked. "It's very good. They even have orange juice."

"Actually, that sounds great. Thank you."

Fran called to the kitchen for another breakfast and it was delivered swiftly. Lewis realised his hunger as it arrived and his eyes widened at the sight of a full Scottish breakfast with glorious coffee and rare, sparkling orange juice. He fell on it and gulped a taste, the first orange juice he'd tasted in at least two years. It was like swallowing pure sunshine and he couldn't help but smile.

He ate quickly yet relished every morsel. It was the tastiest food he'd had in years and despite a vague guilt at not being able to share with the kids or Maggie, he finished it without delay. With a final slurp of coffee, he let out a huge, satisfied sigh. Fran watched him from her seat behind her desk.

"That was the best, thank you," he said, patting his stomach, a grin on his lips.

"I'm glad you enjoyed it," she said and looked at her watch. "Now get out." Her tone was frosty, her demeanour cold and angry once more but she held up a set of keys which he recognised as belonging to Don's Land Rover. "Take this. It's parked on the street. You'll not get back out in my car. Leave my keys. Just take the baby and go."

Lewis pulled a face. "Alright, I'm off," he said and stood up, taking the keys, "Jeez, Fran, you're a strange one." He placed the book on the desk in front of her and she placed both hands reverentially on it. He picked up Amy's bassinet and turned to the door.

"Listen, now you're back here and you have at least some leverage, try and do some good this time, huh? I mean try to do something that …"

"Get out!" she stood up and pointed at the door. Her face quivered and she stared wide eyed at him. "Take the truck and go! Quickly, go."

"Fine, nice doing business with you," he mumbled and left the room. Shortly afterwards, Fran picked up her bag and her book, slipped out and walked the opposite way. She didn't have a lot of time and it was crucial she finish before they all started to take their seats in the meeting room.

As Lewis negotiated the corridors, he passed many faces that looked vaguely familiar. Some groups spoke in French or German, others in broken English with a variety of accents. Lewis moved as fast as he could, before anyone tried to stop him, but presumed they were all the scaffolding for a big, decisive meeting. Good, he thought, get it done, get it stopped. He found the front door and nodded at the guards as he left. He took the front steps two at a time and walked hurriedly to Don's Land Rover.

Lewis drove towards the checkpoint where they'd let him through earlier but stopped abruptly. Out there in greater Edinburgh it was still a free for all and now that the sun was up who knew what the Sec Units got up to. He was still a wanted man, a draft dodger, implicated in theft, accessory to murder and at this stage possibly international espionage, who knew? In for a penny, and all that. He chuckled despite himself but frowned. Not far away was the main shopping area; deserted, unmanned and curiously unprotected. The Scottish Army soldiers were all involved with keeping the blockade in place, keeping everyone out, Scottish and English alike.

Lewis shrugged to himself and turned the wheel.

"Time for some new nappies, Amy," he said, and headed for the nearest shops.

.oOo.

Fran slowly washed in her bathroom and brushed her hair. Then she sat for a moment with a sticky bottle of nail polish that she found in the bathroom drawer and slipped the red shiny liquid across her damaged nails. The ground in dirt would come off eventually, she was sure of that. She found a lipstick in her desk and applied it liberally. She hadn't had lipstick on for months, not since she was chased out of Edinburgh Airport by the braying mob. Now it was time to put all the records straight and she wanted to look as professional and serious as was possible. No-one was going to ignore Fran MacDonald anymore. They were going to see that not only was she not a criminal, she was also the obvious choice as Taylor's successor.

A knock at the door dragged her from her internal monologue and she answered with a sharp, "Come in."

"Todd Horton, Minister for Rural Land and the Environment, stood in the doorway. We need to talk." he said.

"Yes," Fran relied. "We do. But it has to be quick."

.oOo.

Half an hour later, Andrea Taylor swept through the corridor, greeting each minister and dignitary in turn as she passed, her voice short, her face grim. Her secretary, Damian, walked alongside her, his arms full of files and papers, his lanyard fluttering over his shoulder.

"Wait here," she ordered and Damian stopped outside Fran's door, still struggling with his load. He knelt and put some of the files on the floor, grateful for the pause.

Andrea opened the door to Fran's office without knocking and closed it behind her. Fran now sat at her desk, feet up, chair leaning back so that she looked up at the ceiling. She blew gently on her still wet nails. Andrea frowned. She had never seen Fran

222

adopt such a languid pose, she was usually wound tight and stiff, her professional demeanour masking all humane sensibilities.

"Fran, there are a few things I would like to discuss before this morning's meeting," she said as she stepped into the room onto the deep pile carpet and closed the heavy door behind her.

Fran didn't move.

"No baby?" Andrea said as she sat opposite her, surveying the room.

"Nope. She's gone home where she belongs," Fran said but didn't move.

"Right. Then let me tell you what's going to happen this morning." Andrea crossed her legs and brushed a hair from her skirt. Fran let out a deep sigh and Andrea couldn't prevent her face twisting into acute irritation as she spoke from straight, tight lips. "We need to broker a deal for Scotland. I want independence, and you are going to help me get it. You are wanted for war crimes by Holyrood but you are far too useful to be sitting behind bars. This will stand in everyone's favour. Understand?" Andrea stopped. Was Fran even listening?

"Sure," Fran returned but continued to look at the ceiling.

Andrea cleared her throat and continued. She was not used to being so roundly and rudely ignored.

"I'm not sure you fully understand, Fran," Andrea peered at her. "You are wanted by the Scottish Government for causing the deaths of everyone on board that relief flight from London to Edinburgh. We can hand you over to the international criminal court, who will try you as a war criminal in The Hague, or we can keep you, and all the evidence, and you can help procure a deal which sees us back in Europe on our own terms. You would save your country, Fran."

Fran didn't move.

Andrea went on, "You have one hundred and twenty-two counts of murder to your name. We are considering it a war crime of the highest order. You'd never be released. By your actions, the civil war between Scotland and New Britain began and hundreds, perhaps thousands of lives have been lost. This is all your fault, Fran. All of it. This deal could make it all right again."

"None of that's true," Fran said simply.

"What does that matter, you can't prove otherwise."

"Can't I?"

"Well, you …" Andrea Taylor faltered. Her face darkened and her tone changed. "I'll nail you right to the wall, MacDonald," Andrea growled.

"Delighted to return the compliment, I'm sure," Fran waved at her with a newly manicured hand, took her feet off the desk and turned to look straight at the First Minister.

"I don't care what evidence you think you've got, Fran, no-one can touch me. No-one can assail my position. Not Westminster, and certainly not you," Andrea gripped the arms of the chair.

Fran chuckled, "No." she said, "There is no-one alive who can provide the evidence to put you out of power, Taylor."

"That's right," Andrea said, although warily and with a little fluster, "No-one. No-one has anything on me."

"And if you want to keep it that way, I suggest you do anything possible to keep me out of The Hague," Fran said.

"Only if you help me get the deal. You're the closest we have to a European Ambassador. They know you. They trust you. And if you help me, then I have no reason to tell them all one hundred and twenty-two reasons *not* to trust you."

"And if you do," Fran said, "I'll be obliged to tell them all one hundred and one reasons not to trust *you*."

Andrea Taylor frowned. What did Fran mean? She stood up and strode to the door.

"So we understand one another?" Andrea said. She was unsure if Fran had acquiesced or if she'd tipped the balance in her own favour, and she did not like the feeling of uncertainty. However, the meeting had to start soon and it had to be the beginning of the end, one way or another.

Fran nodded and Taylor left. Then she straightened her shirt and jacket, picked up her blue leather-bound book, placed another notebook on top and left the room for the last time as the Minister for Europe.

CHAPTER 35

The sea became less choppy as they rounded the headland into the shelter of the wide, south facing beaches of the island. Izzy slept whilst Callie cradled the newborn and watched out of the tiny, grimy windows.

"Time to get up, Izzy," she shook her friend awake and went back to the window. The white sandy beaches looked very inviting even in the cold winds and she could see marram grass and dunes forming mounds on the horizon. She thought it might be low tide but couldn't be sure.

"Are we there?" Izzy asked, rubbing her eyes.

"It won't be long now," Callie replied.

They both peered at the beach as it passed.

"We can't land there, can we?" Izzy asked. "Do we go right into a harbour? Or do they ..." she looked at Callie in horror, "They're not going to make us swim are they?" she asked.

Callie continued to look out.

"Bloody hope not," she said simply.

Inside the cramped cabin, people began to shuffle and prepare. The smell was overwhelming, from unwashed bodies overcome with stress and fear. Boots were laced and people helped one another into coats and sweaters. They murmured and coughed, patted pockets and zipped up small bags.

In the front, the captain steered as close to the beach as he could without grounding his boat. He had done this a dozen times before and hoped the next one would be the last. He had a family in Eyemouth, it was their turn next. For the first time since he left the Scottish harbour, he switched on his radio and picked up the microphone to speak.

"Callie," Izzy asked.

"Hmm?" she replied.

"What happens next?"

Callie looked at her, "No idea."

Just then, a booming sound permeated the boat and Callie and Izzy jumped. The deep rumbling noise continued for a few seconds more and then stopped with a clank and a bump and a softening of the engine noise. They had stopped.

"What's going on?" someone called.

From the front, there was no reply. The boat bobbed and swayed on the water. The horizon shifted and dipped in the windows.

"Why have we stopped?" the voice called again.

The captain cleared his throat. "We, uh," he began, "We are going to wait here for a … while," he said.

People turned to one another, fear and worry etching their faces. Were they going to land? Had they been caught? Did they have to go home? Was he scamming them?

"Why?" asked a cautious voice.

"I think there may have been … developments," he finished then refused to speak further. Two days at sea, these people could stand a few hours more.

CHAPTER 36

When Sophie awoke from a fitful sleep, Aaron had already left the van to walk with Pip. The dog had taken a drink from a puddle and scampered off to dig at a mouse hole by some gnarled tree roots, but Aaron whistled her away, she had work to do.

Sophie opened her tear crusted eyes and pulled her greatcoat closer around her. Her long hair was bundled on top of her head but the windy quad ride and a troubled sleep in the sweaty van had done it no favours. She flipped down the sun visor to look in the mirror and blinked at her reflection. Before, the messy face looking back at her would have led to a scramble for the cosmetics bag but all she saw was a deep well of sadness that no amount of foundation could cover up.

She switched on the van radio and it crackled to life. It was still tuned to the station they listened to before they were chased into the hills and found Don's house where the coverage was patchy at best. She didn't recognise the music but was sure her mum would have. It occurred to her that she didn't know of any new music from the last two years. There must be some, somewhere, she thought and wondered if she would ever find out.

She sat back and closed her eyes, listening to the tune. They'd tried so hard to keep it all together and work as a team and keep one another safe, she thought, yet here they were, Don was dead and Maggie, Pauly and Mol had almost certainly joined him. They couldn't even go back and check just in case the Sec Unit was still hanging about. A year ago she would have complained that it was so unfair but she was just too tired now. Sophie didn't know how much longer she could carry on. How much more could either of them take?

She considered her family and wondered where they were now. Could they risk a visit home, she thought? No, she shook her head, she couldn't risk being seen anywhere right now. There didn't seem to be one official group in Scotland that *didn't* want her dead. Sophie raised her eyebrows at this thought. Only 16 years old and already a criminal, wanted by Scotland, New Britain and the police. All armed. All really, really cross. It would be so cool if it weren't so horrifically real. She chuckled ruefully and sighed.

Half an hour later, from her position curled up in the front seat, Sophie watched as Aaron and Pip returned, with a dead rabbit dangling over Aaron's shoulder.

"Yum, lunch," she mumbled and jumped out of the van.

"Get a fire going, mate," he called. "I'm going to see if there's a knife or something in the back."

Sophie gathered wood and expertly created a firepit as fast as she could by the side of the van out of the breeze. She set the kindling and the flames caught quickly as Aaron returned with a bag in one hand and water bottle in the other.

"Remember these?" he said and held up the bottle. It was from one of their old Duke of Edinburgh expeditions with Mr Jack, a bottle with built in filter, which would purify any river or stream water.

"Useful," she said and marvelled at Aaron's ongoing ability to keep going and smile even in the face of death, destruction and seemingly hopeless situations.

He held up the bag, "Found a knife too," he said and went to work skinning the rabbit. Pip watched closely, then carefully accepted the leftover carcass when he'd finished. She trotted off under the trees to settle down and gnaw at the bones.

Sophie filtered water from the burn then rummaged in the bag.

"Oh my god!" she exclaimed, "Protein bars! How old are these?" It brought a smile to her face despite her sadness, and she shook her head. Aaron balanced freshly skewered meat onto stones in the fire and it began to pop and sizzle. The radio began to play the first song she actually recognised and they both joined in with the chorus.

Within a few minutes, they were eating fresh rabbit and sugary protein bars. A little food made Sophie feel better and she felt her head clear. There was always something they could do, always a path to follow, and she knew they'd find it.

"Sophie?" Aaron began, "Do you think we could …"

"Wait!" Sophie shot up off her log seat and lunged at the radio. She turned it up when she heard the newscaster say the name, "… Fran MacDonald …"

CHAPTER 37

The room filled up slowly. Each official was accompanied by an equally harassed secretary or assistant and they filed in haphazardly, the ministers and politicians at the large, oval table, the assistants in corners or on low seats, their work balanced on their knees. Monsieur Janvier whispered to his secretary, Rene Faure, and they looked deeply serious. Murmurs blew around the table in a variety of languages, nods and handshakes, small laughs, and shuffles. Fran sat with her back to the window. Finally, the Right Honourable Andrea Taylor MSP swept in and took her seat at the head of the table, as Fran knew she would, squarely in front of the large fireplace which was now hot and glowing with crackling yellow flames. The heat radiated into the cool room along with the fragrant smell of pine sap. Today, Taylor had requested eucalyptus leaves be scattered on the wood pile and the menthol smell cleared their collective heads. She sat down, satisfied with her morning's work so far and assured of the outcome ahead.

She began. "Good morning, ladies, and gentlemen, and welcome to Scotland. I hope to engage in full and open debate about Scotland's future presence in Europe and the need for ..." but she was halted by a raised hand the other side of the table.

"Ms Taylor, thank you for your hospitality," Monsieur Francois Janvier interrupted. "But you must agree that we cannot consider your position in the EU until we have reached a deal on the civil war here in New Britain. If you don't mind, and with respect to Assistant Secretary Zukic who sits as Security Council mediator, I will chair the meeting and I will call on you when necessary and appropriate."

Andrea Taylor's face flickered but she didn't miss a beat.

"Of course, Monsieur Janvier, I understand, and of course all of our information and our Minister for Europe, Fran MacDonald are entirely at your disposal." She eyed Fran with a steel stare.

"Yes, Miss MacDonald has already been incredibly useful to us since we arrived, and we thank her for all she has done," Janvier remarked as he shuffled his papers.

Andrea Taylor couldn't hide her ire this time. She looked from one to the other. She took a sip of water with a trembling hand but it didn't seem to help. Useful? How had Fran been 'useful' to Janvier?

"Now," he continued, all humour and pleasantries drained from his face. "We need to address several matters. One, the raising of an illegal army against the elected government in Westminster, two, erecting an illegal border and three, creating and enforcing an illegal compulsory draft of New British citizens, both of age and minors."

"Of course, Monsieur Janvier," Andrea Taylor sat bolt upright. His tone and demeanour told her everything she needed to know about how the wind was blowing on this one. She was on the back foot already; she could feel it. This would take some serious spin to resolve in her favour.

Janvier looked at her and down at his notes in turn. "With respect to point one, two and three, before we can go any further, the EU requires that there is an immediate ceasefire, a resumption of talks with Westminster, the dismantling of the hard border and a total stop on the draft in Scotland."

Andrea Taylor sat back in her chair and eyed each of the officials in turn. She coolly regarded the Home Secretary Marcus James, who smirked at her from his reclined position. He had one hand on the desk and the other waved an expensive looking pen in the air. Field Marshall Llewelyn-Hoult, the head of the armed forces in New Britain; Secretary Zukic from the Security Council, Commissioner Janvier and Fran amongst other UN officials who Taylor had decided to ignore on account of their apparent lack of importance. Then she noticed Todd Horton and narrowed her eyes slightly. He was a junior minister and a man of little consequence. What was he doing here? He never liked me, she thought. She took a deep breath.

"I can, of course, order a ceasefire," she began. "And I can stop the draft. The border *may be* negotiable but I have nothing further to say to Westminster. We are a separate country. Why would we remain tied to a country that would wilfully bomb citizens of Europe? Even you must admit that no-one wants to be associated with terrorists. Also, they have invaded and engaged our troops. They need to retreat before I will speak to anyone south of the border."

"Thank you, Mrs Taylor," Janvier continued. "But I was not expressly asking you. This is an order, from NATO and the UN. And on the matter of the Strasbourg bombings, you have been effectively removed from power pending an investigation into war crimes for orders given by you in April and in November of last year." He looked directly at her; hands clasped in front of him.

She returned his stare and tried to swallow, but her throat was too dry.

.oOo.

Lewis, Amy on hip, found the baby section and held his fists aloft in triumph. There were still packs of nappies! Disposable ones! He wouldn't have to wash another one for ages! He was ecstatic for a moment, then dragged as many packs as he could from the shelves, followed by food and milk. Then he looked deeper into the baby section and smiled to himself. Buggies. He kissed her cheek and tucked her into a new buggy with a blanket, then threw as much as he could underneath, hung bags onto the handles. He raced out as fast as possible around the broken glass and debris; it didn't for one moment escape his notice that he was stealing in broad daylight and these days that was a shoot on sight offence, then emerged outside. The wide city street was empty. There was movement up by the castle and down the road at a checkpoint but he was essentially alone. He piled his bags into the back of the Land Rover and folded the buggy. Then he placed Amy back into the bassinet and tucked her in. As his fingers slid down the side of the thin blanket, something crinkled against his hand. He finished tucking but the crinkling continued as he moved. He leaned over and pulled out a sheaf of paper, folded into thirds, like a letter. It had his name on the outside, written in Fran's distinctive, cursive hand. He opened it and began to read;

Dear Lewis,

Please keep the enclosed files safe. Whilst I am aware you owe me nothing, you may find them interesting reading. They both implicate and exonerate. This is the tricky thing about having power or knowledge. Eventually, both corrupt.

Best Wishes,

Fran MacDonald MSP

Lewis pulled out a larger file from under the mattress. He peered at the papers within it, opened his eyes wide and breathed out a low, slow, "Wow."

Lewis jumped at the knock at the window. He rolled it down to see a soldier standing there.

"Dr Jack?" the soldier asked.

"No," Lewis replied.

"But this is his Land Rover?"

"Yes," Lewis looked at the soldier and the suited officials behind him.

"Are you Lewis Sinclair, from Muirbridge, latterly Wolf Craigs Farm?"

"Yes."

"Could we have a minute of your time?"

.oOo.

Andrea Taylor eyed the door. It was guarded both inside and out, there was no escape that way. She glanced at her secretary, but

234

Damian just sat, grimly taking notes. He looked exhausted, unshaven and pale.

"What do you mean, 'War Crimes'?" she asked. "If Westminster …"

"We have a list of crimes in which you have recently been implicated."

"You can't do this!" she cried. "I was merely defending my country!"

"One: Raising an illegal army against an elected government."

"They refused to acknowledge our referendum!" Andrea Taylor half rose from her seat.

"Two: Drafting minors into a war."

"In Scotland we can vote at sixteen in matters of Scottish concern! The draft is an extension of that privilege!" She raised her fist above her head, face trembling.

"Three: Erecting an illegal border."

"Pshaw," She sat down, waved the accusation away and half turned from the table. She stared into the fire behind her, her face stiff with fury.

Across the room, two uniformed officials approached Damian and gesticulated for him to get up. He rose, picked up a large briefcase by his side and handed it to one of them. Then they escorted him from the room. Andrea Taylor watched as they crossed the room, then turned back to Commissioner Janvier.

"You have *nothing* on me!" she hissed. "Nothing!"

Fran leaned forward into her line of vision; hands clasped delicately on the table.

"We have everything we need," she smiled and opened her blue, leather-bound book.

CHAPTER 38

After his release, Lewis passed through the inner checkpoint with no trouble. The soldiers on duty all seemed very preoccupied with walkie talkies and phones. They waved him through with a mere glance and he nodded as he passed. Once in outer Edinburgh, he sped up, determined not to be stopped by the Sec Units, but the roads were once again deserted. Where roads intersected and major confluences came together, he was sure the Sec Units would gather to make trouble, every corner he turned had been abandoned. His speed increased with every passing minute. The sweat trickled down his forehead as he got closer and closer to the outer checkpoint and he struggled to come up with a plausible story for his journey this time.

"Here goes, Amy," he mumbled as he crossed the bridge over the southern bypass. He slowed, then sat forward in his seat. "What the ...?" he asked himself.

The checkpoint was empty, the gate open and no-one manned the booth. No-one was in sight, anywhere. Lewis sat back and pressed the accelerator, a long-held breath escaping his lips. He was not going to question it, just go. Glancing in the mirror dozens of times a minute, he sped off into the Pentlands towards home.

.oOo.

Aaron and Sophie listened wide eyed to the van radio, its volume turned way up so that they didn't miss a second of the news cast. Sophie cupped her hand around her ear to make sure she heard and understood everything.

"...it is understood from sources in Bute House that alongside information from Fran MacDonald and representatives from NATO, the UN Security Council, the Home Secretary, Marcus

James and Commissioner Janvier from the EU, a ceasefire has been declared and is effective immediately. All combatants, both in the Scottish Army and all other guerrilla units have been instructed to lay down their weapons and dismantle all borders, checkpoints, and barriers. It is believed that New Britain troops are already withdrawing from the area. Further details to follow, as they arise."

Sophie turned the radio town and turned to Aaron.

"So he got there!" she said with a grin. "Stupid, pointless Mr Sinclair actually managed to get the book to Fran! How the hell did that useless radge do it?" She laughed and grabbed Aaron's sleeves.

They danced up and down on the spot for a second or two, before Aaron spoke quietly. "Do you think that means he's got her?"

Sophie gripped his jacket tighter and leaned towards him. "He *must* have, Aaron! He *must* have!" She stared at him for a second, then her face opened wide as realisation spread across her face, "Walkie talkies!" she yelled, "In the van!" she turned and scrambled into the driver's seat and threw herself over to the glove box. She clicked it on and a small green light glowed on the top edge.

"Remember? Don always made us carry them everywhere when we went out! If Lewis took a bag of any kind, he must have one!"

"He won't be in range, though, will he?" Aaron asked.

"Maybe not, but if he's got Amy he'll be heading home, I mean, Muirbridge home. And if he does, he has to come this way. Sooner or later, we'll catch him!" Sophie beamed then spoke into the device.

"Lewis! Lewis are you there?" she said, trying to keep her voice as even as possible.

"But if he's going to the farmhouse ..." Aaron began.

Sophie looked at him over the microphone.

"Oh shit," she breathed.

"We have to try," he said. "Try and get him first."

Aaron sat back down by the fire to wait. The dog joined him and they sat together for a while, as Sophie spoke the same words repeatedly. Each time, the crackle of static told its own story and the sound of the dead air pierced at his heart. What if they got to the farmhouse and saw the mess? What if the Sec Units decided not to let him out, or worse still, lay in wait for him to return and just shot him? What would they do with his little sister? What if he's already there? What if he was arrested and was never coming back?

.oOo.

"Please sit down Mrs Taylor, you need to hear all the charges against you. It's the law."

She scoffed, "Huh!" but sat down in her chair. "Who's law, exactly?" she spoke with sarcasm and bile.

"The International Court," Janvier looked directly at her and she stilled for a moment.

"Number Four: the shooting down of flight AN 3006 from Heathrow to Edinburgh at 12.11pm GMT on the 9th November of last year."

Andrea Taylor looked at Fran who placed a hand onto her blue diary and smiled.

"What did you tell them?" she sneered.

"Mrs Taylor," Fran replied, "With no secretary of my own, sometimes I had to borrow yours ..." she said and drummed her fingers gently on the book. Andrea Taylor opened her mouth to speak but Janvier stopped her.

"Number Five," he continued and looked up significantly. "The bombing of the Louise Weiss building of the European Parliament in Strasbourg on 1st April , and the murder of 101 people therein."

Everyone in the room took a collective sharp breath. The air in the room seemed to solidify with the silence as the news burrowed deep into their collective consciousness.

Lewis drove as fast as the old Land Rover would allow. The suspension was tight and harsh, and he jiggled in his seat with every pothole and jumble of rubble strewn across the road. Amy burbled and fussed at the constant movement, and he reached a hand out to her for reassurance.

"Don't worry, littlie, we'll get you home, we'll see big brother soon, don't worry," he mumbled, as much to sooth himself as the baby. "Let's listen to the radio, shall we?" he asked himself and leaned to switch it on. As he moved, he heard a familiar sound, the crackle of static from a walkie talkie. He was momentarily confused, where was that coming from?

Again, the familiar crackle. From under the seat. He realised.

"Holy shit!" He slammed on the brakes and stopped at the side of the road. He pushed a hand under the seat and waved it about before he found the walkie talkie. He clutched it in both hands, grinning, then stopped. It might not be ...

"Lewis, are you there?" a faint voice spoke. It was Sophie!

"Oh my God, Sophie, are you all ok?" he cried and tears began to fall down his cheeks as he flooded with relief.

.oOo.

"I've got him!" Sophie yelled to Aaron, who jumped up to listen. "Where are you? Come back to the school van! Have you got Amy?"

"Yes, she's here, but I'm on the way to the farmhouse, I'll meet you there," he said.

Sophie clutched the walkie talkie, "No!" she cried, "Come here to the van! Please! Don't go to the house!"

"Sophie? What happened?"

Silence. Sophie closed her eyes as she prepared to tell him.

"Sophie is everyone ok?" he pressed.

She sniffed away the tears as she replied, "No, they're not ok, Lewis, the house, there was an explosion, I think Maggie and Pauly ..." she stopped.

"Explosion as in Don's basement?" Lewis asked.

"Please just come," she sniffed.

CHAPTER 39

"What did you say to me?" Andrea Taylor stood up and balled her fists at her side. The uniformed guard by the door took a step forward.

"The Strasbourg bombings, Mrs Taylor. We have evidence linking you to the bomb that caused the destruction of the Louise Weiss building in April of last year."

Andrea Taylor looked from Fran to Janvier then across at Marcus James, the Westminster Home Secretary. He cleared his throat, smoothed his tie and, eventually, smiled at her with a wide, smug grin.

"What the hell are you talking about?" she swallowed audibly. "What evidence?" She continued to eye the Home Secretary who held her gaze as she sat down.

"The bomb that was placed in the central atrium of the Louise Weiss Building did not detonate properly, as we all know, limiting the loss of life to 101 people from the bomb that went off just inside the main doors," Janvier began.

"A bomb that does not go off is not only a blessing, it is traceable," Fran finished.

Fran stood up and walked around the table towards the First Minister. She stopped by Andrea Taylor's chair and placed a large, blown-up photograph in front of her.

"This is the bomb that didn't detonate in the Louise Weiss building in Strasbourg," she said and tapped it, then continued towards the fireplace. Andrea Taylor looked at the photo then turned to watch her stride towards the huge open fire surround. All eyes watched as Fran pulled out, from behind the large stone dog statue sitting beside the fireside, a black, taped shoe box. She brought it back to her seat and opened the lid.

Voices rose and people jumped from their seats in horror as they saw what Fran had brought to the meeting. The uniformed guards rushed towards her but Janvier rose and stopped them.

"It's ok!" he bellowed, over the scramble of terrified noise, "I know what this is! Please! Listen, ladies and gentlemen!"

Carefully, Fran took out the contents of the box, piece by piece. As she lined up the pieces of the bomb in front of her, it became clear that what she had was identical to the picture in the middle of the table; colour and grade of wire, tape, detonator and a couple of sticks of explosive material. The officials looked from the picture to the bomb and back again.

Fran continued, "When the bomb went off, I made it my business, as Minister for Europe, to know everything I could about it to try to bring those responsible to justice, despite no longer being a part of the European Union. Even though I had only been to the European Parliament a few times, after my extensive investigations and collaborations with European colleagues, I knew every last thing about the Louise Weiss building; who worked there, who had which office, who contracted whom."

Andrea Taylor looked up at Fran, then at the device. Fear stole across her face for the first time.

"The English New Nationalist Party were implicated because it seems they contracted someone to do some work for them, supposedly in the clearing out of their telecommunications in their offices after Brexit sometime in April. Actually, the beginning of April." Fran continued.

"Except the person they contracted didn't turn up. He had been stood down and someone else sent in his place," Fran paused. "By you." She paused again. "In orders you made sure came not from you but from Steve Lister in the Scotland Office in Westminster, ably assisted by members of the Home Office who may have sympathised with you."

"And he's dead, thanks to you, Fran!" Taylor sneered, "Dead and gone on that plane you had destroyed!"

Fran sighed sadly, "Yes, Steve is dead I'm afraid, but even if he were here he wouldn't have known who he was being asked to send, or why he was being asked to send them. Steve was just another pawn. See, you asked Steve to send a man to Strasbourg who knows just about everything about everything. This man could pose as a telecommunications engineer, no problem."

"This is absurd!" Andrea Taylor cried, "Commissioner Janvier, please!"

He shook his head.

"But he wasn't an engineer, was he Andrea?" Fran said.

Andrea Taylor squirmed.

"He was a chemist."

"Lies!"

"Andrea Taylor, you told Steve Lister to send Dr Donald Drayforth-Jack. The chemist of Wolf Craigs."

CHAPTER 40

Sophie stopped him with a hand on his arm. They were sitting around the fire beside the van, as it crackled and spat with new wood from the copse.

"Wait. So? It was Don?"

"Looks like it," Lewis sniffed and wiped his cheek with a sleeve.

"Is this real?" Aaron asked. He cradled Amy and she lay on his chest, chewing on the leather bookmark Fran had given her.

"From what I can see, I think so, yes."

"Just a minute," Sophie rose and grasped at her hair, trying to think. "Don, our chemistry teacher, is the man who did the Strasbourg bombing?"

The two men looked at her. Lewis nodded.

"But ... he was ... but ... Don was ... why?" Sophie sat down with a thump.

Lewis looked back at the extensive letter that Fran had written and shuffled the pages.

"I gave the rest to the men who stopped me on Princes Street, but I kept her letter."

"Here," he said, and began to read once more.

"... As you can see from the contracts enclosed, Maggie's care and equipment was bought, maintained and paid for entirely by the government. Her two full time carers weren't just Polish helpers, they were fully trained stroke nurses with access to the latest drugs, therapies and equipment. The collapse of the NHS meant that a simple High School teacher would never have earned enough credits to put her through the extensive surgeries and treatments that she had, nor pay for her ongoing care. His debts were huge when she approached him, all to take care of his wife. Maggie's stroke nearly killed her, however by acquiescing to the demands of Taylor he was able to hold onto his beloved wife for a bit longer."

"He did it for Maggie," Aaron said, simply.

Lewis nodded and looked back at the letter. "Fran wasn't just the crazy lady we lived with who wanted revenge, she really was putting two and two together."

They sat for a while in silence, staring at the flames, minds racing.

"Didn't he know he was going to kill loads of people?" Aaron asked.

"I can only presume he did," Lewis shrugged.

"She made him do the bombing so she could blame New Britain?" he continued.

"That looks likely, yes," Lewis replied.

"Does that make us, Scotland I mean, the bad guys? Are we the baddies? Are we guilty?" Aaron asked in a dismayed tone.

Lewis took a deep breath. He had to answer this one as carefully as possible; more carefully than anything he had ever told a student before.

"It's complicated," he began, and Sophie rolled her eyes.

"Adults *always* say that when they don't know," she said and poked a stick into the fire.

"No, I want to hear," Aaron turned back to him. "What is complicated?"

"Well," Lewis grimaced, "Scotland and England have had an alliance for hundreds of years, you know that from history lessons, but we are two very different countries. I think when Andrea Taylor won the independence vote in IndyRef2, she was happy, as we all were. Then the courts didn't uphold the vote, so we couldn't go. I think she used Don's expertise to make it look like New Britain were, you know, a bit mad and New Nationalists were *'those mental bomber people from Westminster'*, and that they were holding us against our will, which they kind of were. Who on earth would want to be a part of a crazy state?" He paused for breath. "I think she just wanted to make absolutely sure this time that we got out – by any means - and to make sure that Europe helped."

"It all went wrong, though," Aaron said.

"It all went wrong, son, yes."

"So the New Nationalist Party in England aren't the ones to blame?"

Lewis chuckled, "Holy shit, kid, I said it was complicated, and I meant it. They are and they aren't. We are the bad guys in that our politicians committed a despicable act of aggression – there is never any excuse for terrorism. There are always so many sides to each story, it's never easy. The ordinary Scottish people aren't the bad guys though – we rarely get to change things. Then again - this time, I think we did. What I do know is that we aren't at war anymore and surely, surely, from here the only way is up."

Aaron and Sophie stared into the flames for a moment or two. Whether they cared or not, there were still mountains to climb. The bigger picture had encroached on their lives and it looked like it wasn't quite over yet.

Eventually Sophie spoke. "So Don started this whole thing," she said.

Lewis shuffled in his seat and sighed.

"I don't think we can completely blame him, no ... but ..."

"And it looks like Fran finished it."

"In a manner of speaking."

"Adults, I swear to God, man." Sophie shook her head.

The clouds obscured the sun and the sky darkened with rainclouds as they sat looking at the flames. The breeze lifted their hair and Pip's fur. Amy began to fuss and wriggle and Aaron let her go so that she could take a few steps.

Aaron looked at Lewis. "We have to go back to the farm, Sir," he said.

"I know."

"I need to get Amy inside, too. She can't sleep in a van."

"I know."

Lewis took a deep breath and stood up. "Come on then," he said.

CHAPTER 41

The hours dragged. Izzy had to feed little Caroline several times, and each time she latched on was more painful than the last. Izzy gritted her teeth and fed the baby regardless; it was clear the little thing was hungry.

"It'll get easier, Iz," Callie whispered. She continued to look out of the window. Occasionally, from the front, they could hear small noises from the transceiver and low murmurs from the captain.

Izzy sighed, "It's ok," she said. "But the minute we land, she's on a bloody bottle."

Callie laughed gently. "Baby milk! Now that is something we haven't seen for years!"

Izzy grumbled, "Yeah, well, that was Scotland. This is Holland. Nearly. I hope."

Just then Callie inclined closer to the dirty window and peered out.

"What the ...?" she began as the noise of the approaching boat started to echo through the cabin. Others began to crane necks or stand up. Murmurs and cries of dismay rose through the stale air.

"That bastard! He sold us out!" one voice shouted, and a man began to lumber towards the front of the cabin.

"No!" the captain replied and emerged with his hands up. "It's the police! We don't have a choice, we must let them board!"

The man stopped. "What do we do now?" he asked the room. "Are we going to be arrested?"

Outside, the police boat came alongside and a voice bellowed, "This is the police, prepare to be boarded."

The captain backed out of the cabin, stepped out on the deck and threw a rope to the boat beside them. Immediately booted feet jumped aboard and entered the cabin. Several people whimpered and adults clutched at children at the sight of yet more uniforms. Izzy held Caroline to her chest and squeezed her eyes shut. It was too much to ask that they would get away and be free. She heard the Captain talking urgently to the officers and waited for the inevitable arrests to happen.

The man who entered first, tall and silver haired, held up his hands.

"Are you all from Scotland?" he asked.

There were nods and murmurs. Several people began to cry.

"I am Captain Hoogstraten," he continued, "I will be taking this craft to shore. There are people there who will help. Do not try to get away. We have the boat surrounded."

"Are we going to be arrested?" Izzy asked Callie in a whisper.

"Probably," came her simple reply. A tear trickled down her cheek.

There were complaints from around the room. "You can't arrest us!"

"Please don't send us back!"

"We'll be killed!"

"It's a war zone. It's not safe!"

"We were starving! We are still starving!"

The noise became unbearable as the dirty band of refugees pleaded for their lives. Izzy tried to cover her ears but it wasn't possible. She groaned in distress, the stress pressing on her from all sides. One way or another, please just let this be over, she thought. She clutched at Callie who held her just as tightly.

Individual officers entered the cabin and took people off one by one. A young woman took baby Caroline and wrapped her in a foil blanket before she took Izzy and her child off the boat. Izzy looked back at Callie as she stepped outside, to see that she hadn't moved. Izzy held out a hand and beckoned to her but Callie was lost in the crush of bodies moving towards the door. She had no choice but to keep going, to accept the police officers extended hand and leave the boat.

Despite the circumstances, Izzy relaxed slightly. The police boat was warm and comfortable, the blankets a welcome addition. She sipped water and nibbled a bread roll, twisting her head to see when Callie was going to join her, but the engines roared into life and the boat turned away.

The police boat rumbled towards the shore and they eventually came alongside the dock in Texel Harbour. With the baby, Izzy was disembarked first and taken inside to a small building where they asked her to take a seat. She was offered a hot drink and water, food and baby supplies. Izzy nodded or shook her head as appropriate, whilst scanning the room at each face in turn, looking for Callie. Her mind buzzed with all the new information, and she found it hard to concentrate on the questions posed to her. The room was over-bright and painted in a dirty off white, the lights overhead sharp and piercing. Izzy blinked at the brightness after hours at sea and weeks in a dim corner of a room in a sports centre.

After a while, she was led into a smaller room with a desk and low chair. She sat and looked around herself. That was it. Nothing else graced the room except the person, another young uniformed woman in front of her. It reminded her of the medical waiting room after the NHS collapsed and they had to use doctors set up in mobile units. The walls there were thin and the floor spongy and insubstantial.

"Miss? Are you ok?" a voice floated to her after a while. "I asked you, do you want to claim asylum in The Netherlands?" the official sitting in front of her peered at her face and Izzy suddenly became aware of how grimy she was. She rubbed her forehead with a hand and realised she was probably just making it worse.

"Um, yes, yes I do, of course," she replied. Did she? She wasn't sure.

"Do you want to return to Scotland?" the woman asked.

Izzy thought for a moment. She wanted that more than anything in the world. She wanted to celebrate Burns night with Haggis and whisky, she wanted to smell the coconut aroma of the gorse bushes in the hills, she wanted to attend a wedding with kilts and heather and a ceilidh and cranachan on the menu. She wanted Scottish raspberries and salmon and beer and pubs and streams and pheasant and beaches in the snow. Then visions of blast holes, barbed wire and dead bodies in pools of blood, riddled with Sec Unit bullet holes pressed into her consciousness and she groaned. The tears prickled her eyes once more.

"Do I have to go back?" Izzy asked.

"Do you want to?" the officer replied.

"I ... I don't know." she said, frowning.

The official leaned on the desk in front of her and clasped her hands.

"I can tell you," she began with a smile, "That as of a few hours ago, there has been a ceasefire declared in New Britain. The fighting has stopped, at least."

"Ceasefire?"

"All over."

"England and Scotland not fighting anymore?" Izzy asked. Her mind raced.

"Nope. One big happy family, it would seem. All finished. Your government has been, ah, disbanded," she finished, but struggled to find the right word.

"So England won?" Izzy frowned at this idea.

"Well, no, I don't think it is as simple as win or lose but as far as the civil war goes, it has come to an end and the Scottish government has stood down, I think."

"So there's no more Scottish government?"

"Not the old one. There will be someone new in charge."

"But that's not right!" Izzy cried, "That's like, like ... England have taken over again! Have they?"

"I don't know, honey, I am sure it will all come clear very soon." She smiled and began to fill in the paperwork in front of her.

"We voted for independence," Izzy said quietly. "We wanted to join Europe. No-one seems to care. No-one understands. No-one tried to help us when New Britain wouldn't let us go."

The officer looked at Izzy with sympathy, then nodded her head at Caroline, "Was she born at sea?"

"Yes," Izzy replied, "Yesterday."

"Then you have a choice," she beamed, "The law states that any child born in international waters can take the residency of the country where they land," she shrugged. "More or less. You have the option to stay, at least."

Izzy looked at her.

"We might not be able to save Scotland right now but we can save you and your daughter. You could go back and rebuild your country, or you could stay here and build a life with us. Both choices will be hard. I know that."

Izzy thought about Lewis. He was a distant memory, getting fainter all the time.

"Do you have family still in Scotland?"

Izzy didn't miss a beat, "No," she replied. Her mother and brother were still there, but Izzy could already see the benefits of being in Holland.

"Then think about it."

She was escorted out of the room and to a plastic chair in a corridor with other pre-processed passengers. The long room was lined with dirty glass windows and through them, Izzy could see the dirty old fishing boat as it bobbed up and down on the water in the harbour outside. The captain stood on the dock with several police officers and officials. Beside him, Callie stood with a blanket around her shoulders. Izzy rose and walked outside into the chill, sweeping wind.

She walked as fast as she could towards the dock edge, gripping Caroline to her chest in her large blanket. The wind whipped the blanket edge around her legs and tousled her hair backwards and forwards. The cold wind off the sea bit at her face.

"Callie!" she called and her voice disappeared into the air.

"Callie!" she called again.

Callie turned and started towards her. "Izzy!" she yelled, "Get back inside, it's too cold for her!"

"Why aren't you coming in?" Izzy said, as she stumbled a little.

Callie caught Izzy and held her up - she was still exhausted from the birth.

Izzy continued, "They're saying there's a ceasefire and it's all over and if I want to, I can go back. But that I can stay because she was born here, or something." Izzy drew the hair from her face and tried to pin it behind her ears to no avail. She continued to babble, "What do I do? Callie, please tell me what I should do?"

"Izzy, calm down," Callie soothed, "I can't tell you what to do. Only you know."

"But I don't! What are you going to do? Are you going into Belgium? Can I come with you?"

Callie looked over her shoulder at the boat.

"The ceasefire changes it," she said. "I think ..."

"What are you going to do?"

"I have to go back, Izzy."

"What!? You come all this way only to go straight back?!"

"I know, but now that there is an end to the fighting, I can go get my Elliot and Matthew. I can get my boys," Callie smiled and Izzy saw both sadness and strength behind those eyes.

"But you brought me all this way ..." she said and began to cry. "I thought we were a team."

"You are a team, you and Caroline. And you can come back with me but I'm not sure an unstable post war territory is the right place for a baby. I'm a nurse - so it's probably exactly where I should be. Stay. Stay and be safe."

"Where will you go ... what will the boys do?" Izzy sniffed.

"Now, that I don't know."

Izzy barked a laugh, "You always know what you're doing!"

"What I want might not be what they want. But at least they are free men now, not drafted and we can make a decision for us, not for what politicians want."

"Callie!" The captain called her over and she turned back to the little crowd.

A uniformed official approached to escort Izzy back inside.

"Can I confirm that you are claiming asylum?" he asked.

Izzy looked at Callie's back, "Yes," Izzy replied. It was the safest option. She was saving herself. She was saved.

"Come with me then. You're our priority. We need to find somewhere for you both. Let's get going, it's cold out here."

Izzy turned to go but needed to say goodbye.

"Callie!" she called, "I have to go." The words caught in her throat and she sobbed.

"Good luck, Izzy. I hope it all works out for you." Callie ran back to hug her. A tear spilled from her overfilled eyes.

Izzy paused, the tears prickled her own eyes. It was all moving so fast, and the final act of asylum was here, leaving her friend for good.

"I ... I ... thank you, Callie. For everything."

Callie nodded sadly, reached into her pocket and pulled something out.

"Here," she said and placed something in Izzy's hand.

Izzy looked down. It was her engagement ring, the one she used to buy them passage.

"The captain gave it back," Callie wiped her eyes. "Said he thought you might need it more than he did."

Izzy pushed it back on her finger. It was loose but familiar. It would be handy. Izzy just had to work out for what.

Callie hugged her once more, turned away and Izzy watched as she and the captain jumped onto the boat.

"Goodbye, Callie," she said and her eyes filled once more.

The official led her away and this time she went fast, just as the tears began to flow.

CHAPTER 42

Andrea Taylor stood up and straightened down her skirt. Two uniforms stood at her flank and one took her elbow.

"This way, Mrs Taylor," he said.

She pulled away in irritation and shot him a look, he grasped her arm once again, more firmly, and steered her towards the door. She stalked out, head high, her face a mask.

"Well, finally New Britain has been exonerated." Marcus James shifted in his seat to drape his arms over the table. His voice was loud and blustering, his tones incredulous. "I expect the sanctions and blockades to be lifted immediately. I refuse to let the citizens of New Britain be subjected to this outrageous treatment any longer. Take down that ridiculous border and return all rule in New Britain to Westminster." He turned to the European delegates and pointed a thick finger at the Commissioner.

"Commissioner Janvier, I trust this will be your first priority. We cannot run the risk of this sort of carry on happening again."

Several voices rose at once as the implied insult sank in. Todd Horton spoke,

"Mr James, despite having found Mrs Taylor to be less than honest, she is not alone in her double-dealings and political tricks. Your refusal to acknowledge the legal referendum and independence of Scotland has led to all of this. Every last move by Taylor and others was to free themselves of your insular, selfish, isolationist stance and you used the courts to stop it and in the meantime, grab oil rigs and power stations. You may not be 'to blame'," he held up his hands to emphasise his point. "But your behaviour just proves our point more. We want out. We are leaving."

Marcus James opened his mouth then snapped it shut. Everyone around the table looked at him. He did not see any obvious allies. He sat back again, looked towards his lap and fiddled with his tie.

There was a pause in proceedings as Todd Horton's words sank in.

After a moment, Fran stood up.

"Thank you ladies and gentlemen for your assistance in bringing peace to our country. I know there is much to do and I am eager to get started. Might I offer my services by creating an interim cabinet, and ..."

Commissioner Janvier held up a hand and stopped her. "We shall support Scotland in her endeavours in this tricky time, of course, and we shall call upon all the expertise in Europe to help to rebuild it. If they need anyone in particular, they shall ask."

"They?" she asked.

"Mr Horton here will be nominally in charge and will put together a suitable strategy and administration team," Janvier continued.

"Todd Horton?" Fran said with disbelief, "But he's a ..." she stopped herself before the word 'nobody' slipped past her lips.

"I will help any way I can," Fran said, but with less confidence and she slid back down in her seat. She clasped her hands on her blue book.

"But we shall," Janvier continued, "be needing this book, if it is, as you say, filled with all irrefutable evidence of guilt," he leaned across the table to take it from her.

Fran grabbed the edges and pulled it off the table.

Janvier's hand stopped mid-air as she clutched the book to her chest.

"No," Fran said reflexively. "It's ... mine. My book. Just tell me what you want," her eyes widened.

Janvier sat back and his hand floated back to the tabletop. "Give me the book, Ms MacDonald," he said simply.

Fran looked at everyone around the table in turn as they all turned to peer at her. Her strange behaviour piqued their interest.

"No," She stood up quickly and two uniforms twitched by the door.

"It has become central to knowing the full details of Mrs Taylor's and Dr Jack's involvement in the bombings and the shooting down of the plane."

She shook her head and backed away.

"Or is there something in there you would rather we didn't see?" Janvier asked.

Fran gripped the book tighter.

Janvier sat back in his chair and it creaked. He regarded her with a knowing eye.

"Did you think we wouldn't try to reach the chemist? The minute you told us of his involvement?" he asked, slowly.

"And what did he say?" Fran narrowed her eyes at him.

Janvier held her gaze. "We spoke to someone else. Apprehended him on Prince's Street. I believe you know Lewis Sinclair?"

Fran took another step back. She swallowed. So they knew everything. Why the hell didn't Lewis get out of town when she told him to!

"Rene," Janvier spoke to his secretary, "Did you go to Dr Jack's house yet?"

"Not yet."

"Take a team. I believe Mr Horton," he gesticulated towards the Minister for Rural Affairs and the Environment, "has already indicated who we can trust. We need as much evidence intact as we can find. Ms MacDonald, there is no escape. We will find everything we need."

Fran turned to Horton in a fury. "Horton, I trusted you with that information!"

"No, Fran, you thought I was just a messenger boy."

"This country needs a strong leader, Horton, and you do not have what it takes. You're a nobody," she pointed her red nail at him and this time spat out the word with ire.

"This country needs people to stop fighting and talk. And a nobody like me has to be better than a murderer or a terrorist."

They regarded one another for a long moment. The silence in the room was complete.

"Arrest her," Janvier finished then picked up his papers and tapped them into a neat pile.

"And bring us more coffee," Todd Horton said as Fran was also escorted from the room. "We have a lot of work to do."

CHAPTER 43

The ruts in the track were still there, the gates open and the sheep roaming on every hillside. Aaron looked in dismay as he saw three dead ewes and at least five dead lambs dotted around the crags. After the explosion, they had bolted and run scared and eventually succumbed to fright, or predators or the elements. Sophie kept her eyes on the road ahead and gripped the seat in front of her. They could all see a small column of smoke coming from the base of the valley and although Sophie prayed the smoke was from the fireplace, and Maggie was sitting up in bed, and Pauly was miraculously better and his leg on the mend, she knew in her heart that it was not going to be that way.

As they rounded the last crag, they saw it. The farmhouse had been completely demolished. In the place of the two storey, stone built home, they was a haphazard pile of stones and debris, glass and twisted metal. It was all burned to a blackened mess, strewn across a wide area where Don's chemicals had exploded. It was unrecognisable as the house they called home. A trickle of water had cut a groove into the yard, where the mains water pipe had cracked and breached. The small curl of smoke came from the north corner of the yard, Sophie couldn't imagine what it was. She turned away and sobbed, she didn't want to know. Her home had gone and the people she loved all dead and she didn't want to imagine what had gone through Maggie's mind as the house exploded around her.

"She blew it up," Aaron said and kicked out at a small stone.

"She sent us away so she could ..." Sophie couldn't finish. "The Sec Units were going to ... and she ..."

"She was a brave woman," Lewis said. "She adored the both of you. I'm so, so sorry. I wish this all could be different."

The three of them stood in the yard and surveyed the mess. The barn was damaged and the cattle had long since disappeared. Lewis sat on a pile of stones and closed his eyes. Pip ran off over the yard and into the rubble.

"Come on, let's get you home," Lewis kicked at a stone and stood up.

"I'm not sure what home is," said Aaron. "The animals. They need me here. I kind of, you know, I like this life. Me and Amy, we could do worse. I think I want to carry on, work the land. It saved us before, it can keep us going."

Lewis nodded. Aaron. Always the responsible one.

"Pip!" he called, "Come on!"

There was no movement from the dog.

"Pip! Come on!" Lewis whistled. Still nothing. He squinted at the mess before him, where the kitchen yard had been. "Pip?" he called, then saw movement from under a pile of stone. "Pip, come on, girl."

The stone moved once again and Pip emerged, tail wagging.

"Good girl, come on." he said, but she stopped.

"Pip, let's go."

Pip wouldn't move.

"Pip? What's wrong?"

She whined and looked at the hole behind her.

Lewis saw a small movement and heard a soft scraping.

"What is it girl?" Lewis got onto his knees and began to pull stones and debris away from the faint noise. Under a beam he saw two green eyes. As he adjusted to the gloom, he could see a dark shape which whimpered in recognition. It was Mol, alive, but filthy, lying on top of Don's grave.

"Come on, girl," he said and hoisted her out. She shook her fur and scratched at her neck. Pip sniffed and curled around her, a smile on her furry face. "You just couldn't bring yourself to leave, huh?"

Aaron stood, hands on hips. "I don't think I can, either," he stated.

Sophie joined him. "Me neither. Not yet."

They exchanged looks.

"You know people are going to come, don't you? From the Government. To get evidence for what happened."

"I know."

"Wouldn't you both be safer at home in Muirbridge?"

"No."

"Don't you want to see mum?"

"Of course" she rolled her eyes at him. "But this job isn't finished yet. We need to find Maggie and Pauly. Anyone who comes from the government can help for a change."

Lewis patted dirt from Mol's fur and she licked his hand. "Wolf Craigs. The safest place in the country, right?" He sat on some rubble and wiped his face.

"It is now," Sophie sighed.

"I have to find Izzy," he said.

"Yeah," she replied.

"But we'll be back."

"We know," Aaron smiled as they both turned and began to clear the rubble, one stone at a time.

AUTHORS NOTE
GWEN GATES PARKER

Wolf Craigs has been sitting at the back of my mind for years. It started with the crash in 2009, developed with austerity, and then the first failed IndyRef. Brexit finally made me put pen to paper as I followed events through to their unsettling conclusions.

I have lived in Scotland for 17 years.
Despite all, Scotland will survive. She will thrive.
She will rise again.

Social Media:

Facebook:	www.facebook.com/gwengatesparker/
Twitter:	@GwenGatesParke1
Goodreads:	Gwen Gates Parker
TikTok:	gwengatesparker

If you enjoyed this book please give it a review on Amazon. Also you may be interested in another book by Gwen Gates Parker – *Charm Offensive*:

Gregor is the sweetest, kindest man in the school. The children worship him, the women adore him. Everyone loves him.

No-one can quite work out why Corinne left him. But Jen knows why. Tied up, bruised and pregnant, sitting very still on his cold bedroom floor. She's trapped, in a prison she helped to create. But through her befuddled, punch-drunk thoughts, she knows that someone will help her escape.

Someone. Anyone? Hello?

⭐⭐⭐⭐⭐ **Thrilling. Couldn't put it down. Highly recommended**
Reviewed in the United Kingdom on 6 May 2021
Verified Purchase

I couldn't put this book down, I was hooked from the first paragraph. A well written book with plot twists that had me on the edge of my seat. I can't wait for this author's next offering.

⭐⭐⭐⭐⭐ **Not my usual reading**
Reviewed in the United Kingdom on 30 April 2021

It's not what I usually read but the story caught.my attention. From wanting to shout at the women concerned for being so stupid, the author had me hating Greg with a vengeance. So much happens in this book that it makes it a really good read.

⭐⭐⭐⭐⭐ **Thrilling and impossible to put down!**
Reviewed in the United Kingdom on 19 July 2020

This is a tightly plotted and unputdownable read! Set in both the U.K. and Australia it is a tense exploration of coercive control and gaslighting with a well-drawn cast of characters. This high tension tale stayed with me long after I'd finished reading it....now looking forward to reading much more from this talented author.

⭐⭐⭐⭐⭐ **Gripping read**
Reviewed in the United Kingdom on 18 July 2020

Really enjoyed this book, really gripping storyline especially towards the end. Strong vivid characters , made me hold my breath, made me shed a tear , recommended.